Fifteen Years With The Outcast

By

Fflorens Roberts

Double 9
BOOKS

Fifteen Years With The Outcast
by Fflorens Roberts

ISBN: 978-93-61423-96-3

Published by

DOUBLE 9 BOOKS

2/13-B, Ansari Road
Daryaganj, New Delhi – 110002
info@double9books.com
www.double9books.com
Tel. 011-40042856

ABOUT THE AUTHOR

Fflorens Roberts, a prolific author, is renowned for his literary masterpiece "Fifteen Years with the Outcast," a poignant and insightful narrative that chronicles the transformative journey of a marginalized individual over a decade and a half. Through rich prose and profound storytelling, Roberts captures the essence of human resilience and redemption, illuminating the complexities of societal exclusion and the enduring power of compassion. Set against the backdrop of urban life, the novel delves deep into the psyche of the outcast, offering a compelling exploration of identity, belonging, and the quest for dignity in the face of adversity. With sensitivity and empathy, Roberts portrays the struggles and triumphs of the protagonist, inviting readers to reflect on their own perceptions of social justice and humanity. "Fifteen Years with the Outcast" stands as a testament to Roberts' literary prowess and his unwavering commitment to shedding light on the marginalized voices often overlooked by society. Through this timeless work, Roberts leaves an indelible mark on the literary landscape, challenging readers to confront the harsh realities of inequality while embracing the transformative power of empathy and understanding.

CONTENTS

PREFACE

A missionary, upon returning from his field of labor in India, was making an effort to stir up the sympathies of the people in behalf of the heathen. By telling his countrymen of the influence of the gospel upon the Indians and of the hundreds, even thousands, of them who had become Christians, he succeeded in creating an interest among many of his friends. He told many stirring experiences of the difficulties encountered in the missionary work, and gave affecting accounts of the persecution of the native Christians because of their turning from their idolatry and former beliefs.

A noted English hunter had just returned from a hunting tour in Bengal. These two men were invited to speak at a certain assembly. The large audience listened attentively to thrilling experiences of the hunter as he related the hairbreadth escapes in the jungles and told of the many Bengal tigers seen and killed. After he had finished his account of his hunting tour, he was asked to give a report of the missionary work as he had found it in India. He stated that in all his travels in Bengal he had not seen a native Christian and, further, that he did not believe there were any, but that there were plenty of tigers. He said that he had not seen a missionary on the field and that the missionaries were deceiving the people by their reports.

The missionary was stung to the heart. He knew that the people were almost ready to cast him down in derision because of the powerful influence this noted hunter had exerted over the audience. When he arose, trusting the Lord for wisdom that he might be able to convince his hearers of the real situation of missionary work in India, he kindly referred to the statements of the eminent hunter and said: "He has related his exciting experiences in tiger-hunting and has told you that tigers abound in that country. Why should I believe his word? Though I spent several years in Bengal, yet I never saw a tiger outside of a cage nor any one hunting tigers. He says he did not see a native Christian or a missionary on the field. I have seen hundreds of them, have lived among them, have taught them, and I am able to verify my statements. Shall I discredit the statements of the hunter because I saw no tigers? I was not looking for tigers; therefore I did not go to the jungles to find them. He was not looking for Christians and missionaries, and for that reason he did not go to the plains where they were to be found." The words of the missionary had the desired effect, and the cause that he represented was sustained.

It has often been said that the world is growing better and that the places of vice are few; but if the veil is drawn aside only enough to give a glimpse of the pitfalls of darkness and sin, one is made to stand aghast and lift the hands in horror. How little is known of the next-door neighbor! In our cities many people do not even know the names or the occupations of those living in the next room or in some other apartment of the same house. Oft-times dens of vice are almost at our door, and we know nothing of their existence until we are awakened by some sad occurrence that might have been avoided "had we known."

Many parents fear to inform their children of the evils of the world and of the dives and pitfalls of vice. This false modesty, or failure to impart knowledge, places children face to face with danger without their suspecting any harm.

There are gambling-dens, houses of ill-fame, and various other places of vice, where young and old are led astray. The "white slave traders" — those who decoy and sell girls and young women for such places—are ever on the alert.

The author of this book has spent years in trying to rescue girls from such a life, and "Fifteen Years with the Outcast" will undoubtedly do much to counteract the influence of these places of vice and infamy.

Fathers and mothers should place this volume in the hands of their children and should encourage them to become sufficiently informed concerning such things not only to protect themselves but also to warn others.

With a desire that the influence of this book may reach the highest anticipations of the author I am

Yours in Him,

E. E. Byrum.

INTRODUCTION

REPLYING TO YOUR QUESTION

"How did it happen that you became so deeply interested in rescue work, Mrs. Roberts?"

Hundreds of times has this question been asked of me in various parts of this State (California). In order, whenever time and place permitted, to answer intelligently, I have replied by relating the story of my conversion, through a vision, which occurred on the afternoon of Sunday, Sept. 13, 1896.

For some time prior to this, with my husband, J. H. Roberts, a mining man, also my son, an only child of fourteen, I had been living about two and one-half miles from Angels, Calaveras County, California.

For lack of means to carry on the development work of the mine which Mr. Roberts was at this time superintending, it closed. In order to increase finances in our hour of need, I gave piano lessons. My health, never in those days very robust, soon succumbed to the severe nervous strain to which it was now continually subjected.

THE VISION

On the never-to-be-forgotten date of my spiritual birth, whilst I was enjoying a much-needed rest and reading a novel, everything in the room seemed suddenly to be obliterated from my view; I became oblivious of my surroundings and was apparently floating in an endless vista of soft, beautiful, restful light.

I was quite conscious of rising to a sitting position, pressing my left elbow into the pillow, and with the right hand rubbing both eyes in an endeavor to see once more my natural surroundings. But no! Instead, suspended in this endless light, appeared a wonderful colossal cross of indescribable splendor. This wonderful cross can be likened only to a gigantic opal. Its rays of light seemed to penetrate me through and through as over my mind flashed the thought, "I must have died, and this is my soul!"

For one brief moment I closed my eyes, then opened them, and now, in addition to the vision of the cross, came an added one of such a glorious Being that words are utterly inadequate to describe him. No writer, be he ever so skilful, could give a satisfactory word-picture, and no artist, be he ever so spiritual, could possibly depict the wonderful majesty of our glorious, loving, royal Redeemer.

His left arm slowly raised. Presently his hand rested on the right arm of the cross. Then the wonderful eyes looked into mine. *That one compelling look drew me—forever—to him.* But that was not all. With the right hand he beckoned, reaching downward toward me, and I saw the sweet smiling lips move. Though no sound emanated from them, yet I knew they framed the one word "Come!" whilst the hand slowly, gracefully moved, pointing upward toward the cross. A ray of light revealed a healed wound extending the entire length of the palm. Soon this invitation was repeated, and so great became my desire to hide (because of my unworthiness) beneath the cross that I must at this time have slipped off the bed, for when once more conscious of my natural surroundings I discovered myself kneeling on the floor.

Then for the first time in my life I saw myself as I believe God sees. What a revelation of selfishness and carnality! What a realization of utter unworthiness! My righteousness was indeed and in truth no better than "filthy rags" (Isa. 64:6).

Could God, would God, forgive?

Mentally I decided that, had I been in his place, lavishing and bestowing innumerable and untold blessings day after day upon one so careless, so heedless of his wonderful love, I should find it very, very difficult, nay, impossible.

Oh, how I *now* longed, *now* yearned, to be different, as I caught the reflection of carnal nature in the spiritual looking-glass! With all my soul I implored mercy and pardon.

Suddenly thick darkness, indescribably thick, seemed to submerge me. I felt as though I were smothering. I tried to find my voice. Presently consciousness returned, and the room appeared as natural as ever. I was crying aloud, "Save me!" At the same time it seemed that something weighty was rolling up like a scroll off either side of me. I felt free, light as air, and from that moment began to experience the New Life, the True Life. *Oh, I was happy! So happy!*

One, only one, desire now had possession—that I might forever remain under this benign influence. Did ever the birds chirp so sweetly! Was ever parched nature or dried-up grass more beautiful! Oh, why did I have to come back to this world! But how selfish! Now came the longing to share my joy with others; I was eager to do so. Would my husband's visitor never go? Finally I heard him making his adieus. Bathing my face and smoothing my hair, I went forth to impart the glorious news to Mr. Roberts.

Well, he listened attentively, as with soul filled and thrilled with divine love, I endeavored to describe my wonderful vision.

"What do you think of it, dear?" I asked.

"I think you were dreaming," he replied.

"Oh, but not so! I heard you talking to Mr. Rouse from the time he came, though I was paying no attention to your conversation. How could I?" I inquired.

"Nevertheless, my dear, it was only a dream," he insisted.

Something (an inner voice hitherto unrecognized) suggested that I ask what he thought of it, even though it might be but a dream. He admitted that it was wonderful and beautiful. (Afterwards he told me that he would not have paid so much attention to my recital had it not been for the unusual light on my countenance. "You can't think how you looked," he said. "Your face shone like satin!")

THE AFTERMATH

Immediately following this God-given experience came the desire to "search the Scriptures" (John 5:39). I regret having to tell you that my Bible lay very near the bottom of a trunk and that the blessed volume had not been opened for a shamefully long time.

It took me, in my spare time, something like three months to read the book carefully from cover to cover. Not one word escaped me. I found it to be so interesting—at first as a matter of history—that I began it all over again. Thus it has been ever since; for to the Spirit-born child nothing will, nothing can, take the place of the Bible. It is always new, always refreshing. It is the voice of the tenderest, most loving of parents, ever ready to answer our questions, comforting when sorrowful, healing when sick, warning when in danger, ever directing, admonishing, and encouraging under any and all circumstances. "Oh!" but you say, "the chastening! You forget that." No, dear one, I do not. All wise parents chasten their offspring. Would to God they would lovingly, wisely administer more corrections than they do. The outcome, I verily believe, would be a wonderful foretaste of heaven on earth. But I find I am digressing.

Immediately following my conversion came the desire to impart the knowledge received, to my friends and neighbors. The result was that a report somewhat like the following was soon circulated: "Poor Mrs. Roberts!

Have you heard the news? Her husband's financial losses have affected her mind; she is going crazy. Thinks she had a vision!" etc. Then I began to realize what it means literally to "forsake all to follow Christ." Heavier troubles followed, but they did not affect me as heretofore. I had had the vision, and it had come to stay.

Illness presently brought me to the very threshold of eternity. With animation temporarily suspended, but my soul and brain never more keenly alive, I mentally implored the dear Lord to spare me for a little while, because I did not now want to come to him empty-handed. Oh! the longing to win souls, as I lay there helpless yet realizing what it might mean to be forever debarred from the things which God had prepared from the foundation of the world "for him that waiteth for Him" (Isa. 64:4). How eager I was to tell the news to any one, no matter to what depths he or she might have fallen! It was the immortal soul that I was now anxious to reach. Lying there, I made an absolute consecration, promising my heavenly Father that if he would restore me to health and strength, I would go to whatever place he thought fit to send me, and never hesitate to stoop to the lowliest for his sake and theirs.

RESTORATION

God takes us at our word. I wonder how many of us realize this?

Returning health and strength found me located with my family in Redding, Shasta County. Here my husband and I, in the spring of 1897, followed our Lord's example in baptism.

In Redding came many delightful opportunities to engage in church and personal work for the Master. While I was visiting in Sacramento in the fill of 1897 and attending revival meetings conducted in the First Baptist church, came my first real knowledge of the unfortunate of my sex.

Previous to this revival the Rev. Mr. Banks, now deceased, anxious for these special services to be well attended, asked for volunteers from his flock to distribute in every house in their immediate neighborhoods a printed invitation. Whoever undertook this work was to pledge themselves not to pass one house nor miss any opportunity for personal work. Not two blocks from the place where I was rooming was a district that I hitherto had never explored—in fact, had purposely avoided. God now gave me strength to take up this cross, for which may I be forever humbly grateful. But I shrank at first; for, unable to persuade any of my acquaintances to accompany me, I had to traverse this neighborhood alone. Did I say alone? Never did I experience a greater sense of guardianship, of protection, of being in the best of company, though these guardians and companions were visible only to the eye of faith (Psa. 91:10-12).

That day I saw tears fall, and heard experiences of which I had hitherto had scarcely any conception.

Touched by a loving hand, wakened by kindness, Chords that were broken will vibrate once more.

Soon after this the first little rescue home for girls in Sacramento was started by some consecrated young people. It was located on Second Street near O. I did not have the pleasure of attending the opening of this "shelter," because of a direct call to service about this time with some traveling evangelists. I assisted them by giving out the "good news" in song.

While I was traveling northward with these evangelists, there came into my possession, in answer to prayer, my treasured, God-given little autoharp, No. 1. My second was at one time the property of a now pardoned State prisoner—his companion in his lonely hours when locked in his cell.

"Where were your husband and your son all this time?" you inquire. The former was away prospecting—his favorite occupation. The latter, because of his love for the water and his desire to see other countries, was an employee on an ocean-steamer.

MY SPIRITUAL MOTHER

On Sept. 1, 1902, there passed into eternal rest one of the oldest members of the First Methodist Episcopal church of San Francisco, Mrs. Salemma Williams.

For more than twenty years this dear sainted friend, though I knew it not, daily prayed and believed for my conversion. Five years before she was made aware of the fact, her prayer had been answered. Her joy, when one day I called upon her to impart the welcome news, knew no bounds, and until she passed away we spent many happy days in each other's company. A few hours before she went home, she gave her children and me her parting blessings. The precious prayer of this dying saint as she held her aged hands on my head comforts, sustains, and encourages me now, even as it did then, and I believe that it ever will.

HER BLESSING

"Lord, I thank thee for answered prayer. Make this, thy child, wonderful for thee, Lord, wonderful for thee! for Jesus' sake. Amen." Though she spoke with great difficulty, yet every word was distinctly audible. About two hours later she sang (with me) the following lines as she passed into eternal rest:

> Oh! if there's only one song—I can sing
> When in his beauty I see the great King,
> This shall my song in eternity be:
> Oh, what a wonder that Jesus loves me!
> I am so glad that Jesus loves me!
> Jesus loves even me.

SUMMARY

Would that it were in my power to relate better, in "Fifteen Years with the Outcast," the few incidents of the many which have come under my personal observation. The real names of the principals of the stories are withheld, but not so the names of personal friends.

Dear readers, I am well aware that this book, judged from a literary point of view, would be regarded as a failure; but I make no pretensions as a writer, nor do I entertain any aspirations for literary fame. My sole object in endeavoring to present faithfully a few experiences of my brief years of service for the Master is to warn many who are in danger.

Interspersed between these covers are a few songs, the words of which, with scarcely an exception, were written in the night, and, for the most part, were culled from incidents of personal observation and experience. Much valuable assistance has been rendered by a dear friend in the transcribing and arranging of the music.

For those of my readers who do not yet know the dear Lord as their personal Savior and Redeemer, my sincere prayer is, May they while perusing these pages catch a glimpse of Him. May they, by faith, "wash and be made clean," determining, God helping, to shun forever all evil and evil companions. The sinful life never pays.

In order to make this book suitable for young people to read, much concerning rescue work has been withheld. Parents will readily understand why and will appreciate the omission. Doubtless they will have little if any trouble in reading between the lines. God grant them love and wisdom to interpret to their questioning boys and girls, and may countless blessings from the Shepherd of our souls attend all into whose hands this book may chance to come.

Yours, in precious service for Him,

(Mrs.) Florence Roberts.

P. S. Since the above was written, I had the occasion to visit one of our California State prisons (San Quentin). I went at the urgent request of a young man whom the officials recommended for parole. I had a portion of the manuscript of this book with me, which the captain of the guard, at my request, kindly allowed the young man and his cell-mates to read. In consequence, we are indebted to one of these dear boys (God bless him!) for some of the illustrations appearing in this book. Others have been contributed by a young brother and sister who are devoting their lives to God's service at the Gospel Trumpet office.

EXPLANATORY

This book was originally prepared for the press under the title, "The Autobiography of an Auto-harp." It was then written in verse and liberally interspersed with foot-notes. Upon more mature consideration and also upon the advice of one of much experience as a writer, I have rewritten the work and given it the title, "Fifteen Years with the Outcast."

Although the change necessitates a continuous repetition of the personal pronoun "I," a word whose avoidance was the primary object in writing under the original title, yet the new form is, I believe, much more interesting. Furthermore, time and experience have occasioned many needful additions.

For fifteen years "I have fought a good fight," though not so good as I would have desired, and although I am in the evening of life, I realize that I have not yet "finished my course." There is still much more for me to do in this sorrowful, sin-cursed world. God has, among other blessings, given me a strong physique. By his unmerited power I am keeping the faith, growing in grace and in the knowledge of our Lord and Savior Jesus Christ.

My greatest longing and ambition is some day to see Him whom my soul loveth, "face to face," especially to have the joy of bringing some priceless trophies to lay at His blessed feet.

Most sincerely yours,

Florence (Mother) Roberts.
Gospel Trumpet Company,
Anderson, Indiana.
September 27, 1911.

CHAPTER I
LITTLE ROSA—A WARNING TO MOTHERS AND GUARDIANS

What I am about to relate is my first experience in rescuing a girl and occurred not long after my conversion.

At this time my husband, my son, and I were living in Redding, Shasta Co., Cal. In the house that we were occupying lived another family also, the little four-year-old daughter of which was an especial pet of mine. While she was acting naughtily one day, thus hindering her mother with the household duties, I bribed her to be good, by promising to go down-town for some particularly nice candy made by a man who sold it every day at a certain street corner, displaying it on a tray suspended from his neck and always handling it with the whitest of cotton gloves. When I reached the place, he had not yet arrived. Desirous of not disappointing my little friend and having learned where the man lived—in a tent on a lot near by—I immediately repaired to the place designated. There I found a disreputable-looking middle-aged woman and a forlorn little girl about twelve years old. The girl was in tears.

Upon my inquiring what was the matter, the woman immediately berated the child in my presence. Turning to me, she said that this girl was one on whom they recently had taken pity, and had hired to do chores.

As there was but one tent, I questioned also as to sleeping accommodations. It contained a full-sized bed and one narrow cot, between which was suspended a thin calico curtain. The cooking, eating, etc., were done out of doors.

The poor little one continued to cry bitterly. With aching heart I laid my hand on her bowed head and bade her to be a good girl and try her best to please and obey her employers, then inquired of her whether she had ever attended Sunday-school or knew anything about Jesus. She did not reply. This caused the woman to accuse her of sulkiness, at which the girl looked up with swollen eyes, full of tears. Oh that look! It astonished and puzzled me at the time. Hatred? Yes, and despair, and misery, and yearning. There was a volume in that look, which I could not then interpret. Beyond words, it troubled me.

Silently praying, I went on my way. I had walked only a few yards toward home, when I heard the quick patter of bare feet behind me, and some one calling, "Lady! Lady!" Turning, I saw the little girl breathlessly trying to overtake me. Quickly she poured into my ears a horrible story of wrong, of indescribable wickedness perpetrated on her for the vile gratification of that man—so celebrated as a candy maker.

Soon I was in the presence of Judge Sweeney (now superintendent of the United States mint in San Francisco) relating the awful story of little Rosa. Immediately after my rehearsal the man and woman were arrested.

Previous to going to live with these people Rosa had made her home with a young married sister. The sister had a family of little children and was poor: so when an opportunity presented itself for an apparently good home for Rosa in exchange for light services, she quickly, gladly availed herself of it, without making the *very necessary inquiry* as to who this man and woman (strangers in Redding) were or whence they had come. Thus thoughtlessly did she relieve herself of a solemn responsibility, the dying request of their mother, who had passed away when Rosa was much younger.

A physical examination proved, beyond a doubt, the unfortunate child's condition, and the law proceeded to take its course. The sister was (temporarily) made responsible as Rosa's legal guardian. Here I quote from "The Morning Searchlight" the article headed:

A SENSATIONAL CASE

A little Girl Held Captive by G— — E— —.

A petition for a writ of habeas corpus was filed in the Superior Court Saturday by Mrs. M— — S— —. This is the process by which she hopes to obtain possession and care of her sister, Rosa L— —. The girl is but twelve years of age, her mother is dead, and she has been deserted by her father.

Somehow, she has become acquainted with G— — E— —, the street candy-vender, and has, of late, been living in his tent in the southeastern part of the city.

The petition further states: "That as your petitioner is informed and believes, and therefore alleges the fact to be, that said restraint of said minor by said E— — is for immoral purposes"

The hearing of the petition will take place before Judge Sweeney Monday morning. If the points alleged in the petition are true, E— — should be dealt with severely.

The trial was held behind closed doors. Poor little Rosa was too nervous and frightened to give her testimony with sufficient intelligence so that the law could deal with the couple as they deserved. Through some technicality they escaped legal punishment, and hurriedly stole out of Redding for parts unknown, fearing the vengeance of an insulted, righteously indignant community.

The child was soon under the kindly care of a consecrated Christian couple, and the last time we saw her she wore a smiling and happier countenance. This dreadful experience, however, permanently wrecked her health, so that she could be of but slight service to her new guardians; but they, through wise and loving treatment, through portrayal of Jesus in word as well as in deed, were doing all they could do for this little shorn lamb, doing their best to aid in helping to eliminate her awful past—a task by no means easy. Poor unfortunate, sinned-against little Rosa! Her life forever blighted through the shifting and shirking of responsibility on the part of the older sister, who had promised the dying mother to carefully guard and guide the little helpless girl. Poor ruined child! Shunned, whispered about and pointed at by her schoolmates, she, sensitive girl that she was, suffered so intensely from such treatment that it was deemed advisable to have her study, as best she could, at home. There she need not be subjected to the thoughtless torture of children, who, as children will, had undoubtedly listened to, and learned from, the conversations carelessly carried on in their presence by parents and other older people, this unfortunate little girl's cruel, heart-rending fate.

Did this experience affect my future career? It certainly did. Let me tell you. I firmly resolved, God helping, to live closer to the Master; to aid in rescuing the outcast at any cost; to see and love their souls, forgetting the sinning exterior; to help win them to Christ, then encourage and further their advancement; constantly to sit so low at the Savior's feet as to be ever able to discern and obey his still, small voice; to be sufficiently strong in body, soul, and spirit, as gladly to respond to his call at any and all times, whether that call should be in the highways or hedges, streets or lanes, among rich or poor, the prison boys or the outcast girls.

Earnestly I prayed, still I pray, for courage to address and warn parents and guardians of the pitfalls concerning which I have, in answer to prayer, increased knowledge, having been granted much practical experience, sharing many a sorrow with others, mingling my tears and sighs with many a parent, many a wanderer, and many an outcast, who have poured their troubles into my listening ears.

The one cry, ever and always, from both parent and child, has been, "*If I had only known*, I should have been less heedless, but now it's too late, too late! O God! forgive me for Christ's sake." Does the bird with the broken pinion ever soar as high again? Only through Christ, the precious Redeemer of souls, the Great Physician.

Are we to take warning from the fate of little Rosa—we to whom our heavenly Father has entrusted the care and keeping of his priceless jewels until he comes to claim his own? May the Lord help us to learn and love our lessons; to learn and love them well.

CHAPTER II
A VISIT TO SACRAMENTO—THE OUTCOME

At the time of the preceding experience I was the organist of Redding's Baptist church and also superintendent of its Sunday-school. Aside from this, there were my household duties—duties never to be neglected, as some erroneously think, because of drinking in the deep things of God. Also, there were now many outside calls to rescue or to warn poor, foolish boys and girls. The heart-aches now commenced in real earnest; for too many refused to heed, and in many cases the home environments were of such a nature as to prohibit even an ordinary moral tone, the unfortunate offspring being the victims of both pre-natal and post-natal conditions.

Business now demanded my husband's absence from home for some time. Taking advantage of the opportunity thus afforded, I, with my son, a youth aged fifteen, made a necessary visit to Sacramento. Here, in the First Baptist church, I taught a class of young men in their teens. Soon after my coming, a revival in the First M. E. church, which I constantly attended, brought me great blessing from the Lord. This revival was followed by a similar one at the First Baptist church.

In order to insure the success of the latter meeting Rev. A. B. Banks, the pastor, now deceased, a most eloquent and lovable man, whom we delighted in calling "Father" Banks, announced the necessity of distributing handbills and asked for volunteers to place one in every home in the districts in which they lived, and also, wherever possible, to give a verbal invitation. It so happened that the district in which my son and I lodged contained the resorts of the wandering girls. Some of these places were less than two blocks away.

NO ONE VOLUNTEERED FOR THIS LOCALITY

There was a prolonged pause, a painful pause. I felt as though every eye were upon me, and I experienced a sharp struggle; but hallelujah! the next moment the Lord had the victory—and my hand went up. Father Banks fervently said, "God bless you for this, my little sister! and he will."

You may be sure I did not want to go alone. I invited several to keep me company; I prayed the greater part of that Sunday night; I visited several

Christians on Monday morning, stating to them that I had never been in such a quarter, and was timid. "They all with one accord began to make excuse." Luke 14:18.

Oh, how I prayed for grace and strength! As I traversed that district, believe me, I felt almost the visible presence of angels, and was soon giving God's message of tender love to inmate after inmate of those awful dens.

How did they accept, you ask? Many with tears coursing down their cheeks. Very few but manifested some feeling. Scarcely any, however, promised to come out to the revival services. Nearly all declared that they did not believe they would receive kind treatment if they did come, and none of them wanted to be looked upon or treated as an outcast. One girl allowed me to come in and pray for her. Later on she was most wonderfully saved and sanctified in the rescue home of which I shall now speak.

Yes, a rescue home for girls was about to be opened and established in answer to the prayers of many, especially some of the dear Christian workers of the "Peniel" Mission situated on K. near Fourth Street. Some of these I had become acquainted with since the revival meetings commenced. I learned that Mrs. Glide, a consecrated lady of much means, had guaranteed the payment of a year's rent on a ten-roomed cottage on Second and O. Streets.

Desirous of seeing this home for myself and of assisting, if requisite, I soon wended my way to the locality named.

The building was old and rather dilapidated, and as yet it contained but one piece of furniture, a cheap washstand bureau. Some of the young men were putting new panes of glass into the windows, others were papering the walls with odds and ends, which had been donated. Sister Jennie Cloninger was busy scraping an old bathtub with a piece of glass, preparatory to painting it, and Sister Eva Shearer had her dress tucked up whilst mopping one of the floors. Every one was busy and happy in the Lord's service.

"Sister Shearer dear, what can I do to help this blessed work?" I inquired.

"Sister Roberts, that washstand is all the furniture we have. Please go in the name of Jesus and ask for donations," she replied.

Prayerfully I started on my errand, and soon had many promises from hotel proprietors and others.

Shortly after this my son, having an ambition to see more of the world, grew restless. All effort on my part failed to keep him near me. I simply commended him to the One who has promised that if we are faithful "our righteousness shall be for our children," and comforted myself with this promise as I sorrowfully bade him farewell and returned to my lonely lodgings. Did I say lonely? I made a mistake. To be sure, I greatly missed my boy, but he was in our Father's keeping, and I was dwelling in "the secret of his presence" who doeth all things well.

Soon afterward I returned to my home in Redding, taking the journey as a singing evangelist with Mr. and Mrs. C. E. Thurston, an elderly couple then in undenominational gospel-wagon work. It was on this trip that, in answer to repeated prayer, I acquired my first autoharp, which I shall frequently mention in connection with my work. "How did I come by it?" I will tell you in the next chapter.

CHAPTER III
MY FIRST AUTOHARP—I FORSAKE
ALL TO FOLLOW JESUS

There it lay, all covered with dust, in that auctioneer's window in Chico. We had just arrived from Sheridan, Sutter County, where we had conducted a successful series of meetings.

In the latter place we had been able to borrow a small organ, and I had a splendid choir of little children, who crowded our commodious wagon an hour each evening before service, that time being devoted to serenading the neighborhood with gospel song. There I saw the drunkard and the saloon-keeper yield to the blessed influence of the singing by these sweet, innocent little children of songs such as "Wash me in the blood of the Lamb, and I shall be whiter than snow." But the time soon came when we must part with the little organ as well as with the dear children.

How I longed and prayed for an autoharp! At this time my pocket-book was well-nigh empty, my husband having met with total loss in mining enterprises. I possessed exactly $2.50 on the day when we reached Chico.

As I looked in that auctioneer's window, somehow I felt that that humble, little three-barred autoharp was to be mine. I stepped in, priced it, and presently told the proprietor what use was to be made of it. He had at the first asked $5.00; now he offered it, *for such a cause*, at half price. Hallelujah! How gladly I parted with my last cent and joyfully walked out with my precious little musical instrument, destined to go with me on my visits to comfort and help save the lost. I will tell you of my present one later on.

Leaving Chico that afternoon, we camped in the evening under some beautiful live-oak trees, beside a clear, running creek. This was in Tehama, Tehama County. There, before retiring, and following our family devotions, I dedicated my little instrument to the Lord's work, praying as I did so that he would use it absolutely, together with me and my voice, in helping to win precious souls for his kingdom.

Soon afterwards I was once more in my Redding home and resuming my former avocations in the church and Sunday-school. But what had come over me? what had wrought such a change? For, strange to say, I was no longer satisfied with simply the church work. I spent evening after evening and all spare time in the humble little mission down-town or amongst the outcasts, though never neglecting my home.

My husband, always a reserved, proud man, one day gave me an unexpected shock. Without forewarning he quietly, coldly informed me that I must decide between the rescue work and him.

"Do you mean it?" I inquired.

"I certainly do," was his reply.

Oh, how I agonized with my Lord in prayer as soon as I could have the privilege! Then I opened his Word for comfort, and my answer was, "Ye are bought with a price; be not ye the servants of men." 1 Cor. 7:23. What did this mean? I was too young a child of the King to comprehend, and therefore could only wait and pray. So troubled at heart was I at my husband's pride and growing coldness that I at last visited the pastor of the church where my name was enrolled. He tried to persuade me to refrain from any but church work, and also did his utmost to effect a reconciliation between my husband and me, but all to no effect. Mr. Roberts refused to listen, and the breach widened. I seldom crossed my threshold those days, yet yearned to be out in God's field. Circumstances, which it is neither pleasant nor profitable to relate here, soon necessitated the breaking up of my home. I was looking to God for guidance. I did not have to wait long, for a door was soon opened. A letter from Sister Belle Trefren, of Sacramento, with whom I had much correspondence, especially relative to the rescue home already referred to, now for several months occupied, informed me of the severe illness of its matron.

"Is it not strange," she wrote, "that in all this great city none come to her aid excepting for a few hours at a time? If help does not arrive soon, I fear she will die. Why could not you spend a while with her, and thus relieve her of this very heavy burden until she is sufficiently recovered to take her accustomed place again? Besides, dear Sister Roberts, I have long felt that the Lord wants you to cut loose from the shore-lines and 'launch out into the deep,' where are to be found the biggest, best fish. Pray over this, as I am now doing, and the light will surely come to you."

I prayed, and the light came quickly. I wrote Sister Trefren that I might soon be looked for in Sacramento, and that I was simply waiting on the Lord.

I soon resigned my church office, and early one bright, beautiful morning I bade farewell to Redding. Just before the train drew out of the depot, I opened my Bible. My eyes were focused on these words (many friends had gathered to bid me Godspeed): "And let us not be weary in well-doing; for in due season we shall reap, if we faint not." Gal. 6:9. I stood on the rear platform of the train, holding up the open Bible, and soon Redding and friends disappeared from my vision. I was indeed and in truth now alone with my Lord and on the road to the little rescue home in Sacramento, with my precious autoharp lying by my side.

In the afternoon, as time seemingly dragged and many passengers showed signs of weariness, I picked up the little instrument. Soon from one end to the other of the car different ones sang with me familiar song after song of Zion. The journey ended joyously, some being strengthened in their faith on that trip, and more than one acquaintance being made which later ripened into warm Christian friendship. Praise the Lord!

CHAPTER IV
I AM INTRODUCED TO THE RESCUE
HOME FAMILY—A GLORIOUS TEST

My cherished friend, Sister Trefren was at the depot to greet me, and I spent that first night under her roof. Early in the morning came a message from the home, requesting that, if I felt sufficiently rested, to come to them as speedily as possible.

She was a beautiful girl—I mean the one who responded to my ringing of the door-bell. Oh, how she surveyed me (though not rudely) from head to foot! We shall hear Leila's story in another chapter. Soon I was at the bedside of the sick matron, who, though hardly able to speak, greeted me lovingly and tearfully. In a few minutes a trusted girl was given some directions, and then I was invited into the sitting-room. There were assembled all the inmates of the home, and I was soon warmly greeting, first collectively and later individually.

"My, what an opportunity to study character!" I said to myself as I observed the twenty-four faces into which I had a bare glimpse. I presently asked them if they would please kneel and pray with me and for me, and soon I found myself, for the first time, listening to the humble, earnest petitions of these precious jewels in the rough.

Brokenly and tearfully, they thanked God for rescuing them from lives of sin, shame, and despair; for providing so good a home, food, and shelter (it was all very modest and humble). Some praised Him for sanctification as well as salvation. (Perhaps my reader does not know the interpretation of that word, "sanctification." Briefly, it refers to a second blessing, following justification, or the forgiveness of sins; a second work of grace, whereby the nature becomes purified and kept free from sin by the operation and power of God's Holy Spirit—now the indwelling presence.) Then how fervent were the prayers for the healing of the sick matron! and now, "O God, please bless Mrs. Roberts for coming to her aid and ours," ending by thanking him for answering their earnest appeal for help in their time of great need.

I forgot all my own heartaches as I drank in and indorsed every word, and then, with all my being, offered the closing prayer. Soon the trials and testings commenced in real earnest.

In such a place it does not require many days, nay, many hours, to discover the subtlety of the enemy of souls. For some time my nerves, never too strong, were so wrought upon that I was under a constant strain, and more than once, fearing a breakdown, felt that I should be compelled to relinquish my arduous duties.

In answer to prayer, our Father, ever mindful of his own, strengthened me and bestowed the necessary knowledge and wisdom, so that I was soon able to cope with the situation, which was this: None of these precious ones had long been established; some were not yet saved. Cravings, in one form or another, for the old life, perhaps a thirst for liquor, would at times secretly take possession of one or another, and frequently some saved girl would come to me, saying, "Sister Roberts, Mamie [or some other] has gone out without permission." Then I would quickly telephone to police headquarters to be on the lookout for her and to have her privately detained until some one from the home could come. Often we were compelled to tell the erring one that the law would have to take its course if she rebelled or refused. Sometimes such a one would almost hate us because she did not comprehend how much we had the interest of both body and soul at heart.

Ah! reader, do you realize what it means to "stand still" in the trying hours? to watch our Father's Spirit working in the lives and natures of the outcast? Truly it is marvelous, marvelous! Soon I will relate the story of one of our family, but before I do so, permit me to give you my first Sunday's experience. I think it will be interesting.

I arrived at the home on Tuesday. On Friday morning, Sister B— —, the sick matron, said as I stood by her bedside: "Sister Roberts, all our family of girls whose health will permit are in the habit of attending Sunday morning worship in one of the churches; in the afternoon, those who wish, attend the mission; and in the evening we have prayer-service at home. I shall not, as you know, be able to go with them for some time to come. That duty devolves upon you, dear, for the present." Imagine, if you can, my feelings. "Sister, I fail to see that the Lord requires any such sacrifice on my part," I impulsively replied. "I think it sufficient to work with and for them *here* in the home. What would my former society friends say or think should any chance to meet me with them?" And the tears of (righteous?) indignation filled my eyes. "My dear," she gently replied, "take a little time in your room alone with God. He will make it clear, what he would have you to do."

Soon I was locked in, where I sat for a few moments on the side of my little bed, as rebellious and indignant as ever I was in all my life.

When I grew somewhat calmer, I fell upon my knees and sobbed out my troubles at the foot of the cross. Painfully, I at last submitted, *provided it was the will of God*; and in my prayer I requested *"Should such be thy will,* please see that none of my friends of social standing chance to cross my pathway on this occasion." Then I arose from my knees.

Sunday morning found thirteen girls neatly clad and all impatiently waiting for my appearance. Never in all my lifetime did I start on a trip more fearfully or timidly. We had not traveled half a block when, on turning a corner, I saw a family whom my family and I held in high estimation. We both received a never-to-be-forgotten shock. I was greeted with a surprised bow of interrogation from the wife, whilst the husband very slightly raised his hat. My girls behaved beautifully, little dreaming the state of my feelings.

Old Adam dies very hard sometimes, doesn't he? I soon met others and still others. Never did I so long for even a knot-hole into which to crawl, but no such place presented itself. Precious Lord, thou knewest what was for my best interest when thou didst in thine infinite love and wisdom thus answer such a selfish prayer.

The next chapter will introduce you to the naughtiest girl in the home.

CHAPTER V
A CRUSHING SITUATION—WONDERFUL VISION—THE STORY OF RITA

We had not been very long in the second-from-the-front pew of the First Baptist church, when Rita, who, at the private suggestion of the matron, I had placed next to me, began to embarrass and disconcert me by her actions, causing the rest of the girls to titter (sometimes audibly) and thus to attract the congregation, also the pastor, so that finally an usher had occasion to whisper to me, admonishing me to retire with her, to which she replied, "I ain't agoing out."

Mortified beyond measure, I let my head sink forward on the back of the pew in front of me. I soon became oblivious of my surroundings, for *I was being blest with a wonderful vision.*

I saw the Garden of Gethsemane. It was night, and sleeping souls lay all around. One there was who was not sleeping. He was prostrate in agony of prayer. As he wrung his hands, the blood started through his pores, and dripped down upon the ground. Then a light shone around him, a glorious light. Presently he arose, and the place filled suddenly with soldiers who led him away, shouting in triumph as they did so. Quickly the scene changed. Christ was now before the high priests. Again the scene changed. He was passing by a man who was strenuously, indignantly denying that he knew or had had anything to do with the man under arrest. Oh! would that words of mine could picture the suffering, sorrowful countenance, as Jesus gave poor Peter that parting, yearning look. Pilate's hall was soon in sight, and the men in charge of Jesus were mocking and smiting him. It was cold, and scarcely dawn of day. What a throng, as they crowded into the presence of Pilate.

Again the scene changes. The Christ is being mockingly arrayed in a once gorgeous, now old, shabby robe. Soon he is wearily pulled and pushed back to Pilate's hall, where they strip the Son of God in the presence of that howling mob, and beat him, until the blood streams down his poor, lacerated back. Surely that is sufficient; but no! they spit in his face. They press a cruel crown hard down upon his brow. Now Pilate has washed his hands, and the Savior of the world is led away. The soldiers are compelling him to bear some heavy wooden beams in the form of a cross. Oh! can't they see that he is too weak, suffering too much, to be able to carry such a weight? They do not care; but look! he has fainted! Some one is helping him now. God forever bless him! 'Tis Simon the Cyrenean who enjoys that precious privilege. Simon, the cross-bearer.

I can not bear to witness any more. But I must. I must watch to the end.

Oh! the awful thud, *thud*, THUD, as they hammer the spikes, the cruel spikes into his hands and feet, and he never once cringes. How can he be so courageous?

I am looking up at him now, and he is looking down with such an uninterpretable look *on me*, and I hear him faintly say: *"For you."*

"Yes, Lord, I know."

"And now won't you try to love my poor shorn little lambs? 'Tis for them also."

"Yes, dear Lord, I am trying to."

"Would you be willing to lay down your life for little Rita, for the sake of her soul?"

"Blessed Savior, surely that will not be required, but fill me full of love, a great love for her soul and other souls. I promise that with thy help I will do my best, for oh, how I love thee now! how I love thee! and I will do anything thou dost require to prove my love."

Some one is pulling my sleeve. I turn my head to find Rita leaning against me and quietly whispering, "Mother, don't cry; I'll be good. Don't cry."

From that time on the change in Rita was unmistakable, and although she had many hard battles to fight, to lose, and to win, she came out gloriously victorious.

"Who was Rita?" I'll tell you.

Rita was a roguish, fun-loving, childish little woman, twenty-one years old, who neither acted nor looked her age. Her mother had been a waitress in one of the dives of a locality called "The Barbary Coast," San Francisco, where are many low, vile haunts of vice. Her father, she never knew. She was very dark, apparently part Spanish, quite attractive, and rather pretty.

Some time prior to my advent she was brought to the home in a semi-intoxicated condition by one of the Lord's consecrated missionaries. Full of mischief and depravity, she was, from the first, a trouble-maker. From her earliest recollection, her companions had all been of the type with whom her mother associated; therefore it would take time, great and loving patience, and a constant waiting on the Master for her to harmonize perfectly with new environments.

This poor girl had seen no other life, up to within a few weeks of my meeting her, than a life replete with vice from one day's ending to another. Much of the time she had participated. But be it recorded to the credit of her mother that, to the extent of her knowledge, she had guarded her girl from criminal assault as long as she was able to control her, and that, when told of Rita's being in the rescue home, she seemed greatly pleased that at last her daughter had found friends who would do their utmost to help her lead a better life.

Rita had an uncontrollable temper, in consequence of which the entire household was sometimes made to suffer keenly; but she would eventually yield to earnest persuasion, then kneel down and ask forgiveness of God and the family. She was very ambitious to learn to read, being entirely devoid of education. Different members would take it in turn to teach her, and it was a proud day when she could decipher a few words in her Bible. I never shall forget the evening of her first realization of the price Jesus had paid for her. It dawned upon her soul so suddenly, so beautifully, following a mid-week prayer-meeting, in which some of the Christians interested in this work often participated, that a great shout of joy went up, and when we retired that night, some of us were too grateful and too excited to sleep. Oh, how the adversary attacked and tried over and over again to get her back to his territory! He once so well succeeded that we finally deemed it necessary to exchange her into another home. I was the one deputized to take her there, and very soon was introducing myself to Mrs. Elizabeth Kauffman, whose noble work for the erring, in San Francisco and other places, is known to the thousands. After placing Rita under her kind care in the rescue home, then situated on Capp Street near Twenty-first Street, in San Francisco, I returned to my post of duty in Sacramento, little dreaming at that time what an important place I was destined, in the future, to occupy with Sister Kauffman.

Erelong I learned, through correspondence, that my little Rita (who, by the way, was the first one outside of my own family to give me the endearing title of "Mother," which title has clung to me ever since) had found a warm friend in a deaconess whose name I have forgotten, but who took a loving interest in her and greatly aided her, especially from the spiritual point of view.

Rita, with the approval of her guardians, married a Christian young man. Together they are bringing up their little ones to know and love the

Savior so precious to them; and, through the daughter's example the mother, so long a wanderer in paths of degradation, was, I have understood, finding purity and peace for her soul. At the time of the earthquake and great fire in San Francisco, Rita and her loved ones, I am told, escaped without so much as the loss of a dish. This remarkable fact proves that God is ever mindful of those who put their entire trust in him and who live as does this precious jewel and her family, on the promises of the ninety first Psalm.

CHAPTER VI
MY FIRST CALL TO THE PRISON WORK

After I had been in the Sacramento home about a month, the matron became sufficiently recovered to go into the country in order to recuperate. In the meanwhile the dear Lord had laid it upon the hearts of two consecrated workers to assist me, so that I was now occasionally free for some outside work. Taking advantage of this, a lady who had been a constant attendant at the jail services for many years, urged me to come on the following Sunday afternoon with my little autoharp. This, by the way, was an every-day friend in our family, for most of our girls could sing, and we were soon learning many beautiful hymns, with either my modest instrument or the parlor organ for an accompaniment. When something would go wrong, the matter would be laid before the Lord in prayer, and singing was the next thing in order. How you would have appreciated and enjoyed hearing our family joining in with all their hearts—

I must tell Jesus all of my trials,
I can not bear these burdens alone;
In my distress he kindly will help me,
He ever loves and cares for his own.

They would repeat it over and over until sweet peace filled their souls once more.

But to return to the invitation to the county jail. I begged to be excused on the ground of sensitiveness. I felt that I could not bear to look upon any more distress than I was a daily witness to outside of prison walls. To see human beings caged up like so many wild animals I thought would be more than I could bear; therefore I unhesitatingly said so. She continued her pleadings, adding, "O Sister Roberts, you will never know how much good you could accomplish or how much precious seed might be sown if you would only come with that little autoharp of yours." But I was unyielding. She left me with sorrow on her countenance.

This refusal was followed by deep condemnation—condemnation which lasted a whole week. When, at last, I promised the Lord I would take up this cross and go if once more invited, the burden lifted.

About two o'clock the next Sunday afternoon I found myself, with a band of about twenty workers, behind iron bars, looking into the faces of nearly two hundred men and boys and a few women. Oh! but the tears flowed from my eyes, especially for the boys, many of whom were so young, as I wondered what would be the outcome of their present association and environment. It seemed awful! awful! I sang song after song; then I was invited to speak. My heart was too full for many words, but when the invitation was given to seek our Savior, many hands went up for special prayer. The meeting soon closed. Then as those terrible but necessary iron doors again unlocked and the prisoners filed past us one by one to their lonely, cheerless quarters, I made up my mind to come whenever I could, and, whenever permitted, to do and say what I could to help he "whosoever wills," also to use my influence in certain quarters for the betterment of the children prisoners, not one of whom but doubtless had been cheated out of his birthright by untutored, ofttimes wilfully ignorant parents or guardians.

Let me call your attention to one of the women prisoners, whose peculiarly repulsive countenance was so remarkable that when we came away from the jail I interrogated one of the workers concerning her. To my amazement, I was informed that the woman (Nell) was regarded as a hopeless case, and also that she had enjoyed musical educational advantages, her people having sent her to Paris to complete certain accomplishments. There, in that wicked capital, she became very gay, soon acquired the absinth habit, and rapidly descended in the social scale, and now she was scarcely ever out of prison. It was very difficult to realize that this poor soul, who now was never known to use any but vile language and oaths, was once a beautiful young woman, a linguist, pianist, singer, also otherwise accomplished person. Though all efforts (there had been many) in her behalf had proved futile, I determined to make an attempt to save her. Accordingly I paid a special visit to the women's quarters. So far as she was concerned, it was all to no purpose; but oh! praise the dear Lord! I found others who would heed, and I had a blessed time of Bible reading, song, and prayer with them.

One of these was a young girl, Anita, who had been arrested at the request of her mother—yes, her own mother. "Why, what kind of unnatural mother could she have been?" you ask. Not different from many others with whom I have been brought in contact. The daughter implored me to call on her mother and beg her not to consent to her being sent to the reform school, the girl solemnly promising good behavior in the future. How she clung to me as I tried to picture the merciful, loving Savior. We knelt in prayer in her lonely, dismal cell, where she followed me in a petition for God to save her soul and show her the way. Anita appeared to be about seventeen years old; but her mother with whom a few hours later I had an interview, and a most distressing one, I assure you, told me that the girl was but fourteen, that she had been so petted and spoilt from her babyhood up (parents and others, please take note of this) as to be absolutely unmanageable, that she was out at all hours of the night, in all sorts of places, with all sorts of company.

The mother appeared to regard herself as a very much wronged, greatly abused parent, and when I gently but firmly endeavored to place the blame where it belonged, she all but ordered me out of her house. Her conduct led me to the conclusion that her daughter would be better off in the place to which she was about to be sent than under the jurisdiction of such a parent.

Sad at heart, I returned to poor expectant Anita, remaining some time to comfort her as best I knew how and promising to write to her and, God willing, to visit her in her new home. The first promise was soon fulfilled, and about one year later I had the pleasure of personally hearing her expressions of gratitude. The discipline had been most beneficial, and, besides, she was learning to be a good cook and housekeeper—something that could never have happened in her mother's home. A few years later, while I was holding a meeting in one of the local churches, many came forward at the close to greet me. Among them was a fine-looking young woman with a pretty baby in her arms. "Don't you remember me, Mother Roberts?" she said. "I'm Anita." Soon she was telling me of her marriage to a young farmer about eighteen months previously. The next morning she came in her buggy to take me to enjoy a few hours in her cozy home.

CHAPTER VII
LEILA

Leila was that beautiful girl, the first to welcome me as I crossed the threshold of the home. She was a rather reserved, high-strung, aristocratic-looking girl, who did not always take kindly to requests made with regard to little household duties required from each member of the family, health permitting, of course.

One day shortly after my advent in the home I had occasion to reprimand her. She turned on me with such language and so evil, so distressing an expression as to shock and grieve me terribly. Presently the dear Lord gained a glorious victory. I hunted her up; for, in her anger, she had gone into hiding, and, putting my arms about her, lovingly implored her to forgive, as I had not intended to offend or in any way remind her of her dreadful past. From that time on we were great friends. Before long she confided to me her troubles, past and present.

Her people were poor and proud, and she did not take kindly to her environments either at home or at school, and did not go quite through the grammar grades. Her mother, from whom she inherited her temper, frequently quarreled with her and also disparaged her. At the age of fifteen, partly because of her restlessness and partly because of her desire to earn money, for she would no longer go to school, she, being quite a tall, well-developed girl, procured a situation as waitress in a wealthy family near her home in the city of San Francisco. She was a Catholic. Because of her duties, she attended early mass. One Sunday morning, whilst she was returning from church, her prayer-book accidentally slipped out of her hand. Upon stooping to pick it up, she discovered that she was forestalled by a well-dressed gentleman (?), who handed it to her with an admiring look and most respectful bow. Raising his hat, he politely passed on.

As Leila never expected to see him again, imagine her astonishment at meeting him the following Sunday, when again, with a glance of recognition, which flattered this poor victim, he most respectfully raised his hat. The third Sunday the same thing occurred again, but now instead of passing by, he politely accosted her with words to this effect: "Good morning, young lady. I trust you will please pardon the great liberty I am taking. I never more earnestly wished to know of some one to introduce me, but because

I do not, will you not kindly take the will for the deed, waive all formality, and permit me the honor of walking at least a portion of your way with you? *I am a gentleman with whom you need not for a moment hesitate to be seen;* and now, may I have the pleasure of learning your name? Mine is Claude Forrester."

Poor innocent, ignorant, flattered Leila began blushingly to confide to this villain her true name, her occupation, and much concerning her home life. As they neared her employer's residence, they parted, she promising to meet him for a walk one evening during the week. Her heart fluttered with joy, her silly head was completely turned at having captured so fine an admirer, and she could hardly wait for the time to come when she was to enjoy that promenade.

You may be sure he was on hand at the designated corner. Leila, in order to keep the appointment, resorted to falsehood. She asked permission of her mistress to be allowed to go home for some trivial article, promising to return by a given time. She kept her word as to the time, but the leaven of the adversary was rapidly working. He led her to believe that he was the son of a wealthy widow who expected him to make "a good match," but that he was in the habit of gaining his point with this indulgent parent whenever he so desired. He intended, he said, to confess to his mother that he had fallen in love with the most beautiful, innocent, and virtuous girl in all the wide world, and to tell her that he should never be happy again unless she would see Leila and eventually consent to her becoming his dear little wife. He told the confiding girl that he intended to lavish on her all his wealth. He pictured the beautiful garments that she was to wear, the jewels, the carriage, the home. He promised also to give her private lessons in order to fit her for her position as his wife. Poor, poor little girl! Who does not pity this worse than motherless child?

How distasteful her position now appeared, and how she longed for Sunday morning when she again would see her grand, wealthy sweetheart! When they met, he informed her that his mother would like to meet her, requested her to look her prettiest on the following Tuesday evening, and to be at the appointed street corner, and said that he would take her to his home and introduce her to the one now so desirous of making the acquaintance of the girl with whom he had fallen so desperately in love.

Alas, poor Leila! By another falsehood she procured permission to go out. She was ushered into a fine-looking room in a house on Mason Street, and soon a grandly dressed lady, young looking to be this villain's mother, greeted her very cordially, asked many questions, and then rang for refreshments, which a Chinaman servant soon carried in on a tray—and *when Leila next awoke it was broad daylight.* What was she doing in this strange room?

It wasn't long before she succumbed to all the vices and evil influences governing the life she was now destined and even resigned to lead.

About a year later, when she was no longer of value to her betrayers, when she was an outcast whom no one wanted—no one but her Savior and some of the consecrated children of God—at this time she was sitting on a table in a "Ladies' entrance" department of a saloon. There one of God's rescue missionaries so lovingly approached her that Leila, longing to get away from San Francisco for fear of being recognized by her mother and friends, was easily induced to come to the home, where she had lived for several months when I first met her.

The time came when she gave her heart to her Savior and then followed his example in baptism. It was one of the sweetest experiences of my Christian life to help prepare her and some others that evening for this beautiful, sacred ceremony. What a happy, happy family returned to our home and retired to our rest an hour later!

But alas! some acquaintance discovered Leila's whereabouts and conveyed the information to her mother. One day, on coming home from some errand of mercy, I was informed by the matron, now sufficiently recovered to be with us once more, that she had a surprise for me, and she asked me to guess. My first guess was, "My darling boy has come back to me."

"No; guess again."

"Then it must be my husband."

"No; I am going to tell you. Listen! Do you hear that loud weeping in the parlor?"

"Yes."

"It's Leila's mother. She is in a fearful state because her daughter is an inmate of a rescue home. Come in and help me to try to pacify her."

It was a difficult task, but on our promising to bring her daughter in if she would be calm, an effort on her part soon proved successful. Soon mother and daughter were alone. In about fifteen minutes Leila called us, and in our presence the mother promised that, if we would only let her dear child return with her to her own home, *under no circumstances would she ever remind her of the past* and also would make her life pleasanter for her in the future. It was impossible to refuse. Leila, with tears and prayers, soon bade farewell to us all.

I would that I might record that in the future it was well with her and her soul, but alas! I can not. One day her mother, because of some trivial offense, forgot her solemn promise. Poor Leila flew into a rage and, without even waiting for her hat, rushed out of the house never to return, and once more the enemy had her back in his territory. Long but vainly did we search for her until she was so far gone that she coldly refused all God's and our overtures of mercy, and no language of mine could describe her awful physical condition. She was only nineteen, but an utter wreck, morally as well as otherwise. Her own mother would not now have been able to recognize her.

We find no occasion to moralize in closing this story. We know that your tears will fall and that your heart will ache, but oh! be warned, and warn others. Full well do we who are rescue workers know there are *thousands of cases today parallel with this one.*

CHAPTER VIII
I BID FAREWELL TO THE SACRAMENTO HOME

God's "still, small voice" bidding me to prepare for other fields of labor came very definitely soon after his Spirit gave me the song entitled "The Messengers," a song which has proven of great value, especially in the prison work. I informed the matron, who insisted upon it that I was mistaken and deliberately laying down my cross, but I knew better; for God's Word makes no mistakes, and the Spirit always agrees with that Word, which now told me what I must soon prepare for, saying, "Go out quickly into the streets and lanes of the city and bring in hither the poor and the maim, the halt and the blind." Luke 14:21. It was most difficult to cut loose from these dear ones, but "to obey is better than sacrifice." 1 Sam. 15:22.

Requiring a rest, I took lodging in my former quarters, where, on first coming to Sacramento, my son and I resided, and there quietly waited on the Lord; for my having received no monetary compensation whatsoever from any one placed me in a most blessed position of faith and trust, which our Father did not long permit to go unrewarded. I told nobody of my needs, but simply asked God for the things needful, which he sent through his children. Soon I was supplied with remunerative work sufficient for my immediate requirements, and, as did Paul of old, I "labored with mine own hands because I would not be chargeable unto the brethren."

During those few days I was a regular attendant each evening at the Peniel Mission, already mentioned, and there once more met Brother and Sister Thurston, who, as you will recall, were using a gospel-wagon. They were now about to respond to a call from Woodland, Yolo County, to open a mission. Again I was invited to join them. Feeling led of the Lord, I accepted, and soon we were in our new field of labor.

THE MESSENGERS

(The Doves.)

Words and Music by Mrs. FLORENCE ROBERTS.

> The messengers tap on the windows.
> The windows of the soul.
> They carry this news from our Savior,

"I died that ye might be made whole."
"I died that ye might be made whole,
I died that ye might be made whole."

The messengers tap on the windows.
And beat their wings on the bars;
They carry the news to the sinner,
"You can become bright as the stars."
"You can become bright as the stars.
You can become bright as the stars."

The messengers tap on the windows.
Three times they come and they go;
Jesus saith, "Tho' your sins be as scarlet.
Trust me. I will make them like snow."
"Trust me. I will make them like snow.
Trust me, I will make them like snow."

The messengers tap on the windows;
Behold, I freely forgive
Whoso-ever will come, let him do so,
Partake of salvation and live.
"Partake of salvation and live.
Partake of salvation and live."

The messengers tap on the windows;
Sweet peace from our Savior they bring;
Sweet peace which is past understanding,—
The windows now open. Come in.
The windows now open. Come in.
The windows now open. Come in.]

It was very precious, very blessed. Erelong, however, my companions in the work received a call to other places, whilst I received a definite call to remain. That first evening alone on the rostrum—shall I ever forget it? All day I had been praying (not always on my knees) for a text for *my first public message* or sermon, but not one could I settle on. Whilst the audience was gathering, we sang many hymns. This was followed by a few voluntary prayers; then came the embarrassing moment. I was compelled to inform the congregation—and it was a large one—of my predicament, and besought them to kneel again with me in brief supplication for a text. "Praise God from whom all blessings flow!" my Bible fell open, my eyes riveted on these words: "And immediately the angel of the Lord smote him because he gave not God the glory, and he was eaten of worms and gave up the ghost." Acts 12:23.

Positively the message came from the Lord. As I spoke I was as though in a trance. The altar filled with seekers, and souls stepped into that precious fountain still open in the house of David. How happy I was! To God be all the credit, all the glory.

Amongst the seekers was one who presently told me that for *forty-one years he had been a drunkard.* He certainly looked as if he had—poor, bloated, filthy, loathsome, ill-smelling creature. I can not find adjectives enough to describe him. Everybody avoided him. It surely was a testing time for me. Also, I had trying experiences thereafter with this particular soul; for, though he certainly found salvation, he was such a weakling that he was ever leaning upon the arm of flesh; in consequence of which I endured much persecution. He haunted me much of the time, morning, noon, and night, so that I was subjected to unkind remarks and ridicule; but, remembering the words of our Master in Matt. 5:11, 12 and Paul's in Phil. 2:7, I endeavored to bear this for the sake of his soul. Much later, when I was in the work in San Francisco, he took up his abode there, and shortly afterward the blessed Lord saw fit to provide him with an earthly companion (he was a widower), a most worthy Christian woman, who tenderly ministered to his needs until Father called him home, little more than a year following the earthquake and fire of that great city. Concerning that catastrophe he wrote me as follows:

San Francisco, Potrero Camp, Opp. S.P.R.R. Depot, Third and Townsend Streets, April 29, 1906.

My dear Sister Roberts:

We are alive and well. Praise the Lord. On the morning of the eighteenth we were roughly thrown from our bed by earthquake, and our house broken all to pieces, and it was afire before we were rescued.

Two men (God bless them!) took my dear wife and me with ropes, and by the time we were in the street the house was burning furiously. Two poor women on the lower floor were burned to death. We lost all we had except the clothes we had on and our Bibles. These we had been reading the night before and had left at our bedside. As we went out, we each took a Bible. I had a very fine collection of religious books, some very valuable, but all went in smoke; but, thank God! he saved our lives. I assure you we have thanked him in prayer many times since we escaped.

We got over on the Potrero and we had to sit in the hot sun all day the eighteenth, nineteenth, and twentieth, and in the cold night wind, and we had nothing to lie down on nor to cover us to keep the cold out. My wife asked a woman to loan her a blanket to throw around me. She would not do it, yet she had enough extra ones for a dozen people. Finally near morning of the second night a lieutenant from the Presidio (regular army) came along and saw us sitting in the cold, and asked if we were so bad off as that. I told him yes. He said he would see about that. He went and took a heavy pair of blankets from that woman and brought them to us. We wrapped ourselves up in them and sat down again. After that we got along comfortably until morning, but the woman took the blankets away as soon as morning came.

Then we got into a Santa Fe car, which kept us out of the wind, but we had no bedding. After two days we all had to get out of the cars, as the company had to send them to Los Angeles to load them with sugar. Then we were out of doors again; but, praise the Lord! Mr. John A. Hedges, a showman, gave us a comfortable house, and he says we can have it as long as we stay. His dear wife gives us hot coffee and food every day, and good coffee and food, too.

They have two fine boys, sixteen and eighteen years of age. The boys have found jobs to work to help their father and mother. There are hundreds of able-bodied men around the camp, but they will not work. They can get from $2.00 to $2.50 a day, but they would rather live off the liberality of others. But when the soldiers find them they are forced to work, and they get no pay, only something to eat....

I am alone in our little house today. My dear one is out visiting some friends. She will soon be with me. Sister, she is a dear one to me. God bless her!

Mr. A. D. Porter, a banker of Woodland [now deceased], came down to hunt me up, and had a hard time to find us; but day before yesterday while looking around and asking for us he met Mr. Hedges, and he brought him to us. He told us to come to Woodland, and we could have rooms without cost. He is going to fit up rooms with kitchen and cooking utensils, etc., so we can live comfortably and without charge.

We will go on Tuesday or Wednesday, first or second of May. He also pays our car fare. We are thankful to him for his kindness. So you can write to us in Woodland.

You have no idea how often my wife and I have said we wished we could see our dear Sister Roberts. We can not begin to say all we want to in a letter. There is so much to talk about at this time. My wife got out in her night clothes. She did not have a chance to get her hat to cover her head. Some of the people are very kind to us.

My wife has got back to camp and is sitting by me while I write. I will not try to say more at this time. Good-by. I hope you had no trouble at Beth Adriel [the San Jose rescue home to be referred to hereafter]. God bless you and your work. With love from

Brother and Sister Mosby.

God wonderfully strengthened me and aided me to be faithful to this aged brother's soul, who through that awful demon, liquor, for years had been well-nigh an imbecile when first we met; and I expect one of the first ones to welcome me when I reach the glory-land will be my old friend, Brother Mosby.

CHAPTER IX
WOODLAND (Continued)—A BOYCOTT

One of the greatest and most agonizing trials of faith and trust occurred shortly after my being placed in charge of the Woodland undenominational gospel mission. The test well-nigh prostrated me. A letter from my son, then in San Francisco, abruptly broke the following news:

Dear Mother:

By the time you receive this I shall be on my way to Manilla. It will be a good opportunity for experience, and to see the world. I go as an employee on board the "Logan."…

Hoping to see you again in about three months, I remain. Your loving son,

Charlie.

To leave me, with only this for a farewell! "O God!" I cried, "I am indeed bereft of all my earthly treasures." No word from my husband had reached me for many months, although occasionally I had, through interested friends, been able to locate him. He never, from the time of my leaving home, contributed one cent toward my support. So I was given, as but few are given, a glorious opportunity to trust daily, hourly, and prove our dear heavenly Father—and he never has, nor ever will be, delinquent, unless I fail in my love and duty.

No collections were taken in the mission. Freewill offerings supported this work, which system gave occasion for some blessed testings; for sometimes rent-day would find us with an empty treasury, together with God's warning not to appeal to any but him. My cupboard was empty at times. I prayed, and he bountifully replenished it.

The first Christmas season in Woodland was a notable one. We were to give a dinner to the converts. Many were the gifts of edibles. Christmas eve found Sister Simpson and me very busy preparing and cooking, aided by two prospective guests. While I was thus engaged, a message arrived requesting me to go quickly to a certain street and cabin, where a girl lay dying. Carrying my Bible and little autoharp, my constant companions, I soon arrived at the place designated.

Poor Nell! How grateful I am that God ever permitted me to meet you, for now—not until now have you felt your great need. We spent a very precious, profitable time in that mean, forlorn abode. Soon Nell gladly yielded to Jesus; then whilst I was softly singing, "Jesus knows all about our struggles," she went to sleep. Commending her for all time and eternity to His loving keeping, I stole softly out.

Early on Christmas morning word arrived that Nell had never awakened, but had passed quietly away, shortly after midnight. Hers was the first funeral service at which I officiated. It was well attended. Instead of eulogizing the dead, as is common on such occasions, I delivered, for the blessed Master, a precious fruit-bearing message to the living. Hallelujah!

The passing of Nell did not prevent our having a happy Christmas. All my guests, save two sisters, who were gospel workers, were wonderfully redeemed, blood-washed men and boys. After all of us had enjoyed to our hearts' content the good things to eat, we lingered round the table relating one experience after the other. Some of the boys had been in prison time and again, and they rehearsed some of their escapades whilst serving the devil. All agreed that the primary cause of their downfall was disobedience to parents or guardians when very young, a continuation of this in youth, then the tobacco and liquor habits in connection with disobedience. Then, nothing but sorrow; now, nothing but peace and joy if they would only remain true to our wonderful Redeemer. Doubtless most of my readers have never attended such a dinner party. Let me tell you something. We had for our guest—the King. To be sure, we did not see him with these fleshly eyes, but the spiritual vision wonderfully revealed his presence, beyond a doubt, to each of us. It was a "feasting with my Lord."

In the days gone by, before becoming acquainted with my Savior, I had both entertained and been entertained sumptuously; but never, never had I so enjoyed a banquet, never had I been more happy than with these guests.

In the summer-time of that year following these occurrences we were boycotted. Strange and various worldly procedures for the raising of money in the different churches were causing much comment. The matter reached my ears, and, like Jeremiah and some of the other prophets of old, I proceeded to tell Father what a stumbling-block this was to both sinner and saint and how it grieved my soul, and besought him to warn them.

He gave me answer from Isaiah, sixth chapter. (Please read it.) He spoke to my soul in the night, saying, "Thus saith the Lord, Say unto these people,

Thou shalt read, mark, learn, and inwardly digest, Ezekiel, third and fourth chapters, also Matthew, sixth chapter, twenty-fourth verse." He brought Isa. 6:6-8 so before my mental vision that I lay on my bed trembling from head to foot.

A union prayer service, the last of the season, was to take place in one of the churches on the following Wednesday evening. I was impressed on Tuesday to announce to the mission audience that we should on that occasion attend this union service. I made no mention to them of the message the Lord was trusting me to give, nor did I know how he would have it delivered. My soul was heavily burdened, and a great fear took possession of me, as I entered the basement of that church, which was soon filled with members and pastors representing the various denominations, also many of the mission attendants. The subject I well remember—"The Forgiving Spirit." It was beautifully discussed and handled, causing me to think that under these circumstances the Lord would possibly excuse me. In order to find out, I reverently opened my Bible. My eyes fell on one word in big capitals—"JONAH." Oh! I must obey; but how? I waited and watched. Soon came a call for voluntary prayer, and I received my cue when Brother Smith of the Seventh-day Adventists prayed. Testimony was next in order. Following one or two brief testimonies, I mechanically arose, and gave out the message just as it had come to me from the Lord, and then sat down—*a great burden now off my soul.* Painful silence followed, but finally a brother (Sunday-school teacher) arose. "Let us see what this means," he said. "I will read Ezekiel 3"; and he proceeded to read. Then a brother on the opposite side spoke—"I will read Ezekiel 4." Pastor M—- next said, "And I will read Matt. 6:21, after which we will proceed with our testimonies." But they did not. They could not. After a long silence only one arose. She gave an honest answer, promising God never so to offend him in the future.

On my way home Satan said to me, "Now you're in for it." Sure enough. I comforted myself by audibly singing as I walked along, "Jesus Lover of My Soul." Maybe you think I was frightened and miserable. Not so. I could not have been happier; for the load was lifted, my conscience was clear.

On the following Monday evening we expected one of the pastors, by previous appointment, to preach in the mission. We waited. He never came. I was sent for to come to his parsonage the following morning, and there I learned this: "At a special ministerial meeting, which took place on Monday morning, the Woodland pastors took action with regard to the attitude assumed toward the churches by the woman, Mrs. Florence Roberts, now in charge of the City Gospel Mission. A motion was made, seconded, and unanimously adopted to boycott said mission and said worker."

Was the mission thereafter a failure? No, praise the Lord! It prospered, and it still prospers in the hands of the various workers the Master sends from time to time. He kept me there three years, and never did I lack for the things needful. In that time was I absent twice for short periods, but the mission nightly continued its precious office work under the guidance of the Holy Spirit.

CHAPTER X
A BRIEF CALL TO SACRAMENTO—I ENTER THE SAN FRANCISCO FIELD

Both those periods of absence were occasioned by the return of my son, who now had made two trips to and from the Philippines. After the second one he decided to return to Sacramento, if I would make a little home for him. His stay was of but a few months' duration notwithstanding our cozy, comfortable quarters, for the spirit of roving still possessed him, and erelong he shipped as an employee on one of the large passenger steamers bound for Australia. Then, at the repeated requests of many, I returned to Woodland, from which place I eventually accepted a call to the rescue work in San Francisco. There I made my home with Sister Kauffman, whose name and calling has already been briefly mentioned. For a long time we worked together for the inmates of The Home of Peace, and each Sunday morning at 9:30 o'clock I, with other Christians, could be found at the county jail, No. 3, adjacent to the Ingleside district and about three and one-half miles distant from the city center. Of this branch of the work we will speak hereafter.

The duties and the expenses of the San Francisco home were great; for there was always a large family, most of whom, on coming, were destitute of decent apparel, and, with scarcely an exception, all needed physical treatment, some permanently, so that we toiled incessantly either in the sewing-room, the sick-room, or the nursery, where were several dear little babies. Who does not love a baby? You can not imagine how attached we were to them, soon forgetting their unfortunate advent, and doing what we could to instruct and aid their untutored young mothers. The feeding of the family was alone often a problem (I mean as to the source), so that we had to be very much in the spirit of prayer.

Sometimes our Father would see fit to test us to the limit, for instance: Shortly after my coming, the one in charge of food supplies said, "Sister Kauffman, we are out of everything. There is only enough for today, and perhaps tomorrow morning's breakfast." The worker whose business it was to visit The Mission merchants for any donations of food, etc. came home late that afternoon with but meager results for her day's hard labor. In the morning, following earnest prayer with the family gathered around that poorly supplied breakfast table, Sister Kauffman and I started out to plead for absolute necessities. All without exception commended this laudable work for the wandering girls, but oh! the excuses. To this day I am amazed at many of them. In one office was a portly, good-natured-looking gentleman puffing away at an expensive cigar. (Reader, there was a time in my life when I enjoyed the fragrance of a good one, for my husband was a smoker.) He declared that he could not afford to assist *one cent's worth, that he was too poor.* I dared to inquire gently how many cigars he smoked daily and if they were not at least twenty-five cents for two. "Worse than that," he proudly replied; "twenty cents apiece. But I only smoke half a dozen a day at the most. I'm not an inveterate smoker; besides, it's my only bad habit." When I told him that the cost of one day's smoking would feed all our hungry family with a substantial meal, he turned his back and began to get busy at his desk, and thus we considered ourselves dismissed. There was excuse after excuse, refusal after refusal, principally on the plea of there being so many appeals for charity equally worthy and only a limitless pocket-book being requisite to meet the many demands.

Noon-time discovered us in front of the *Call* building, corner of Market and Third Streets, both of us faint, weary, hungry, and slightly discouraged, yet still hopeful. We stood on the street corner for a few minutes holding each other's hands, and, unknown to the passers-by, praying for strength of body and soul, imploring our heavenly Father to renew our faith and courage. After resting a little while on one of the stone seats near Lotta's Fountain, we once more began to toil up office stairs or ride in elevators. At four o'clock we were near the city front in the wholesale district. Still our faith was being tested, for most of those from whom we had expected help had either gone for the day or were absent from some other cause. At last I weakened.

"Sister Kauffman, I can stand this awful strain no longer," I said. "Perhaps God has sent in food to the girls during our absence. Let us try to get back home." We could not telephone. That would mean a nickel, and we didn't have it. "Once more, dear, once more we'll try," replied courageous Sister Kauffman. So we ascended a long flight of stairs, only to find the door fast locked. Bless her noble soul! she was just as tired, weak, and hungry as I, but infinitely less selfish.

As we came out on the sidewalk, she suddenly remembered one who had some time previously promised help whenever she happened in that vicinity again. It was but half a block distant. Thither we dragged our weary bodies. When we reached the top of that stairway, a gentleman was just in the act of locking a door. His greeting was:

"Well, well, Sister Kauffman, how do you do, and how are all your family? You're just in time. I was about to go home. Glad to make your acquaintance, Sister Roberts. Ladies, come in a moment and rest after your hard climb." He handed a piece of money (five dollars) to Sister Kauffman, remarking as he did so that he had been saving it for her several days.

Then something happened—something totally unlooked for by any of us three. Sister Kauffman and I burst into tears and wept unrestrainedly for several minutes, whilst the kind friend retired, I suppose, to a remote corner of the large room. Presently, when we had become somewhat calm, we told him what we had endured since early morning. It was not at all strange (now was it?) that this good-hearted man, during our short recital, resorted to frequent use of his handkerchief. But it was now fast growing dark, and we had to hurry.

Many samples of canned goods were upon the shelves. (This was a wholesale commission merchant's office.) He filled my net shopping-bag, made up another package, then forth we went with smiling faces and happy hearts. Presently he helped us on to our car, then left us. "Oh! Sister Roberts dear, we'll have to break our five dollars to pay our car fare," said Sister Kauffman. When the conductor came our way and she inquired whether he had change for five, he answered, "Your fares are paid." God bless that noble-hearted, thoughtful gentleman. I do not remember his name, but I do hope he will read or hear of this. Whether he does or not, the generous deed is, I feel sure, recorded to his credit in heaven.

When we turned the corner of our street, some of the family, disregarding the rules, rushed out to greet us and to help us in with our load. Soon our five dollars was purchasing bread, potatoes, and other things for an immediate meal, to which we all quickly sat down, and, after reverently thanking our heavenly Father ate—shall I say?—yes, *ravenously*.

Reader, do not imagine this as being a common every-day experience. By no means, although we were ever subject to tests in one form or another. This taught us to pray more, and not to labor quite so hard—an excellent and profitable lesson; also, to pray God to reprove those who, though well able to help, had refused. "For inasmuch as ye did it not to one of the least of these, ye did it not to me." Matt. 25:45.

CHAPTER XII
AM INTRODUCED TO THE DIVES
OF BARBARY COAST

Sister Kauffman was well acquainted with the dives of Barbary Coast, she having occasionally to seek some one inquired for, or perhaps a lost member of the family returned to former haunts of sin. The next time she had occasion to go, I requested that I might accompany her. She very gladly consented.

At nine o'clock that night we were in a horrible neighborhood. I had a tight grip on her arm, and no wonder, for we were now where every vice and crime were common and reigned supreme.

Plainly do I still see the first place we entered. It was called "The Klondyke." "Come, sister, don't be afraid: God is watching over us," whispered Sister Kauffman as she walked me through a screen door and into that gaudy, low barroom, where were congregated a most deplorable mixture of degraded men and youth in various stages of inebriety. The place reeked with the vile odors of whiskey, beer, tobacco, uncleanliness of body, etc., so that my stomach revolted, and I felt as if I should be compelled to return to the fresh air; but Sister Kauffman, who had obtained permission from the proprietor (tending bar), took me through another doorway, which led into a dance-hall. Positively I was as though rooted to the spot, and I said to myself, "This is even worse than anything of which I read or hear." I do not dare to describe the situation; for I know that young people are going to read this book and I have not the least inclination to sully their minds. Suffice it to say, I was looking upon a shameful scene of total depravity participated in by both sexes, some of whom were little more than in their teens.

An intoxicated girl sidled up to me. How sickening was that vile breath in my face as she said. "Say, what yer got in that case?" It was my auto-harp. "Sing something for her, Sister Roberts," said Sister Kauffman, at the same time drawing the girl and me into a remote corner. I sent up to the throne of grace a quick, silent petition, and the answer immediately returned, for strength came. Taking my little instrument in my arms. I commenced, with shaky voice, the song that you will find between these pages entitled, "Her

Voice." "Don't, oh! don't! Oh! for God's sake don't!" sobbed and shrieked that poor wanderer as she threw herself upon me and buried her head, with its tawdry covering and matted mop of dirty hair, in my lap.

Andante

HER VOICE

Words and Music by Mrs. Florence Roberts.

1. Hark! I hear the sweet-est music Float-ing 2. Once a-gain I hear sweet voi-ces I've not 3. Years have passed since they have left us, Still the

round me o'er and o'er, Such a min-gling of sweet heard for man-y years, Join-ing in the heav'n-ly ten-der mem-o-ry Of these sing-ing saint-ed

voi-ces, Sing-ing as in days of yore; And I cho-rus; And my eyes are filled with tears, As I loved ones Lin-gers round my heart to-day. Now I'm

feel such peace and glad-ness Steal-ing o'er me ten-der-ly, hear my saint-ed moth-er, With the loved ones free from care, wait-ing and I'm lis-t'ning For the one that I love best.

As I hear my moth-er sing-ing, "Je-sus
Sing a-gain as in my child-hood, Of no
Je-sus, bid-ding me to blend My voice in

loves me, e-ven me, loves me, e-ven me." sor-row o-ver there; sor-row o-ver there, sing-ing with the blest; sing-ing with the blest.

Refrain. 1st Verse.

"I am so glad that Jesus loves me, Je-sus loves e-ven me."

Refrain. 2d Verse.

"There'll be no more sor-row there, There'll be no more

sor-row there; In heav-en a-bove, where

all is love, There'll be no more sor-row there."

Refrain. 3d Verse.

"In the sweet bye and bye We shall

meet on that beau-ti-ful shore; In the sweet bye and

bye, We shall meet on that beau-ti-ful shore."]

This drew the attention of the dancers, causing a temporary halt. One of her companions tried to pacify her and to draw her away, but she resisted and only clung the closer. I forgot the awful surroundings as my heart went out in tenderest pity. Placing my hand on her shoulder, I offered soothing words and inquired if I could help her, if I could comfort her. Presently she said: "Lady, God must have sent you here tonight. I'm sober now; I was drunk when you came in. I want to let you know my mother is dead." How she sobbed! The dancing was resumed, whilst the girl, somewhat recovered, continued her story. "She only left me a year ago. She was a good Christian, my mother was; and just before she died, she sent everybody out of the room so as to have a talk with me. 'Hazel,' she said, 'You've given me a heap of trouble and anxiety, but I forgive you, dear, I forgive you. Now kiss Mother, and promise to be a better girl. I've been praying many a long day for you, my child. I'm going to leave you. The doctor says I may not see morning. Don't cry, dear. Don't cry.' .... And then she prayed aloud. 'O God! make my naughty girl a good girl. Save her soul, O God, and may I some day meet her in heaven. Please, God. for the dear Savior's sake. Amen.' ... Just look how I've kept my word! What's your name, lady?"

"You may call me Mother Roberts, dear, and, furthermore, you may come with me and that other lady over there, to our home if you wish."

Before we left that place, and between dances, a man sitting in drunken stupor on a bench suddenly tilted back his hat, stared at me, and accosted me thus:

"Howdy-do, Mother Roberts."

"My! who is this that recognizes me in such a den?" I questioned myself. "Who are you, my man, and where have we met?" I inquired. Imagine my chagrin at his replying:

"In the jail at Sacramento."

"How awful! What will these people think—that I am an ex-jail bird?" Such were the thoughts that were running through my mind.

"Yep; you gave me a speel there, and I don't forget it. Say, kids, this 'ere woman's all right. I wish I'd a minded wot she said, 'n I wouldn't be 'ere ter night."

Hearing these last words, Sister Kauffman, who had been busy dealing with many souls all of this time, said:

"If you mean that, come with Mother Roberts and me down to the mission, a block away. The dear young men workers there will be only too glad to help you."

Then we immediately wended our way out. I with my precious autoharp under one arm and the infinitely more precious human treasure's arm tucked safely under my other. We soon reached the humble mission, left the man in safe keeping, and took a homeward-bound car, retiring about 2 A.M., grateful and almost too happy to sleep.

Hazel stayed with us some time and then obtained a permanent situation in a Christian family as their trusted domestic.

The ice, now broken, soon thawed, and night after night two or three of us workers went to the slums, dance-halls, and dives, endeavoring to rescue some mother's wandering boy or girl. Did we always succeed? By no means. Often the small hours of the morning found us wending our way homeward weary and disappointed, but never greatly discouraged. At the least, we sowed the precious seed, claiming God's promise in Isa. 55:11 as we did so.

Many a time I have seen a girl quickly tuck away in the bosom of her dress some little tract (we always were well supplied), perhaps bearing these words. "Jesus the Savior loves you, and sent me to tell you so"; for not always, by any means, would the proprietors or proprietresses permit us to converse with their victims. Sometimes we were so fortunate as to procure a girl's lodging-house address; then we had the gratification of calling there in the daytime and privately dealing with her, always with more or less good results. On such visits I took the autoharp; for singing is a great, indeed I may say, an invaluable aid in this work.

On one occasion, when three of us were seeking the lost, making saloon to saloon, dance-hall to dance-hall visits, we went into a place where my attention was immediately drawn to a beautiful, modest-looking young lady (about seventeen years old) standing alongside of a gorgeous bar and trying to repel the advances of a pompous, sporty-looking middle-aged man. The man behind the bar was frowning and saying to her, "Here, none of those monkey-shines, miss. You tend to business. D'you hear?" Sister Kauffman and the other worker had gone into the dance-hall in the rear. Quickly stepping up to the girl, I inquired of her what he meant, what so young and modest a girl was doing there, and whether she did not desire to leave, and implored her to let me aid in rescuing her from her wretched life. Quickly she told me that she was motherless and also that she had been home from an Eastern school only about twenty-four days. "My child, what has happened that you are here?" I inquired, astonished beyond measure. Before she could reply the big blonde man tending bar said:

"Here you" (addressing me), "make yourself scarce. You and your kind are — — — — hoo-doos to our business"

"Please, please go," the girl pleaded.

Just at this juncture Sister Kauffman and her lady companion came through the dance hall double doors. The latter held them wide open and in her loud, penetrating voice slowly uttered these words:

"What shall it profit a man if he gain the whole world and lose his own soul? or what shall a man give in exchange for his soul?" …

"Come, Sister Roberts."

"Yes, in a minute," I replied as I motioned to them I would join them outside.

"I will not leave," I said to the girl, "unless you give me some good reason for not accompanying me, seeing you express a desire to be rescued."

"— — — — —!" shouted the man, "if you don't clear right out, I'll brain you" He held suspended in the air a full soda water bottle, one of the heaviest.

The girl, pushing me away from her, said, "Go! go! He'll do it." And then she whispered:

"He's my father."

I rushed out, excitedly informed my companions, and then quickly sought a policeman, who, when I informed him, simply shrugged his shoulders and remarked: "I can't interfere. The man has a license, his daughter isn't of age, he's her legal guardian. Don't know what you can do about it; you'll have to consult higher authority than me" —a course which we proceeded to follow in the morning.

In the evening we visited that same place, accompanied by an officer in private clothes. A large, showy woman and also a bar-tender stood behind the bar. "Are you the party what was here last night trying to make trouble?" she inquired. "Well, you're left. The bird has flown. Ha! ha! I'm running this place now, and I don't need your help, neither. Don't you come here while I'm in charge of it," etc. Evidently, the policeman first accosted had given the alarm. I have never heard what became of that poor girl and her wicked, unnatural father. A tenderhearted woman in that awful neighborhood, one who had tried to protect her, told me this:

The girl's mother died when she was a babe. The father (not then a saloon man) sent her to New York to be raised by her aunt. When old enough she was placed in school. The aunt died. She was removed to another school, and there she remained until called for by her father, who all these years had been her provider. He brought her to San Francisco, where he now kept a dive and dance-hall. She being a rather timid girl, it can be readily understood why she submitted to his authority and tyranny.

My mind now reverts to two of the soldier boys, returned from the Philippines and seated one night in one of those places where we were permitted to work and also to sing. Toward the close of the song,

> Can a boy forget his mother's prayer,
> When he has wandered God knows where?

I discovered them with their arms about each other's shoulders and both with the tears silently coursing down their cheeks. Setting my instrument on one side and remembering my own dear son, the daily object of my prayers, I essayed, in earnest, gentle tones, to admonish them. Both acknowledged having been carefully reared by Christian mothers, one of whom was dead. Had they been my own, I could not have more earnestly pleaded with them. In consequence of my admonition they soon took their departure, promising as they did so never again to cross the threshold of any place where they would be ashamed to have their mothers find them, and also to seek once more their neglected Savior. Both were soon reclaimed; for I had the pleasure of meeting them later in a house of worship on the Army's camp-grounds, at the Presidio.

Christian parents, you that through death or other means have been deprived of the companionship of your children, why not occasionally join some of the rescue workers in their efforts to save somebody's wandering boy or girl, instead of sitting in a rocking-chair, nursing your sorrows? Speak the kindly, loving word of warning or advice; encourage the wayward son or daughter to reform; and thus better your condition as well as theirs. This will *surely* bring an indescribable peace and satisfaction to the soul, assuage much grief, and help to promote the Master's kingdom. He takes us at our word. We sing:

> I'll go where you want me to go, dear Lord.
> Over mountain, or plain, or sea,
> I'll say what you want me to say, dear Lord,
> I'll be what you want me to be.

Do we mean it?

CHAPTER XII
MARY

Of all the pathetic stories from members of our family, I deem Mary's far in excess of others though all, without exception, are woefully sad God knows.

One day a telephone call came to us from the city and county hospital, situated in a suburb known as The Potrero, inquiring if we had room for a delicate young mother with her three-weeks-old babe. They informed us that her time as a patient had expired and, moreover, that they had just been quarantined for smallpox, but that she had as yet suffered no exposure. The workers were quickly consulted, also a few trusted converted girls, and together we knelt in prayer and then consulted God's Word. Praise his name! we opened it on the ninety-first Psalm. What better assurance than in verses 10, 11, and 12?

Soon we were welcoming one of the most forlorn specimens of humanity the home had ever received. Jack, the delicate-looking baby, had the facial expression of a tiny old man, but oh! such beautiful eyes! We realized that both would require very tender care for some time to come. When Mary became able to work, she rendered valuable service, for she liked to cook and was efficient and economical. Whilst she was thus occupied, her babe was being well cared for in the nursery.

Several months passed by, during which every means was resorted to in order to help Mary learn to seek and find her Savior, but all without avail.

Little Jack, never very strong, was taken seriously ill and soon, from the waist down, was paralyzed. Mary now relinquished all other duties in order to nurse her sick treasure. We never witnessed greater love and devotion. For ten days before he died, she did not leave his bedside one moment longer than necessary, never changed her clothes, excepting once, and never lay down to sleep. On more than one occasion it became my privilege to share the night vigils, for which she was sincerely grateful. How my heart yearned for this poor, hopeless mother! How I longed to impart to her the secret of salvation and of the Burden-bearer!

"Mary," I said, "if you would only try my Savior, dear, I assure you that you would feel better, body and soul, I've never heard *your* story; won't you tell it to me whilst we're watching beside Baby?"

"I've never felt as if I could before, but I will, Mother Roberts, I will."

"I lost my father and mother when I was quite small, and my grandparents raised my little brother and me. I never remember when they didn't have beer on the table for dinner and supper, and if company came in, they always treated them. If I didn't feel quite well or was tired, Grandmother would say, 'Have a drop of beer, Mary child, it'll do you good and put new life into you.' It took some time to get used to liking it. I didn't enjoy the bitter taste at first, but by and by I loved it—yes, really loved it.

"I grew up, and, like many another girl, had my young friends come calling. I liked Tom S— — best of all, and one day promised I'd marry him if the old folks would agree. They were awfully pleased, and *soon let Tom and me go about alone everywhere.* He was a baker, and a good one. Earned fine wages, so that I was expecting to have a very comfortable home.

"*I wish Grandmother or some one had talked plainly and honestly to me about a few things, but they didn't; so what did I know when Tom told me that in God's sight an engagement was as good as a marriage and that we'd soon, for the sake of appearances, and to comply with the law, go through that ceremony.* My God! Why didn't some one warn me? Oh! Mother Roberts, very few girls loved a man better than I loved Tom.

"By and by Grandmother says, 'What's become of Tom? I haven't seen him lately. I didn't know he'd left his job.' So I told her his work was slack and he'd gone away to hunt a place where he could get better pay. You'll not be surprised to hear she soon grew suspicious, and one day I was obliged to confess.

"Did I tell you Tom drank beer? Oh yes, and enjoyed it with me and them many's the time.

"Was he a stranger to me and my folks when I first met him? Well, no, not exactly, although I must confess I knew very little about him before he was introduced by one of my girl friends at the baker's and confectioner's ball. *Oh but he was an elegant dancer! and that got me, in the first place.*

"My! but didn't Grandmother take on something awful! She ordered me out of her sight up to my little bedroom till Grandfather should come home. I sat there listening to her wailing and moaning and asking the dear Mother of God what she had done that such a cruel, cruel misfortune should have befallen her. Poor Granny! Mother Roberts, I was longing to go down and comfort her, but I durs'n't. So all that I could do was to walk the floor, or sit and cry. Sometimes I tried to tell my beads, but I couldn't take any pleasure in them. They didn't comfort my poor, sinful soul one bit. I wished I could die then and there, but what was the use? I couldn't, though I thought fear would indeed kill me when I heard Grandfather come in and knew Grandmother was telling him. I heard him raving and cursing while she was begging him to keep quiet for fear the neighbors would hear.

"Pretty soon he opened the door that led upstairs. 'Mary,' he shouted, 'you —- —— come down and be —— quick about it, I tell ye.' And when I did, he said, 'I'll see whether we'll own any one what will disgrace their poor, respectable, honest grandparents, *what has brought ye up in the way ye should go*, in their old age! Out ye go, and be —— quick about it.' I can see him now, and Grandmother, who was sitting at the kitchen table, sobbing with her head buried in her apron. I crawled on my hands and knees toward him; I begged him not to turn me out; I clung to him so that he could hardly walk, while he, in his rage, was backing along the hall out toward the front door, and then he managed to open it, me still clinging to him, and threw me, with a curse, out into the dark, cold, wet night.

"I lay there on the doorstep until I found I was getting a soaking, and then I went to a neighbor about a block away, who always had been very kind to me, and had a girl of her own a little younger than me. Did I tell her? Of course I did; I had to. So she took pity on me and let me sleep there that night on a shake-down in the parlor, although Mattie (her daughter) had a large bed to herself, and I told her not to go to so much trouble, that I could sleep with her as I'd done before, many's the time. But she said girls would get to talking, and she didn't want her innocent Mattie to know a girl could ever bring such disgrace on honest, respectable parents. But she didn't know how Mattie and I used to talk for hours after we'd get in bed at night, about our 'fellers' and such like, but now, who was I that I should tell her mother this?

"In the morning after breakfast (she kept Mattie out of sight somewhere) she took me into the parlor, shut the door, and said:

"'Mary child, I'm sorry for you, I am indeed, but I can't keep you here. You know where the county hospital is, don't you? Well, you go there, and they'll take you in. They'll take such cases as yours. Here's a quarter to pay your car fare. You needn't let on you stopped with me. You may be sure *I* won't, for I respect your Grandfather and Grandmother highly. I don't want them to find out I know anything about your trouble or that I took you in. Why, they'd never speak to me again. There, there, don't cry. Good-by and good luck to you, Mary.'

"I got on a car and pretty soon was asking the gate-keeper of the city and county hospital how I should apply to get in. 'Patient?' he asked. 'Yes, sir,' said I. So he directed me to the office. A lot of people were there, waiting their turn. After a while a doctor interviewed me in a little office. He asked me a good many questions. No, I didn't lie to him, but I told him as little as I could. He said, 'We can't take you in yet. Come on such a date,' and put my name on a book, then wrote on a card something about admitting the bearer, Mary H— —, maternity ward, with his name and the day I was due there. I told him I'd no place to go; he said I was able to work for a while. So I went out to try and find some work. Before evening I got a job washing dishes and preparing vegetables in a small restaurant, for the sake of my board and bed, and I stayed there until it was time to go back to the hospital.

"I forgot all my troubles for a while when Jack came.... Mother Roberts, how can I think God is good? He's going to take my baby from me; he's going to let him die. I can't stand it. I'll kill myself—yes, I will...."

Two nights later little Jack still breathed, though scarcely perceptibly, and again I shared poor Mary's vigil. About midnight I asked if she felt able to finish her story. Presently she continued:

"When my little Jack was three weeks old, the nurse of our ward took down the card from the head of my bed, and told me I could go now. I was dismissed, and they wanted my corner for another patient.

"I stood outside the big gate that afternoon wondering where I could go and holding my pretty little Jack against my breast. I'd a nice warm shawl, so he was good and comfortable. A thought like this struck me. 'Grandfather is so fond of babies. I'll go there. *Perhaps when he sees the dear, innocent little baby, he'll forgive me and take me back.*' It seemed as though I would never reach their house [in the neighborhood of Sixth and Clara Streets, reader], and I had to rest on some one's doorsteps very often, I was that weak. It was pretty near dusk when I knocked on the door, and the fog was coming in. Grandmother opened it. She threw up her hands when she saw me; didn't ask me in, but hollered for Grandfather to come, and *come quick*, which he did. Oh! Mother Roberts, to my dying day I'll remember how he cursed me when he saw me and my baby's darling face, and then he closed the door with an awful bang. Well, I was dazed like for a little bit, then Baby cried. I sat on somebody's doorstep and nursed him, then kept on walking and resting; going, I hardly knew where.

"It must have been well after seven o'clock when I found myself on Montgomery Avenue and not very far from North Beach. My! but I was faint, although I'd had a good meal at the hospital at noon, but you know a nursing mother needs plenty of nourishing food and often. I saw a light in a little notion shop, and went in and asked the woman if she could spare me a bite to eat. Bless her kind heart, she gave me a big bowl full of bread and milk, and warmed some stew, and helped me make Jack clean and comfortable, but she had no place for me to sleep, which she told me sorrowfully. Her family was large, and she did not have a bit of extra bedding, besides she was poor. I was feeling better now and more cheerful. My! 'tis wonderful what a good meal can do for you when you're hungry, isn't it? I thanked her kindly and told her I'd soon find friends; then went out on the street and began to watch the faces. At last I stepped up to an elderly laboring man, told him I had lost my way, was broke, a stranger, and a widow, and asked him if he could direct me to a respectable lodging-house, which he did (bless his kind heart!) and paid the woman for a night's lodging, she asking no questions; and soon I was in a clean little bed with my Jack. I don't think my head had hardly touched the pillow when I was fast asleep, all of my troubles forgotten.

"Morning came all too soon. And now what was I to do? I dressed, then made baby as comfortable as I could under the circumstances, went down the stairs, meeting no one as I passed out of the house into the street. Pretty soon I'd made up my mind. I'd walk down to Meigg's wharf (not far away) and with my darling would drop quietly off the end of it into the bay; and I was soon looking into the nice quiet water, just about to fall in when I heard a voice, for sure I did, Mother Roberts, saying, 'Don't Mary.' Maybe you don't think I was scared as I looked all around and could see no one nearer than a block and a half away, and that was a man piling up some lumber on a wagon; besides, the voice I heard was a woman's, not a man's. I began to back away from the water, wondering if I'd heard an angel speak....

"Yes; I admit I am naturally superstitious, but don't you think in a case like this, it's a good thing?"

"Yes; I do, Mary, but go on, dear, I'm anxious to hear what became of you."

"I went back to the woman who gave me my supper, and she gave me my breakfast, then advised me to put my baby with the sisters of Mount St.

Joseph. *But I never could do that, could you?* I said good-by to my kind friend and started out for where, I did not know. All of a sudden I said to myself, 'I'll go back to the hospital and offer to scrub and do chores; anything, so they'll take me and my baby in.' It took me till nearly one o'clock to reach there. Every time I sat down to rest and a policeman came along, I'd get up quickly and walk on, for fear he might arrest me as a suspicious character.

"The man at the gate didn't want to let me in; said they had been obliged to quarantine; but I rushed past him up to the office, threw myself at a doctor's feet, and begged him for God's sake not to send me away. He sent for the head nurse; they gave me my dinner, made Baby nice and clean and comfortable, and pretty soon one of the nurses came and told me they had found me and Baby a good home, and here I've been, as you know, ever since. But oh! Mother Roberts, my little Jack is going to die, he's going to die!...

"Four days since you opened your beautiful eyes and looked at Mother, Precious. Four long, long days....

"*Mother Roberts, I think I would believe and trust God if he would only let my baby look at me once more before he goes. I really think I would.*"

"Kneel down with me, Mary, and we'll ask him," I said.

We clasped hands over the foot of that little bed, and if ever I prayed, I prayed then that the merciful Father would, for the sake of his Son our Savior, and for his own glory, open the eyes of the babe once more before the angels took him home. The poor worn-out mother sobbed herself to sleep, her head resting on little Jack's lifeless feet. I watched, earnestly and intently watched, for my prayer to be answered. Toward daylight I observed a slight movement of the little head. "Wake up! wake up, Mary!" I cried, whilst I shook and continued to shake her. The voice awoke many of the family, who quickly hastened to the sick-room. Mary with bloodshot eyes gazed at the baby. Soon his beautiful eyes opened wide, with a long, loving look at the faithful mother, then closed; and now the angels had him forever in their keeping.

"O God, O God, you are good, you are good," sobbed poor Mary. "I'll never, never doubt you any more." And she never did. From that day, and, so far as I know, up to the present time, Mary has been one of our Father's and Savior's loyal subjects.

As soon as able, she took a situation, so as to earn money to pay Jack's funeral expenses and to purchase the lot where lie his earthly remains. I was told that her mistress accepted the Savior because of her faithful daily walk. Later, her brother, returned from the Philippines, claimed and took her back there with him, where, doubtless, she is seeking and finding jewels for the Master's crown.

"What became of the grandparents—the ones responsible before God for her misfortunes?" During the first few weeks of Mary's stay under our roof, Sister Kauffman and I called on them, hoping so to picture the Savior's tender mercy and love as to be able to touch their hearts, to discover to them their self-righteous condition, and to get them to realize where the blame really lay. All our efforts were fruitless. The earthquake and fire of San Francisco swept away all their property, and in all probability they perished in the flames, for they were never again heard of.

CHAPTER XIII
SERVICES IN COUNTY JAIL, BRANCH NO. 3

Come with me this beautiful Sunday morning. Join with me and this faithful band of young workers from various denominations, in the nine o'clock services, and satisfy yourself as to the good they, by the grace of God, are able to accomplish.

Good morning, gate-keeper. Have the rest of the band arrived yet?

Yes?

Then we'll pass in.

We enter the beautifully laid-out grounds surrounding the women's quarters. What lovely lawns! What a variety of fragrant flowers! But we must hurry, for we can not afford to miss the services. We ascend the long flight of steps and are now greeted by the superintendent and his wife, the matron. Next we traverse a long, wide hallway. Turning to the left, we mount a few steps, and then come up against a solid iron double door. Through an aperture in one side of it we get a glimpse of the throng within. The door is unlocked for our admission, and, passing through, we find ourselves facing anywhere from forty to sixty girls and women, for the most part neatly attired in dark blue-print gowns.

"What a heterogeneous gathering we are confronting! Some look so refined; doubtless they are from the better walks of life. Why are they here?"

For offenses of various kinds too numerous to mention. "That dignified, white-haired woman, third row on our left?"

Ask me about her later on. I will tell you on our way home.

"That pretty fair-haired girl about sixteen?"

Vagrancy. Her sentence expires in two weeks. We're trying to persuade her to come to our home, because her own is undesirable. Both of her parents drink; her older sister has taken the downward course and refuses all our overtures; and her two brothers are constantly in drunken bouts and then imprisoned.

"That old, old woman; what of her?"

She's awaiting her trial for malpractice. She'll probably have to serve time in San Quentin penitentiary. But I'll tell you more by and by.

Brother Edstrom of the Y. M. C. A. speaks—"Let us all heartily join in singing, 'Pass me not, O gentle Savior,' Gospel Hymns No. 27." How they sing! and what beautiful voices some of the prisoners have!

"Brother St. John, will you lead in prayer?"

STILL NEARER

Words and music by Mrs. FLORENCE ROBERTS

1. Oh, help me live near thee, my Savior, Oh, keep thou me
2. I love thee, my Fa—ther, and Sav—ior, For what thou hast

close by my side; I need thee, Lord, dai—ly and hour—ly,
done for me; Me, one of the great-est of sin-ners,

My Coun-sel-or and my Guide. I can—not have thee too
I mar—vel, such welcome from thee! Won-der—ful con-
quest o'er

near me, Ei-ther by day or by night; For when thou art nigh
the Sa-tan's Al—lur—ing paths of sin; My Sav-ior, to thee
the

tempt-er doth fly, Thou dost help me to put him to flight,
glo—ry all be, Now help me some lost ones to win.

REFRAIN

Near—er, still near—er, Come to me o'er and o'er.

Near-er to thee, Sav-ior, I'd be, Now and for—ev—er—more]

Without exception all kneel as the consecrated young brother makes fervent, passionate appeal to the throne of mercy and grace.

"Will one of our congregation now call for a song?"

"No. 18."

"Very good, we will sing No. 18."

Rescue the perishing, care for the dying,
Snatch them in pity from sin and the grave;
Weep o'er the erring one, lift up the fallen,
Tell them of Jesus the mighty to save.

You can't keep back the tears as you listen, and this is not to be wondered at.

"Sister Burton, we will now listen to your reading of the fifty-fifth chapter of Isaiah."

"Sister Roberts, I see you have your autoharp with you. Please favor us with one of your God-sent songs."

"Nearer, Still Nearer."

The prisoners sing refrain twice over with me and then request a repetition. It is inspiring to hear them, it surely is.

"We will now spend a few minutes in testimony. Who will be the first to witness for Jesus this morning?"

Three or four are on their feet at once, some thanking God that, even though they are behind prison bars, he has washed away their sins in the precious blood of Jesus, and declaring their intention of leading clean lives, lives that will honor the Lord; adding that they are asking him to give them honest jobs in respectable quarters, so that they need never again be obliged to return to their former environments of vice and degradation. And so on, until time for testimony is up.

"How many desire an interest in our prayers, that you may lead lives that will fit you for heaven instead of sending you down to an awful hell? Please raise your hands. One, two, three, six, ten; nearly all who have not testified. God bless you! Let us pray."

Brother Edstrom so earnestly petitions the loving Father for mercy and pardon for these poor souls that some of them weep audibly. Again we all join in singing; the benediction is pronounced; then those conducting the meeting repair quickly to the men's quarters in an adjacent but separate enclosure. There a similar service is held, after which the majority hurry away to the various houses of worship for the eleven o'clock services.

When not otherwise engaged, I find it pleasurable as well as profitable to linger, but on this occasion I shall not remain. As we walk along, I will keep my word concerning some of the inquired-about inmates.

The dignified, white-haired woman spends the greater part of her time in that prison-house.

She is addicted to the morphine habit, and, in consequence, she resorts to any means to procure the drug. It has made a petty thief of her, thus causing her frequent arrest and incarceration for three or six months.

She was the wife of a prominent professional man, and, so far as this world's goods are concerned, she enjoyed everything that a loving husband was able to lavish on her. At the time of, and following, the birth of her third child, the attending physician, in order to assuage her excruciating pain, administered morphine. She continued to resort to it, and *soon she was its slave.* Everything known to human skill was done to cure her of the habit, but without much effect. She began to inject the drug into her flesh with a hypodermic needle and also to mix it with cocaine. Thus she soon became a mortification to her husband, relatives, and friends, and erelong they felt that she had forfeited all claims to their consideration. They forsook her, absolutely refused to recognize her. In process of time the husband procured a divorce and sole guardianship of the children.

Soon she disappeared from her home neighborhood and for the future was lost sight of by all except police judges, and officers, prison companions, and habitue of morphine dens. Every home missionary I know of in San Francisco had made some attempt or sacrifice for the redemption of this unfortunate woman, but apparently with little, if any, effect. One day she told me that *I was wasting my time, for she loved her drug better than her God.* I wondered if she really meant it.

You ask if this is an exceptional case? Not by any manner of means. I am able to relate many others, all different in detail, but all alike in the main, the family physician being primarily responsible.

My heart goes out tenderly for the younger inmates of the prison, most of whom are there for a first offense, and who are now in great danger of contracting bad habits, such as cigarette-smoking, from older offenders. "What!" you exclaim, "do they permit women and girls to smoke?" I'm sorry to tell you it is only too true. Furthermore, the weed is procured from those in authority over them. And from that habit and others acquired during incarceration, deeper demoralization results, so that many come forth worse than they ever were before their imprisonment. Nevertheless, realizing the limitless value of even one soul, the home missionary keeps, ever keeps in view Gal. 6:9—"And let us not be weary in well doing; for in due season we shall reap, if we faint not."

With but very few exceptions the prisoners of both sexes admit that liquor or drugs, or both have cursed their lives, made every type of criminal out of them, forfeited them their liberty, some for life, aye, even life itself. I have dealt with some of the ones condemned to die. I learn this from their own lips.

When, oh! when will that awful octopus, that curse of the world be destroyed? When, oh! when will our lawmakers and our officers eliminate forever the accursed poisons that ruin men and women both physically and morally?

What chance do God's consecrated workers have, with this band of demons confronting them on every hand, dragging souls down to hell every hour of the day, yea, every minute?

'How long, O Lord, how long?' Psa. 94:3.

CHAPTER XIV
LUCY—A REMARKABLE EXPERIENCE

Following the services one Sunday morning, several of the inmates waited on me in a body. "Mother Roberts," the spokesman began, "there's a dying girl in one of the cells in the smaller dormitory. She's spitting blood something dreadful, and she's so bad. Bad and all as some of us are, we're scared the way she goes on. Her language is just awful! She never comes out to the services, yet she's been here for months. Says she has no use for 'them hypocrites,' and 'don't want none of 'em near her.' Says she'll curse 'em if they do come. Say, Mother Roberts, couldn't you make some excuse to get into her cell? We haven't the heart to see her deliberately go to hell."

For a few minutes silence reigned, whilst I thought and inwardly prayed. Then I felt it to be of the Lord to carry out an impression to walk quietly into her cell as though by mistake, trusting the Divine Director for results....

Propped up in one corner of her bunk, wrapped in grey blankets, reclined a hollow-eyed, ghastly-looking girl, gasping for breath. Some blood was trickling from the corners of her mouth. She glared at me, tried to speak, but failed. Quickly I took out my handkerchief, dipped it into the granite ewer close by, and wiped her poor face and mouth; then she whispered, "Again." Repeatedly this was done, the Spirit of God all this time impressing me not to utter one word aloud, yet giving me a wonderful, most blessed realization of his presence and power. After I had made her as comfortable as surroundings would admit, she presently slept. Then I quietly tip-toed out; exacted a promise from her companions not to reveal my identity, which promise they faithfully kept, though under difficulties; had a conference with Mrs. Kincaid, the matron; then went away.

I returned the following morning and for four more consecutive days. Still the dear Lord did not permit me to speak. On Friday afternoon as I was about to leave her (by the way, she had observed almost stolid silence so far), she called me to come back.

"What is it, dear?" I asked.

"Say, do you mind telling me who you are?"

"Why? Why do you wish to know?"

After a prolonged silence I once more was about to depart, but she called again:

"I'll have to say it."

"Say what, Lucy?"

"Say this: *you act like a Christian.*"

Oh! praise God, praise God! the ice was broken, and my pent-up soul gave vent to a copious flow of refreshing tears, as I bowed in gratitude at that prison bunk, beside that wandering sick girl, and poured out my heart in earnest prayer for the dear Father to guide her into all truth, and to make me ever-wise in my administrations to the needs of herself and others. Then, kissing her on the brow, I left her.

WAS IT YOU?

Words and Music by Mrs. FLORENCE ROBERTS.

Some one spoke to me of Je—sus, Said he'd come to call on me,
Some one told me how he suf-fered, Said, "For you and me he died."
Some one gave the in—vi—ta—tion, And we bowed in humble prayer;
Lov—ing Sav-ior, how I thank thee Some one came to me that day-Oh,
I know that man-y oth—ers Would be glad if "some one" came.

Said no mat-ter how I'd fall—en, He from sin would set me free.
"Does, oh, does he love so dear—ly? Tell me more of him," I cried.
Soon I felt my sins for-giv—en; Thro' his grace I'll meet you there,
Some one rep-re-sent-ing Je—sus, And I turned thee not a—way.
Bring-ing lov—ing in—vi—ta—tion From their lives of sin and shame.

Some one told me how he loved me, And was knocking at my door;
Some one told me he is com-ing Soon to take his loved ones

home,—

There in mansions bright with glo-ry. Oh,'tis won-der-ful to me

Bless, oh, bless that loving some one, Sent by Je-sus Christ our Lord;

In—to lives of peace and glo—ry, Thro' the blood of Christ the Lamb:

He had oft-en stood there plead-ing, Had been man-y times be-fore.

Told me he was there to par—don, If I now to him would come.

That the vil-est he is seek-ing From their sins to set them free!

Help me, now that I am blood-washed, Wit-ness to thy precious word.

Send me pray-ing, bless-ed Je—sus, With that song, "Just as I am."

Was it you? Was it you? Was it you?]

On the following Sunday I returned and found her eager to see me, also much improved in health. After our greeting she told me that she had been trying to discover who I was, but that no one would inform her. "Ain't they the limit?" was her smiling expression.

"You'll tell me, won't you? Say, who was that singing out in the big dormitory a while ago?"

"Every one was singing, Lucy."

"Oh, yes, I know, but I mean some one sometimes alone and playing something that sounds like a guitar-mandolin like we have at home?"

"Would you care to hear her?"

"Sure I would. Please go ask her to come in." Soon I returned with my precious little instrument.

"Is that it? Wouldn't she come?"

"Of course she would. Listen. Lucy."

Oh! those blessed tears she shed as she pillowed her head on my breast; those blessed, blessed tears!

"Come tomorrow, please come."

"God willing, Lucy, yes."

"Why do you say, 'God willing'? Of course he'll be willing."

And I went forth, scarcely able to contain myself for very joy.

The next morning I returned and spent many hours with this precious, very precious jewel. There was no longer any restraint. She listened eagerly whilst I imparted choice portions of the Word. (Reader, the utmost precaution had to be used, for she had not yet accepted her Savior. Believe me, there is danger of excess in surfeiting with the Bible. I lovingly admonish you to seek earnestly for divine wisdom with regard to dealing with souls. My lessons on those lines have thus far been dearly purchased; for I have ignorantly, zealously, made many mistakes, thus for the time being, hindered, more than aided their spiritual progress. To illustrate: A janitor's child has a toy broom. Papa has just swept one part of the hall and is about to remove the accumulated dust. "Papa, let me help you," and forthwith the child sweeps a large portion of the dust over the already cleaned floor. Papa sighs, sadly smiles, says nothing, but patiently proceeds to clean up again. Reader, I'm sure you see the point.)

Not many days thereafter, when Lucy was again able to be up and dressed, she asked me to pray for her, and before we rose from our knees, she knew my Savior was hers. Even so, yet she still smoked cigarettes. This grieved my soul, but I waited until of her own accord she inquired whether I thought it a sin to smoke. She excused herself on the plea that smoking quieted her nerves and also induced sleep. She told me, however, that she was now trying to curtail, as she had hitherto indulged in as many as twenty a day. I asked if she would wish her dear Redeemer to see her rolling and smoking cigarettes, referred her to Rev. 22:11, and soon, without further comment, took my departure.

She was able to attend services the following Sunday. I still see her eagerly absorbing everything said and sung. As soon as the meeting closed, she took possession of me, marshaled me to her cell, kissed and seated me, and then said:

"I want to tell you something so badly, I could hardly wait until the others were through. Mother Roberts, after you left last Wednesday, I got to thinking about my filthy habit, so I went on my knees, and did what you told me; I prayed, if it wasn't right, for God to make me hate it. My! but I was nervous an hour later, and *had* to have a smoke. I woke up in the night wanting another, so rolled my cigarette and was just in the act of lighting it when something seemed to say, 'Lucy, if you'll let it alone you shall never need one again!' I put out the match and lay down, but I couldn't sleep. I was that nervous; so I reached over to the window ledge, picked up my cigarette, put it between my lips once more and struck a light, when again I distinctly got that impression. Oh! but I was tempted, so for fear I would weaken I got out of bed, and with my bare feet crushed the dirty weed all to smithereens. I slept soundly till morning, and woke up smelling the odor of tobacco-smoke. Mother, I want to tell you the strange part of it; the smell actually made me sick at my stomach. How do you account for that? To be sure, I'm very nervous, but nothing on earth could tempt me to smoke again."...

Dear Lucy grew in grace very rapidly. Erelong she confided who her family were, also read me portions of their letters, and at her request I wrote to her mother, who soon replied at length.

The time was approaching when my dear spiritual daughter would soon have her freedom; but I learned that, for good and sufficient family reasons, it would be impossible for her to return to them for some time to come. The mother wrote, asking if it would be possible for me to assume temporary guardianship.

Owing to impaired health, I was not at this time residing at the Home of Peace, but instead was occupying quiet quarters in the cottage of a sister missionary, who was absent much of the time and who, in return for light services, gave me the use of a nice large room furnished for light housekeeping. I asked and obtained her permission to have Lucy share the room with me—this with the proviso that Lucy's identity be closely guarded. Also, I obtained sanction from the judge (who, when sentencing her, ordered her removed from San Francisco at the expiration of her term) to keep her with me, but under close surveillance.

Lucy joyfully placed herself in my keeping, without knowing what disposition was to be made of her. Frequently she petitioned to be lodged in my immediate neighborhood. In reply, I simply smiled. You can not imagine how much I was enjoying my delightful secret nor with what pleasure I prepared new clothing purchased with the money sent by her own dear mother. Lucy and I were now counting the days, soon the hours.

My pretty room, with its folding-bed, organ, sideboard, decorations of glass and chinaware, underwent, the day before her freedom, an extra cleaning in preparation for my guest, and I arose at three o'clock the following morning in order to add finishing touches and also to prepare for an immediate meal on our return. At five o'clock I boarded a car, which shortly before six landed me in front of the long driveway leading to the prison grounds.

Lucy was ready even to her hat and gloves. She was regaled with such remarks as, "Oh, but you're the lucky girl!" "Wish some one would take a like interest in me," "Come back and see us once in a while," or, "Won't you write me? It'll be such a comfort to hear from you, Lucy." Next she received very kind, parental advice from the Captain and Mrs. Kincaid. Then we went down the steps and terraced walks, the door in the prison wall swung wide open, and once more Lucy was free.

But why does she stand stock still? Why inhale such long, deep breaths?

"Isn't it lovely, Mother Roberts, lovely, lovely!"

"The air is just as fresh in the garden we have just left, Lucy dear."

"No doubt, but this is freedom! Praise God, this is freedom! Good-by [this to the guard on the lookout]. When I come again, it will be to preach the gospel. God bless you. Good-by. Come, Mother, I'm ready."

I was loathe to check her enthusiasm on the way home, but had to do so, in order not to attract the attention of the passengers. We reached our street. I opened the door with my latch-key, led the way up-stairs, entered my room, and bade her welcome in the name of the dear Lord. She had prostrated herself at my feet, but I quickly raised her, and we knelt in prayer and thanksgiving. *It was worth all the gold in the Klondyke to me to hear that girl's prayer.* She couldn't eat, and I didn't do much better. The rest of the day Lucy spent in writing a long, long letter to her parents. If I remember right, she covered thirty pages of ordinary letter paper.

Bedtime arrived.

"Where am I to sleep, Mother dear?" Lucy inquired. "With me, Lucy, here in the folding-bed," I answered.

"Mother, do you mean it? Would you let me sleep with you?"

"Why not, dear? You're my honored guest. You're my spiritual daughter. Jesus says, 'Inasmuch as ye have done it unto one of the least of these, ye have done it unto me.' Don't you understand, Lucy? In entertaining you, I am entertaining Jesus."

"My! Mother, how you must love me! Oh but God will bless you for this!"

Sure-enough he has, over and over, countless times, aye, even up to the present moment. We shall hear more of Lucy in the next chapter.

CHAPTER XV
WE PLAN FOR A HOME FOR RELEASED PRISON GIRLS

Hours had slipped away. We had both been silent, but I wondered whether Lucy, like myself, was not sleeping, but simply resting quietly for fear of disturbing me. One-thirty, then two o'clock. I whispered:

"Are you asleep, Lucy?"

"No, Mother dear," she answered; "I haven't slept a wink for thinking of the goodness of God and wishing lots of other unfortunates had such good luck as me tonight."

"I also, Lucy; furthermore, I'm pondering how to proceed to procure them a home with nice large grounds in which they can work and take pleasure, but I haven't any means. All I now own is my bicycle. I left it for sale in Woodland. Perhaps God will soon find a purchaser; if so, I will take it as a sign that he wants me to travel from place to place in their behalf. Give me your hand, Lucy." She clasped mine under the covers whilst I prayed in a low tone, "Father, art thou impressing us to seek a home for the girls, a home removed from city temptations and environments? If so, I pray thee, seal the impression with thy Word. In Jesus' name I ask this"; and Lucy fervently echoed my Amen. Next I lighted the lamp on the little stand by our bed side, on which lay a writing tablet, a pencil, and my Bible. Reverently opening the latter, we found ourselves looking down upon Genesis, twelfth chapter, first and ninth verses. Thus did our Father seal the impression of the Holy Spirit with his Word. "We will prepare for a long trip, Lucy," I said, "and when we start we will journey toward the South."

Without further notification, I received by mail, within the following fortnight, a cheque for twenty dollars (purchase price of wheel). This amount procured us some necessaries, paid a few small bills and our fares to Redwood City, leaving us with the sum total of sixty cents.

Before proceeding on this undertaking, we occupied every hour of the day, with but few exceptions, in active preparation; our evenings and Sundays we spent in church or prison, or among the outcasts. I am indebted to Lucy for admission into many heretofore forbidden places, where she would be invariably welcomed with such a greeting as this:

"Well, hello, Kid! glad to see you. When did you get out? How's all the rest of them?"

"This is my dear Mother Roberts," she would say. "Please welcome her for my sake. I want to tell you I'm not one of you any longer. I've found my Savior. Don't I look different? Don't I look happy?"

"You bet yer life y' do, Kid. Say, we don't mind being preached to if you'll do the preaching. Go on girlie, pitch in, we-uns would like to hear from the likes of you, cause we know you," etc.

The precious girl! How she enthused all of us as she told the wonderful story and implored them to seek the Savior! Always we finished with prayer. Even bar-tenders, saloon-keepers, and women overseers over the girls in the various dives were touched by Lucy's brief messages from God. The time was all too short on these occasions. As we said our final farewells (July 1, 1903), it was impossible to count the number of those who said: "Y've done me good, Lucy, Y've done me good. Yes, I mean to heed what y've said. I know it's right. Stick to it, girlie, stick to it." And not a few said they had sold their last drink or had drunk their last drop.

I wish you could appreciate how wonderful all this is to me now (Sept. 5, 1911) whilst recalling and writing it, here in my quiet, pretty room in the Gospel Trumpet Company's home for their consecrated workers. It seems as though but a few days, instead of years, have elapsed since that marvelously profitable time.

In the interval between her coming to me and our departure we visited, as frequently as possible, the prison, the place of her incarceration. once taking a modest treat, purchased by a little of Lucy's pocket-money. I can not describe the appreciation of each prisoner as they received, at her hands, a small package of something toothsome done up in a pretty paper napkin, with an appropriate text inscribed thereon. This distribution was followed by a special meeting, for the most part conducted by my dear Lucy.

After the tearful farewells had been said, we went into Captain and Mrs. Kincaid's quarters, where the latter furnished us with the names of some for whom she desired our special interest in the event of our coming in touch with them. They were all ex-prisoners, some of whom we will hereafter mention.

As though to give us a specially bright send-off, the sun arose in glorious splendor on that second day of July. Following a very light early breakfast, Lucy and I, accompanied to the depot by some Christian friends, one of whom was the late Brother Mosby, soon boarded the train at Twenty-fourth and Valencia Streets, and in a short time arrived at Redwood City.

"What are we going to do next?" inquired Lucy. "You don't know any one here, do you, Mother?"

"No, dear. I'm going to ask the depot-agent if he can tell me who is the most consecrated Christian in this town."

Imagine, if you can, his astonishment.

"Say that over again, madam," he said.

I repeated my inquiry, whilst he scratched his head and pondered over this simple but no doubt perplexing question, and also glanced at us as much as to say, "I wonder if you are altogether right in your minds?"

Leaving in his keeping our two telescope baskets, containing all our earthly belongings, we soon reached the residence of the Congregational minister, only to discover that he, with his family, had left that very morning for his summer vacation. His neighbors directed us to the Methodist minister, an old gentleman, who received us very cordially, said many encouraging words on learning of the nature of our errand, and wished us God's blessing as we took our departure to the next place, at that moment unknown.

I now decided to make our errand known to the editors of the local papers. We found two, in close proximity to each other. They received us kindly, inspected the letters of endorsement with which I had provided myself before leaving San Francisco, and took notes.

Noon-time found my faith not sufficient to invest our capital or even a portion of it for the food we now so much needed. Moreover, it was extremely warm, and we were clad in heavy garments, suitable to the colder climate from which we had come. I made the same inquiry of the editor of the *Gazette* as I had made of the depot-agent, and I shall never forget the editor's surprised smile as he replied: "Really, Mrs. Roberts, I'm the last one of whom to inquire, as I make no profession whatsoever of religion. There is a lady living on the edge of town, formerly of the Salvation Army; she might do."

It was a long walk, or rather seemed so. We soon discovered that this lady was in no position to entertain us over night, and as it was long past noon, she must have taken it for granted that we had dined. Before leaving I requested a season of prayer. Her aged mother preceded her, I followed, then Lucy, who drew tears from our eyes by her fervent petition for guidance. After we had made our adieus and had walked a few yards, the daughter called and ran after us, to inform us that she had just thought of the landlady of the Tremont Hotel (Mrs. Ayers). "Her dining-room is closed for the season. She is a very kind-hearted woman. I have no doubt of her inviting you to remain under her roof when she learns your errand," said this newly-found friend. I thanked her most sincerely, and we proceeded once more to town.

I again called upon the *Gazette* editor, for I had it in mind to hold a street-meeting that evening and make public announcement of our errand. He promised the presence of himself and of others in the event of my doing so.

"Mother dear," inquired poor, tired, hungry, over-heated Lucy, "I wonder if God really wants us to hunt a home for the girls, after all? I can't stand much more."

"Neither can I, dear child," I replied, "but we'll ask him. Give me your hand." (We were walking toward the hotel.)

"Father," I prayed, "hast thou sent us on this errand? If so, please seal it with money before the day ends. I ask in Jesus' name." And Lucy sighed, "Amen."

May God forever bless dear Mrs. Ayers, who cordially welcomed us, giving us one of her best rooms and expressing her regret for inability to supply meals; God abundantly bless her and her dear ones.

We shut ourselves in, knelt together at the bedside, and wept—wept tears of gratitude, hope, and joy. Still weeping, both of us, in broken language, thanked the One who never makes any mistakes for guiding us aright and raising up friends in our trying hour, and closed our prayers by imploring his pardon for our having not better stood his testings and by promising with his aid to be braver in the future.

I now invested a quarter to have our baggage immediately brought from the depot, then refreshed ourselves, and soon I crossed the street, returning presently with a nice fresh loaf of bread and a dime's worth of bologna. On these and water, we humbly, gratefully dined. I have partaken of many costly, delicious viands, but never in all my experience have I enjoyed a meal as I did that simple one. Hallelujah!

The sun was gradually disappearing when Lucy and I crossed the street and stood on the corner in front of Mr. Behren's bank. We had carried one of the hotel chairs over with us, for I have never yet learned to play on my autoharp while standing. I now sat at a convenient angle in the street. Lucy composed one of my audience on the sidewalk. At first I felt somewhat timid and very nervous, but not for long. While the crowd was gathering, I sang the song,

I know my heavenly Father knows
The storms that would my way oppose
But he can drive the clouds away
And turn my darkness into day.

The people gathered so fast that before I had finished the second verse I was well surrounded.

There was a fair sprinkling of women, also carriages. Before singing another song, I took advantage of the situation to tell my audience why I was in Redwood City and on that street corner. If God ever gave me liberty of speech this was the occasion. After I had finished my address, which was not very long, one of my audience, named Lewis as I soon learned, stepped forward, took off his hat, and spoke as follows:

"Ladies and Gentlemen: I for one am convinced of this stranger's earnestness and the needs of such a home as she desires to get. Let's give her a collection. We're going to squander lots of Fourth of July money day after tomorrow. Here's my quarter, whose next?"

The money kept dropping, dropping, dropping into that hat, nickels, dimes, quarters until the sound made me nearly shout for joy. It was all I could do to contain myself.

Then some one in a carriage sent a request for me to sing again. I gladly responded, after which my audience bowed with uncovered heads whilst I thanked the loving heavenly Father and pronounced the benediction. Thus gloriously ended my first street meeting conducted without other human aid.

We were the happy possessors of $13.20 toward the fund for the promised home, and no mortals on earth retired that night more grateful and happy than dear Lucy and her "Mother" Roberts. To God be all the glory and praise forever.

CHAPTER XVI
SANTA CLARA EXPERIENCES.
THE SAN JOSE HOME

All the next day we remained in Redwood City in anticipation of receiving mail, and our hopes were realized. There were letters of cheer and encouragement from Mrs. Dorcas Spencer, State Secretary W.C.T.U.; Mrs. Augusta C. Bainbridge, State Superintendent Purity W.C.T.U.; Mrs. Elizabeth Kauffman, matron of the Home of Peace; the chaplain of the Sailors' Home, in which place I had held frequent meetings; Mr. and Mrs. George S. Montgomery; Judge George Cabaniss; Captain and Mrs. Kincaid, the superintendent and matron of the county jail, Branch No. 3, and other friends alike interested. Also, Lucy heard from her people. It gives me pleasure to copy one of my letters:

622 Golden Gate Avenue, San Francisco, Cal June 30, 1902.

Mrs. Roberts.

My dear Sister:

How I do praise the Lord for laying that burden on you! I have prayed for it so long. I knew he would lay it somewhere soon. The Woman's Christian Temperance Union have a special department for jail work, and some lovely Christian women in charge. The State, county and local superintendents of jail, hospital, purity, mother's work, evangelistic and other departments would be glad to help you. I am State superintendent of purity. Let me know now I can help you…. If you want the directory you can get it at headquarters, 132 McAllister Street. You can show this letter to either of the ladies there, and they will know I endorse you and your work….

Yours in love,

A. C. Bainbridge.

We decided to go to Santa Clara on the morrow. Accordingly, the next day we were mingling with a great throng of merry-makers—*with them, but not of them.*

Mr. Lewis' mother, with whom we had dined the previous evening, had recommended a certain private boarding-house. Hither we repaired, and were fortunate in finding a Christian hostess, who made us very welcome. Lucy helped her, she having a great Fourth of July crowd for meals, whilst I rested.

On the following day I went forth in quest of means to help swell the fund started in Redwood City. I walked and talked all day; toward evening I returned to our boarding-house with only a poor report. Lucy greeted me cheerfully and said:

"I'm going to earn your board and mine, Mother dear. The landlady needs help; so as long as we're here, it will not be necessary to touch the fund. You needn't think you are to bear all the burden. No, indeed. I'm going to do my part, too."

"God bless you, Lucy! I'm so thankful!" I replied. "How good the dear Lord is and how wonderfully he provides!"

At the end of nearly a week of toil, I had apparently made little impression. One night as I sat in our room, too tired to go to the dining-room, Lucy came in, took off my shoes and stockings, cried over the swollen, blistered condition of my feet, bathed them, made me retire, and brought to the bedside a tempting meal.

The next day, after making a few calls and receiving some small sums by way of encouragement, I felt impressed to return to our room and then go to a handsome home directly across the street from the boarding-house. Soon I was ringing the bell. A lady greeted me with a lovely smile, bade me enter, and encouraged me in making known my errand. Calling her husband, she asked me to repeat my story. When I took my departure, after receiving overwhelming kindness and a cordial invitation to return when convenient, I held in my hand my first gold piece for the fund. The donors were Mr. and Mrs. Chas. E. Moore, who have been my warm, interested, personal friends from that time to this. They did all in their power to aid me, particularly through introductions to people of means in their home town.

Soon I was led to make myself known to the pastors of the various churches, one of whom agreed to give me an opportunity of addressing an audience from his pulpit. His name was Thurston, and I shortly learned that he was a nephew of the people with whom I had traveled in gospel-wagon work. The following notice in the Santa Clara News of July 7, 1903, heralded the prospective meeting:

FOR A RESCUE HOME

Mrs. Florence Roberts, who is known in San Francisco as the Rescue Missionary and Singing Evangelist, will address the public in the

Baptist church next Sunday on the subject of the establishment of a non-sectarian home for women near San Francisco.

She comes highly endorsed by prominent citizens and Christian societies. There are, she states, thirty-five thousand women on this coast to be reached, and she is endeavoring to procure funds for a home to which they can come for reformation. A free-will offering will be taken at the conclusion of the address.

Prior to this meeting I learned of a little rescue home in San Jose, the adjacent city, and one afternoon Lucy and I visited it. We went without previous announcement, for I wanted to satisfy myself as to its merits. It was a pretty old-fashioned cottage of about eight rooms, located at 637 East St. John Street. There were but two girls—one a mother, the other a prospective one—and, sad to relate, a most inefficient matron. I quickly took in the situation, and, for the sake of the inmates, privately decided to accept erelong her invitation to sojourn temporarily under that roof.

After I had thoroughly canvassed Santa Clara, I, acting upon divine directions, took Lucy and went to the San Jose rescue home.

Before long it became my sorrowful duty to report conditions as they existed. The president of the board of managers, Rev. J. N. Crawford, was absent on his summer vacation. Upon learning that the vice-president, Mrs. Remington (now deceased), was sojourning in San Francisco, I boarded the train and a few hours later was in earnest discussion with Mrs. Remington and her friend, Miss Sisson. This consultation terminated in their sincere plea for me to take upon myself certain responsibilities, concerning which I promised to pray. The result was that I felt led to go further south for a while, but not before some better conditions existed for those two poor girls and others who might follow.

CHAPTER XVII
CALLIE'S WONDERFUL STORY

One day while I was visiting Mr. and Mrs. Helms, Sr., in Santa Clara, good friends of the cause, the latter said:

"Sister Roberts, have you ever met Callie— —?"

"No, Sister Helms," I answered, "but I have heard of her. She was often, before my missionary work there, an inmate of the county jail, Branch 3, and gave much trouble when a prisoner."

"I want to let you know she is wonderfully converted and one of our most remarkable missionaries. Try and take time to call on her. She works in the R— — boarding-house and will be glad to see you, for she knows of you quite well. Ask her to tell you her story. You never heard anything equal to it; furthermore, you never have, I doubt ever will, meet any other like her. She is *a living marvel of God's power to save to the uttermost.*"

The following afternoon, leaving kind-hearted Lucy (without offense to the matron of the home) to administer to the comforts of the inmates, I went to the place designated. Soon there came into my presence a smiling, healthy-looking woman about forty years of age, who told me that she was the person for whom I had inquired. No sooner did I mention my name than she threw her arms about me exclaiming, "God love you, Mother Roberts! God love you! It's good for sore eyes to see you"—and she rattled on. When I told her the nature of my errand, she replied that she would come to the home that evening and would then relate the story of her life and wonderful conversion. She was on hand at the appointed time, and soon Lucy and I were listening to what I will now relate.

"I first saw the light of day in the slums of St. Louis, Mo. I never knew, nor did any one ever tell me, who my father and mother were. All I know about those days and up to my fourteenth year is that one or another of the women of that neighborhood fed, clothed, and sheltered me. I had no schooling; didn't know how to read or write till a few years ago. I never heard much besides bad language, seldom saw anything but drinking, gambling, and so forth; never saw the inside of a church and seldom saw the outside, 'cause I wasn't out of my own neighborhood very much. It was too much like a fish being out of water. Never heard the name of God or Jesus

Christ except when they were taken in vain, and never troubled my head to find out who was God or who was Jesus Christ.

"Before I was fifteen years old, I married a gambler. He was a fine-looking fellow, considerably older than me, and sometimes had a pile of money.

"Yes, he gave me what I asked for. Sometimes I spent quite a bit on dress and treating my friends, 'cause there ain't a stingy bone in my body. I've no use for stingy folk, have you?

"Tom wasn't a heavy drinker, but he used to 'hit the pipe.'"

"What is 'hit the pipe', Callie?" I inquired.

"Don't you know? Why, smoke opium. Also, he had the morphine habit, and if anything, that's the worst one of the two, but, between you and me, there's little or no choice. It wasn't long before I, too, commenced taking morphine, and kept it up until two years ago. Look here!"

With that she stripped up the sleeves of her dress, and we were gazing at arms which from the shoulder to wrist were one mass of tiny bluish spots. I doubt if there was room to place a pin between them.

"Oh! Callie, what are they?"

"Shots—shots from the hypodermic needle that we used to inject the morphine.

"Hurt? No, not much; besides, we get to be such slaves to it that we'd gladly hurt our bodies for the sake of it. It's the most demoralizing, hard-to-break habit on earth. But glory to God! I'm saved and sanctified now, and I'll tell you how it came about.

"I suppose I'd been serving my fifteenth sentence, to say the least, in Branch No. 3, and they'd put me down in the dungeon, as usual, as they most always had to do for the first few drays, 'cause I wanted the drug so bad (they give you some there, but it never was enough) that I used to disturb everybody, and besides, was very troublesome. I'll never forget the day when I tried to knock my brains out on the dark cement floor, but couldn't; so I cried, 'O God! if there is a God, and some of these missionary folk that come here say there is a God, and a Christ what can save, *save me, save me, please save me*! I don't want to go to hell! I've had hell enough! I don't want to go to hell!'

"There was a little quiet-looking old lady visiting the jail that day, and she asked Matron Kincaid if she couldn't go down and try to help that poor afflicted soul in the dungeon, and Mrs. Kincaid gave permission.

"Mother Roberts, her very presence was soothing, and pretty soon she put her arm around me and prayed. Oh, how she prayed to her God and Savior to come, and come quickly, to help and save me through and through! By and by she told me of Jesus who died for sinners. I couldn't bear to part with her, but I had to let her go soon, she promising to come back again. I was still suffering, but after hearing her, and her being so kind to dirty, loathsome me, I made up my mind I'd try to 'grin and bear' the misery if it took my very life.

"Next time she came, I was out of the dungeon, up on the next floor in my cell. Say, Mother Roberts, you wouldn't have known me if you had seen me then and as I look now. I didn't weigh ninety pounds. Now I weigh close onto one hundred and seventy. Praise the Lord!

"I was always a mass of filth and rags whenever the cops [police] would run me in.

"What did they arrest me for? Why for stealing of course. We'll swipe anything to supply ourselves and our chums with 'dope' [morphine, cocaine, opium, etc.]. That last time I'd been sentenced for three months. When my time was up, my missionary friend called for me, and we came down on the train to San Jose. She hired a hack at the depot; wasn't she considerate? God bless her!

"When we reached this home, the matron [Sister Griffith] met me at the door, and, said she, 'Welcome, dear child, welcome in the name of the Lord.' Then she put her arm around me, and led me into this very room we are sitting in now. I fell in love with her right on the spot. She had a lovely face and the beautifullest white hair I ever saw.

"I asked her to please let me go to bed, and would she gave me a room where I couldn't escape; also to please take away all my clothes, all but the bedding and a nightdress. I told her I'd come there to fight it out, that I'd been in hell on earth for years, *that for twenty-seven years I'd been a 'dope' fiend*, and that I wanted all of them who knew how to pray to pray for me, 'cause I knew there was a Christ and a God, but I hadn't found him yet. She did as I asked, and after a while tried to get me to eat, but I couldn't. Did you know the 'dope' fiends lose their appetites for everything but the drug? Yes, they do. I often wondered what kept us alive. It surely wasn't the food we ate.

"My, what a struggle I had! what a fight for the next three weeks! for I was determined from the time my sentence expired, never, if it killed me, to touch the poison again, and I was bound to keep my word. God alone knows what I suffered. One morning a little before daylight (I'd heard the clock strike one, two, three, somewhere) all of a sudden the room was lit up with a strange soft light, and somebody was whispering (or it seemed like whispering), 'Daughter, be of good cheer. Thou art healed.' Oh but I felt beautiful, beautiful! and soon slept the sweetest. Not an ache or pain. Just like a new-born baby. When I woke up I could tell the girls were at breakfast. I took my stick and knocked on the floor. Pretty soon Sister Griffith came up, and I told her. She cried with me for very joy, and knelt by my bedside to thank God for answer to prayer, then went down to tell the family. Glory, glory be to God the Father, Son and Holy Spirit! I was saved and I knew it—saved through and through.

"From that on I gained rapidly, enjoyed my meals, and pretty soon was able to go down-stairs. No fear any more. I've never wanted the drug from that day to this, and I'm trying by the grace of God to help other poor souls like afflicted. Say, Mother Roberts, when you go to San Francisco again, will you let me go with you? I want to surprise the folk at the jail and in the morphine dens; besides, I'll show you a place you never have seen or heard tell of, where these poor souls live—a place condemned by the authorities, but not torn down yet."

I told her that, God willing, I should be very glad to have her accompany me. Then she took out of her pocket a letter, saying, as she did so, "I wrote this to some one you know." (Here she described one of the poor prisoners.) "You can take it up to your room and read it if you like, and mail it for me tomorrow, please."

Soon we joined the rest of the family in their evening devotions, and Callie went back to her place.

I read and reread that wonderful letter before retiring, and as soon as convenient the next morning I telephoned to Callie to ask whether I might copy it before mailing it. She gladly gave me permission, and now I give you the letter almost word for word:

San Jose, Cal. Aug. 18, 1903.

Dear Nan:

No doubt you will be somewhat surprised to receive this from me, but it is surprising—and wonderful the way God has of lifting us up out of sin. Now what has been done for me will be done for you if you will only let him have his way with you. Surely "the way of the transgressor is hard," and the devil is a poor pay-master. I know you are so tired of that life that you will be willing to say, "O Lord, anything but this; 'better a dry crust of bread with quietness than a house full of sacrifice, with strife.'" The truth is a bitter pill, and many have choked to death on it, but while "the mourners go about the streets," the truth goes on just the same. Now my greatest sacrifice was — —. With him the house was full of strife, for I had to produce for it all, and no peace in the end; so to get away from the whole thing and keep out of San Quentin [one of the State prisons] I had to not only die to him, but myself. So now, glory to God! I am sanctified and my sins and dead yesterdays are under the blood, and Just as the branch is to the vine, I am joined to Christ and I know he is mine.

Nan, as I look back to Mrs. J— —'s time [a former jail matron] and the hell we had, trying to live through, and of poor Minnie B— — and Minnie E— —, who have gone out in the darkness—[Minnie B— — was dead, Minnie E— — dying, when the trusty rushed into the room where the matron, Mrs. J——, was engaged in a game of cards, and begged her to come quickly, to which she replied, "Let her die; 'tis a pity a few more of you don't go the same way" and then coolly continued the game she was playing.] If we had continued along on that plane, such would have been our fate also; but he, our Lord, is so patient and long-suffering that the moment we are willing to give up and let him have his way with us, then the work begins for our good. Now, Nan, I am only too glad to be able to help you in any way I can.

I owe the H— — of T— — $10. I stole $40 for "dope" from them while in the "hypo" state. I have now paid back $30, and when your time is up, I will be able to pay your fare down here, and your board until you can see and know for yourself what real liberty there is in Christ.

Everything did not go just as I liked at first; but, as you know, a good thing is not easily gotten, and if you will only try half as hard for liberty in Christ as you do for those you love, it will not be long ere you are out and out for Christ, and your dead yesterdays will be as though they never had been, and if you will let me be a mother to you, I would divide my last drop of blood to save your soul.

O God! bless my erring sisters, "who love not wisely, but too well," bearing their sorrows alone in silence with an anguish none can tell." Now, dear, weigh this well, and "choose this day which you will serve,'" God or mammon. T am not the only "hypo" fiend that the Lord sees fit to take out of hell; so be of good cheer, for he has said, "I will never leave thee nor forsake thee."

Start in with a fervent prayer, saying, "Create in me a clean heart, O God, and renew a right spirit within me." Just as soon as you are willing to take your Savior for your satisfying portion every door of hope will be open to you with outstretched arms. My strength is in God and I want you to feel some of it. I do not know the extent of it.

Poor M—! I feel sorry for her. Mrs. Roberts called on me. She is O K, and her heart is in her work. Dear child of God, she is sowing seeds of kindness all along her line. May God bless her! The little lady who is with her [Lucy] speaks highly of you. Nan, and we all see the Lord in you if you will only give up all to him. Tell Mrs. —— I still have faith for her [the dignified-looking white-haired prisoner already spoken of], for God is still looking around for the impossible things, to move mountains. Love to K—, G—, Mrs. S—, Mollie R—, and all the rest of the girls.

Now, Nan, we have seen the tough side of life together, so come on out and up, and say, "With the help of God I will be a woman." That is not your element by right, Nan, so the sooner you seek, the sooner you will find.

Now, good-by, and may God and his holy angels guide and protect you, and may your whole spirit, soul, and body be preserved blameless until the coming of our Lord Jesus Christ.

Give my love to all the girls. I pray for you all every day.

Callie ——

P.S.—To Mrs. Captain Kincaid. I know you will be happy to know I am still true to God. It pays in the end for if we sow to the flesh, we reap corruption, and if to the Spirit, everlasting life. I am a Bible student, and as soon as the Lord can trust me with the seal of the Holy Spirit, I am to preach the gospel of Jesus Christ, the power of God unto salvation Glory, glory, glory for liberty in him!...

I still have your present in mind. It is forthcoming in the near future.

Respectfully yours,

Callie ——.

The only alterations I made in this remarkable letter were in some real mines, the spelling, capitalization, and punctuation. Otherwise it is her language, word for word.

Oh! bless the dear Lord forever! What an example of

"Whilst the lamp holds out to burn,
The vilest sinner may return"!

Later we paid our proposed visit to San Francisco. Our experience on that occasion will be found in the next chapter.

CHAPTER XVIII
CALLIE AND I VISIT THE JAIL, MORPHINE DENS, AND THE MISSION—THE OUTCOME

Some time elapsed before we took that trip together. I have much to relate regarding the occurrences during the interval, but first let me write about our San Francisco trip.

Shortly before Christmas occasion required my presence in San Francisco. I notified Gallic, and one morning bright and early we reached that city. We immediately repaired to Branch No. 3.

(Before I give an account of our experiences, please allow me to relate an incident that occurred on the train. In a seat almost parallel with the one we occupied sat two women, one of whom was richly dressed. She repeatedly looked my way. Her face seemed familiar. Presently I ventured to accost her with that fact. She smilingly replied: "Of course it is. I'm — — — —. You came to my house in Santa Cruz dressed in a Salvation Army bonnet. If it hadn't have been for that, you would never have got in. One of my girls left because of what you said and did that day. I'll be glad to have you call. I always want to help save a girl if I can. Perhaps you can persuade her sister." Hallelujah! "It came to pass" less than a month later.)

The gate-keeper passed us into the grounds, and soon I was being warmly greeted by Mrs. Kincaid. Presently I inquired if she recognized my companion. She smilingly shook her head.

"You've met her many times, Mrs. Kincaid," I said.

She guessed any but the right person. Finally she said slowly:

"It might be Callie——; but she was nothing but a bag of bones; as forlorn-looking a specimen of humanity as I ever looked upon, whereas this woman is fine-looking, robust, and has a splendid expression. Surely it can't be Callie!"

"But it is Callie. Look!" And Callie proved her identity by pulling up her sleeve—convincing evidence beyond a doubt. Never did I see matron more delighted. Presently, following some rapid questions and answers, she said, "How would you like to surprise your former companions, Callie?"

"Just what I was hoping for, Mrs. Kincaid," Callie answered.

"Very well; I'll have all of them called into the large dormitory. You wait here a few minutes."

There was an enthusiastic welcome for me, but no one recognized my companion—no, *not one*. She stood beside me, speechless and trembling. Finally I said:

"Speak to them, dear."

"I can't," she whispered, and the tears were in her eyes.

"Girls, I've brought some one with me today whom you all know and know well, but I see you do not recognize her." (A long silence.)

"Who is she?" some one asked. (Another long silence.)

"Show them who you are, Callie."

"Callie? Callie — —? Surely not, Mother Roberts. She was," etc., etc.

But she was showing them; choking down her sobs of joy, or rather, trying to, as she rolled up her sleeves to convince them. Even so, they found it very difficult to believe, very, very difficult.

I gladly retired to a remote part of the dormitory, a grateful observer temporarily forgotten, whilst Callie was being questioned and overhauled by about seventy delighted women and girls. They went into raptures of joy, they shouted, they wept, they hugged and kissed her, until she was obliged to say, "Sit down. I want to talk to you. Do, please."

Intense silence reigned whilst she related the wonderful story of her conversion and sanctification. There was not a dry eye present. Then she gave an invitation. Without one exception all responded and then knelt. She prayed—oh! how she prayed! and some of the women wet the boards with their tears whilst they, too, called upon Callie's Savior for pardon and mercy. How I wish we might have stayed there the remainder of the day! but we could not, for my time was limited. Feelingly and reluctantly we said our "farewells," promising to come at some future time if God so willed.

Before we left, they all lovingly inquired for Lucy, sending her many kind messages of love and remembrance.

When we returned to Mrs. Kincaid's quarters, she inquired if I should like to see a photo of Callie as she formerly looked?

"Indeed, I would," I replied.

Well, to this day I do not wonder at their failure to recognize her. *In that picture she looked like a dirty, emaciated, old vagabond.* This is the best I can do in the way of description, dear reader. I wish I had a copy of her "Before and After" to put in this book. You would be sure to say, "Mother Roberts did not exaggerate one iota." If any of you know Mrs. Kincaid, go to her and ask her whether she won't please show it to you....

We were soon on the street-car, and then downtown, where I quickly transacted my business, after which I was once more at Callie's disposal.

I followed her to a place on the south of Market Street, to a building which resembled a deserted, tumble-down stable or blacksmith's shop plastered with old hand-bills and posters. There were some dirty old window-frames in the second story, but I do not believe there was one whole pane of glass left.

"This is the place, Mother Roberts," said Callie.

"Surely no human beings dwell in such a terrible place as this, Callie," I replied.

"You come with me and see for yourself," she rejoined. "Don't you remember what I told you? I said I would take you to a place you didn't dream existed. This is the one."

Sure enough. *And this was once her home!* She opened a disreputable door, and we climbed a dirty and fearfully rickety stairway; next we groped our way along a dark passage. "Mind, there's a broken board! Look out you don't break your ankle," said Callie. She spoke none too soon. I narrowly escaped an accident. Now we turned a corner and got a little better light, this disclosing another old partly-broken-down stairway with nearly all the balustrade gone. Up these we climbed, hugging, as we did so, the filthy wall, for safety. On reaching the top she rapped gently an a cracked door, but received no answer. She rapped louder. Still no answer. Presently some one called from somewhere below. Then she rapped still louder. This time a man's voice inquired, "Who's there?" There was the sound of shuffling footsteps, and then the door opened, disclosing two women, one young, one old, and three men, all young, but all old-looking, cadaverous, starved, ragged, filthy, and indescribably loathsome. Furthermore, the odor issuing through that open doorway was almost intolerable.

Callie knew all, with the exception of the young girl, and called each by name; but, as usual, they did not recognize her, and, in the same manner as heretofore described, had to be convinced, whilst she again rehearsed her wonderful experience. Presently she said: "I'm going to hunt up some of the others, and I'm going to ask this lady to sing for you while I am gone. She's brought her autoharp with her."

THE SONGS MY MOTHER SANG

Words and Music by Mrs. FLORENCE ROBERTS.

DUET Or SOLO.

1. One day I found a precious book
   Containing many a gem
   Of song my mother used to sing
   It takes me back again
   Across the vista of the years,
   When, by her loving voice,
   Melodious invitation came
   To make the Lord my choice.

2. She sang about the previous blood
   Christ shed on Calvary;
   And how, to save our souls from hell,
   He died in agony. "Come, sinners, to the gospel feast"
   Methinks I hear her still
   Singing, as silently she prayed
   "Lord, break that stubborn will."

3. This blessed soldier of the cross
   To her reward has gone;
   But oh, the tender memories
   She left in sacred song.
   And, tho' I wandered far from God,
   And wasted many years,
   The songs my mother used to sing
   Will oft-times bring the tears.]

Up to this time I had not uttered a word. The scene had practically rendered me temporarily speechless; but now I took a few steps into the room, whilst one of the men found an old soap box and turned it upside down for me to sit on. At a glance I saw vermin crawling in the cracks of the filthy floor. Oh! it was awful! Soon, however, I lost sight of my loathsome surroundings, for in answer to silent prayer the dear Lord was giving me a message in song. Never was there closer attention than while they listened to the song which you will find between these pages, entitled "The Songs My Mother Sang." Then I knelt and prayed, and prayed. "On that dirty floor?" you ask. Yes, dear reader; I quite forgot the dirt and the vermin. I only saw souls going to hell if they didn't get help from God. (Afterwards I observed that neither vermin nor dirt clung to me.)

When once more conscious of my surroundings, I discovered how dirty their faces were, for now there were clean channels on many cheeks. Their tears! One girl and two men agreed to forsake sin, and I was happy in the thought of conveying her to San Jose on our return next day, whilst Callie planned for the men. We did what we could for the time being and then went out into the fresh air. I asked Callie how many lived under that roof. To my amazement, she said, "All told, about forty just at present."

Her next mission was to the various places from which she had pilfered, and they were many. One was a harness-shop. She addressed the old man thus:

"How d'you do, sir? Do you remember me?"

"No, mam, I don't. Who are you?"

"I'm a woman who once stole a dog collar from you while your back was turned. I've come to pay for it. I'm converted now, but I used to be a 'dope' fiend."

"You were? You don't look like it."

"No, because God, for Jesus Christ's sake, forgave all my sins, cured me of all my bad habits, and has set me on the solid Rock, and I'm on my road to heaven. When you knew me I was on my road to hell."

"But I never knew you."

"Yes, you did. I'm Callie — —."

"What! You don't say so! Well, well! wonders will never cease. It's enough to make a man believe there is a personal God, I declare it is!"

Callie availed herself of this opportunity, and when we left there, the harness-maker had promised to serve her wonderful Savior and he kept his word.

Next we visited the rescue home, where we were received with open arms by dear Sister Kauffman. After having a precious time with her family and partaking of her hospitality, we went down-town again. There we spent a glorious evening at a street-meeting. Callie testified. Afterward we went to the Emmanuel Gospel Mission, where she gave a message from that most precious parable, "The Prodigal Son." When the invitation was given, the altar filled with seekers, most of whom went from there with victory in their souls.

We were the guests of the mission superintendent and family over night. Callie was my room-mate. Then it was that I saw what the hypodermic needle had done for her. *There was no place (save down her spine) that was not marked*, and no wonder, she had been a morphine slave for twenty-seven years—its abject slave.

The next morning, as soon as we could politely leave our kind host and family, we returned to that 'dope' den, Callie to prepare the two young men, I to take charge of the girl, and all of us to return on an early train to San Jose. Alas! my girl weakened, and nothing would induce her to part with her drug; but the men went with Callie to an adjacent barber-shop for baths, hair-cutting, and shaving. During these operations Callie and I quickly went to the Salvation Army's secondhand shop, where Callie procured the men complete outfits of respectable clothing. What a transformation when we beheld them again! Then we took them to breakfast; but they ate sparingly, and were not satisfied until they had taken some of their favorite drug.

Two and a half hours later Callie and I were it home once more, and our young men were in the safe keeping of two sanctified brothers. Although these brethren were severely tried and tested time and again, they so held on to God for these precious souls that they are now saved and sanctified and on their road to heaven.

Gallic kept her situation for some time longer and then went forth to preach the glorious gospel. The last time I heard of her, she was being wonderfully blest in preaching in southern California. May God forever guide this precious woman and keep her true until Jesus calls, "Well done, thou good and faithful servant, enter thou into the joy of thy Lord."

CHAPTER XIX
STILL SOUTHWARD BOUND—SANTA CRUZ—LUCY RETURNS TO HER HOME

The occurrences of the previous chapter took place several months after the happenings now to be related.

The latter part of August found Lucy and me in Santa Cruz, one of California's beautiful ocean resorts, where again we were fortunate in securing lodging with a Christian landlady, Mrs. Hedgepeth, who took pleasure in furnishing much information. She also introduced us to several, who, later on, became warmly interested in the cause we represented.

In the main, ours was now a house-to-house work. Lucy would take one street, and I another, seeking for means to be applied to the home fund. For days we met only at noon and eventide, weary in body, often somewhat discouraged, but always with new and varied experiences. A few of these we will relate.

One evening Lucy said: "Mother, I called at a lovely home today where were a great variety of beautiful birds and strange little animals in big cages in the yard. The gentleman who was feeding and caring for them seemed pleased at my interest, leaned over the fence and conversed with new about them, telling where he had discovered some, how costly were others, what special care and food most of them required, and much more; but oh! Mother dear, he had no use, no time for Jesus, or anything relating to him. He turned away and left me when I tried to tell him. Isn't he to be pitied? I had better success a few doors higher up. The lady was very kind. She put her name down for one dollar. I've collected $— — for the fund today," and she smiled with joy as she handed me the money.

One reputed wealthy woman, after hearing my story, highly commended the enterprise and said, "I would be glad to help you, but all I can spare I contribute to the Salvation Army." I pleaded further, but in vain. Later, and quite by accident, we learned that her contribution consisted in occasionally purchasing a *War Cry*. What a sad, sad accounting will have to be given by many on that day when the Judge of all the earth shall sit upon his throne!

Several of the local pastors manifested most kindly consideration, some gave lists of names of charitably disposed people, and a few invited me to share their pulpits.

Never shall I forget the day when Lucy and I called at a handsome residence on Washington Street. The door was opened by one of the most spiritual-countenanced young ladies I have ever had the pleasure of meeting, and from that day to this she has been one of my warmest, most loyal friends—Sister B— — G— —. More times than I can count I have acted upon and profited by her wise and kindly advice, and never did she fail me with sympathy and help in a trying hour. Her widowed mother was the first large contributor to the fund. Only God knows my heart's gratitude the day she handed me that cheque for one hundred dollars.

Through the daughter I learned who had spiritual charge of the jail work, and soon, acting on her suggestions, made the acquaintance of Mrs. Mason. She invited us to attend the following Sunday morning services at 9:30 o'clock. In consequence of my responding, the next chapter will relate the sad story which came to me from the lips of a youth sentenced to Folsom penitentiary for ninety-nine years.

We soon located the neighborhood of the poor wandering girls, where many gladly bade Lucy and me welcome. Also, we were informed that, owing to circumstances at that time, the only religious people who would be admitted to certain houses were Salvation Army lassies. Learning our errand, one of these kindly disposed women of God accompanied us, we wearing bonnets loaned for this occasion. The landlady of one of these houses was the one we met on the train, when Callie accompanied me to San Francisco on that important trip.

At this time a gospel-tent was pitched in the rear of the court-house and city hall. Each night there congregated large numbers of people, most of whom came from the humble walks of life. In that precious little tabernacle many souls sought and found salvation. At this time the services were conducted by Brother Williams and his wife, whilst I served as organist, and also, occasionally, as the Lord would lead, delivered His messages.

One night whilst a girl was at the altar pleading for pardon and mercy, she was suddenly seized by a dark-haired, portly woman, dragged off of her knees, and hurried away. This unusual procedure took us workers off our guard and so startled us as temporarily to disable us from acting as we otherwise would have acted. The woman ran down the aisle, firmly gripping the speechless, frightened girl, declaring as she did so that it was her daughter, that she would see to it that this would not happen again; then both disappeared in the darkness. How subtle, how powerful is the adversary of souls! Later we learned that that poor, poor girl had just escaped from this madam (the pretended mother), who, suspecting her victim's whereabouts, had stealthily followed. We worked for her release, but in vain. The girl being of the age of consent, the authorities could not act. Besides, she was now once more subservient to the devil's hypnotic power and influence. All we could do was to hope and pray that the tender Shepherd would, in his own wise way, set her free from her wretched life and save her from the fate awaiting her.

When it became known that two newcomers, practical rescue workers, were in town, we were soon overwhelmed with responsibilities too many to shoulder. Moreover, the San Jose and San Francisco rescue homes, hitherto but little heard of in Santa Cruz, began filling to overflowing with wandering girls.

One day Lucy received a special letter, requesting her immediate presence at home on account of the sudden illness of her mother. We temporarily parted, I promising to join her (God willing) in October, in order to spend my birthday with her and her dear ones. How much I missed my ardent, loving companion I can not say; but as "the King's business requireth haste" (1 Sam. 21:8), I stifled my feelings and busied myself more, if possible, than heretofore in meeting representative people, calling on unfortunates, and, as often as permitted, visiting the prisoners.

In one of these I became so greatly interested that I am sure you also will as you soon read his story.

Before I left Santa Cruz, the Lord had graciously raised up many friends in that place. Time and again it has been my pleasure to return there, always to be warmly welcomed in many homes, and especially entertained by Sisters Green, Mary Perkins, Van Ness, and Brother Westlake and wife. The latter were traveling in gospel-tent work when first I met them. It was when making my home in Redding, where occurred the rescue of little Rosa.

Whilst I recall these precious times, so many instances of special seasons of prayer, special answers, personal kindnesses, and loving considerations come before my vision that I more than ever desire to bow humbly before the wonderful heavenly Father in thanksgiving and praise for graciously permitting so many, many of his loved ones to cheer, advise, and help me;

also for enabling me to look past the sinful exterior and to see, by faith, the priceless souls of humanity, souls that are starving and perishing for lack of proper nurture.

And I am still praying for more strength, more grace, more wisdom, more love, to aid me and his other chosen missionaries in the winning of souls and the rescuing of the perishing, for I do not want to go into his heavenly kingdom empty-handed. Do you?

CHAPTER XX
JOE'S STORY

In giving you Joe's story, I realize that I am taking considerable liberty, having not asked his permission, but I am confident of his willingness because of the lesson of warning to other boys—and they are so many—whose early lives correspond to his. I am one of Joe's interested friends. I have frequently visited him in the prison adjacent to Folsom, near Sacramento, Cal., and have learned from Warden Reilly that he is a model prisoner. I am hoping, and praying that, if it be the will of God, he will soon be out on parole.

Whilst he was detained in the Santa Cruz jail awaiting a rehearing of his case, it was frequently my privilege to visit that place through the week and, with my little autoharp for accompaniment, to sing for the prisoners. One afternoon, whilst I was sitting by the bars in front of Joe's cell, and just following that blessed song, "Tell Mother I'll Be There," he broke into agonizing sobs and tears, and for a long while could not control himself as he lay prostrate face downward on the cold stone floor. I waited and prayed, my very soul in agony for his, as I began to appreciate and realize his awful situation. Stretching forth my hands through those iron bars, I reverently placed them on his head, and with all my heart implored our Lord for comfort, mercy, and pardon for the soul of this stricken young man, who that morning had learned that the sentence already pronounced at a former trial had been confirmed and that it was immediately to go into effect. There was no escaping his fate now.

I was permitted, by the kind-hearted sheriff, to spend hours with Joe on that occasion. When his grief had somewhat spent itself, this is what he said:

"O Mother Roberts, Mother Roberts! if I only could recall the past! If I only could!

"I started in wrong from the time I can remember. Lots of naughty little things I would do even when I was quite a small shaver. *Some things I did the folks would think smart and cute. They would laugh and brag of me to the neighbors, right in my heating, too, and that's where they made a mistake; for, young as I was, it only made me bolder, also saucy.*

"Some of the youngsters in our neighborhood were awful. I do believe they were born bad; anyhow, I knew they swore, and so did some of their parents. They gave them many a cuffing, but they didn't care, only swore worse than ever. My folks used to forbid me to go near them, and when any of them came into our yard, used to say, You go right home; I don't want you here. Joe can't play with you.' But Joe did, and that's the reason Joe has to suffer now." …

"Poor boy! don't tell it, if it distresses you so badly," I said; but he continued.

"The time came when I was old enough to go to school. These same kids went to the same one I did, and do you think I could shake 'em? No, mam; they stuck to me like leeches. They were now harder than ever to get rid of. In fact, I couldn't, but managed never to let my folks see me with them if I could help it, and they knew they dare not come near our house. It didn't take me very long to learn to swear like them, when in their company. I thought it sounded big and smart, although deep down in my heart I knew it was wrong. One day one of them got hold of a deck of soiled playing cards, and the oldest kid undertook to teach the rest of us how to play casino. It didn't take long to learn. I used to often get home late from school now, and when asked what kept me, always told a lie. I hated to do that at first, but it soon got to be easy. The folks so loved me, had such confidence in their 'smart little Joe,' that they never suspected, because I learned my lessons quickly; besides, always had a pretty good report from school.

"We used to play sometimes in a vacant lot. There was a saloon near by, and sometimes the man would treat to soda-water, sometimes we paid for it, and by the time I was thirteen I had learned to love beer and whiskey, also to smoke cigarettes, which we would make from the tobacco we kids stole from our fathers' and other people's pockets when their backs were turned, though sometimes we'd buy it.

"It began to be hard work to get up in time for breakfast and school of a morning, and I'll tell you why. When the folks thought, after I'd said 'Good night' that I'd gone to bed, I'd lock my door, then pretty soon, in my stocking feet, holding my shoes in my hand, I would drop quietly out of my window into the garden, and as quick as I could, by previous arrangement, would join the others in a game of cards for the smokes or the drinks. Father more than once said, 'Joe, I've heard you're keeping bad boys' company. I hope it isn't true. If I have your word for it that it isn't, I'll believe you, because *I've never yet caught you in a lie.*' I confess I used to feel awfully ashamed and guilty as I'd say, 'Whoever told you that told you a lie. You know where I am at nine o'clock, sir.' And he'd say, 'That's so, my boy. They must have mistaken somebody else for you.' But I knew better.

"When I was about sixteen, I went to work driving a bakery wagon, so that I didn't see quite so much of my former pals, but delivering bread took me into places where no honest or moral man or boy ought to even dare to set his foot, let alone one like me; so I fell still further.

"For all that, a pure, good girl fell in love with me, and I with her. I hated to deceive her, but made up my mind that I would cut it all out when we were married, if she'd promise to be my wife; and so we became engaged. But—I didn't cut it out. More than once she said, 'O Joe, you've been drinking! I smell it.' I'd laugh, and make some kind of an excuse, and she'd forgive me every time. Say, Mother Roberts, I hated myself from head to foot for lying as I did to that pure, sweet girl."

"Go on, Joe, I'm listening."

"One night I joined the boys in a game of cards in a saloon on Sequel Avenue. It appears that Mr. L— —, the proprietor, who, by the way, was a veteran G. A. R. man, had received quite a sum of money that day—his back pension. *As God is my judge, I did not know this when I went in there that evening.* We had a round of drinks after the first game, and after the second, another round; then I said 'Good night' and went home.

"Father and I slept in the same room, and I hadn't been in bed very long when a knock came on our door.

"'Who's there?' asked father.

"'Me, Constable — —, where's Joe? I want him.'

"'Joe's out, Constable. What do you want him for?' asked father.

"'No, I'm not out, Father. Here I am,' I said, at the same time jumping out of bed. 'What's up?'

"'Joe, my boy, I'm sorry for you, but you're my prisoner. Dress as quick as you can and come with me. Mr. L— — was murdered tonight. He isn't dead yet, but he's dying. You were in his saloon a while ago, drinking and playing cards, and you are one of the three accused of the crime of murdering him for the sake of robbing him.'

"The shock was so awful that I couldn't speak, and oh! poor old father! He shook me, saying, 'Speak, Joe. Tell the constable it's not so.'

"'Constable, my boy doesn't drink anything to speak of, and I don't suppose he knows one card from another; do you, Joe?'

"Nobody answered this, and pretty soon we were in the presence of the dying man. Oh! Mother Roberts, it was like a horrible nightmare. I was dazed with the shock and the fright of it all. I could hardly get my voice when some one asked me where I had spent the evening, and at what time I had left that saloon. He must have been murdered right after I left. They tried to rouse him to see if he'd recognize me. He claimed to, but I'm sure he didn't; for he couldn't see and didn't know what he was talking about."

"What of your two companions, Joe?" I asked.

"One of them was there, in charge of the sheriff; I don't know where the other one was. From that night up to this we have been here in prison, though we haven't met. He's in a cell on another floor. He's sentenced to San Quentin for life.

"Father mortgaged our pretty home [he afterwards lost it, the mortgage being foreclosed] and has done everything under the sun he knows of to clear me, so have my lawyers; but they've failed! Mother Roberts, they've failed! and I'm to be sent to the penitentiary for ninety-nine years. Think of it, ninety-nine years! That means that unless the real murderer turns up, some day I'll die and be buried in a dishonored grave—and *all through starting out wrong to begin with, then keeping it up."*

My heart felt torn all to pieces for this poor unfortunate lad. How I should have liked to sit beside those bars all night in order to comfort him! but as that could not be, I presently, after commending him to an ever-merciful God and Savior, whom he could not, as yet, accept or understand, took my departure, as sad and burdened a soul as ever walked the earth. As the tears coursed down my cheeks, I resolved to try to help him, and, moreover, by repeating his story, to warn mothers and fathers to guard their little ones closely every hour of their young lives. Also, I purposed not to spare myself in addressing them, whether individually or *en masse*, but to confess my own carelessness and shortsightedness, when, as a young mother, I was much of the time heedless with regard to my little spoilt son, for *whose soul and body God was some day going to hold me responsible.* Had it not been for God's tender mercy and love in pardoning and directing my future life, in answering my earnest prayers for his tender watch-care over me and mine, who knows but that my only and well-beloved son might have shared a similar fate? If he had, I alone would have been to blame.

Many and many a time I have been used of God in trying to comfort stricken mothers who were visiting their children now behind bars. "O God!" they have cried, "what did I ever do that my child should get into such trouble as this?" Poor mothers! You were guilty as was I, but you haven't recognized that fact. Yes, you were; and now you begin to realize it when well-nigh too late. But it isn't yet. Just kneel down and throw yourself on the mercies of a merciful, loving God. Confess to him. Plead with him to forgive you. Ask him to direct every hour, every moment, of your future. Surrender your children to him; tell him you've made a blunder of their lives as well as of your own; then wait on him. Listen to what he says: "Come *now*, and let us reason together,… Though your sins be as scarlet, they shall be as white as snow, though they be red like crimson, they shall be as wool. If ye be willing and obedient, ye shall eat the good of the land; but if ye refuse and rebel, ye shall be devoured with the sword: for the mouth of the Lord hath spoken it." Isa. 1:18-20. "They that wait upon the Lord, shall renew their strength; they shall mount up with wings as eagles; they shall run and not be weary; they shall walk, and not faint." Isa. 40:31. I have proved, daily am proving, all this, to my constant peace and satisfaction. So may you, dear reader, *if you will*. God bless you and yours.

Not long ago I visited Warden and Mrs. Reilly at Folsom and had a long interview with Joe. He told me that his poor old father was dead and that he was now alone in the world. I asked him if he wanted to apply for parole. "No, Mother Roberts," he answered; "parole is for guilty prisoners. I want a pardon." "But, Joe," I replied, "if you are paroled, in two years afterward you can apply for and receive your pardon." … I did not prevail, but I am hoping that before finishing this book I shall receive good news concerning Joe. If so, I will surely tell you.

CHAPTER XXI
I DEPART FOR PACIFIC GROVE—MEET
LUCY AGAIN—HER BAPTISM

Not very long after poor Joe was removed to Folsom, the call of God took me to another beautiful ocean-resort—Pacific Grove. It was only a short journey. There was no one to welcome me, for I was a stranger, but in less than twenty-four hours one of the Lord's loved ones, a widowed sister, Mrs. Hill, now departed to her eternal home, welcomed me under her roof. On the following evening I was introduced to Miss Fannie Rowe and her mother. The former lady, in gratitude to God for wonderfully raising her up instantly from a state of helplessness and affliction of many years' duration, had consecrated her all to him, and, in addition to innumerable responses to calls for prayers and financial aid, had opened and was supporting a mission in the Grove, another in the adjacent town of Monterey, and one for the Indians, situated at The Needles, Ariz. I gladly responded to her kind invitation to address the patrons of Bethel mission one evening. She gave liberally toward helping to procure the home for the wandering girls.

Many were the private requests for personal work with those who were too young and inexperienced to realize that their attitude and heedless words and deeds were having a demoralizing tendency upon themselves, their schoolmates, and others. This work, let me assure you, dear reader, calls for special prayer for wisdom, diplomacy, and deep love. Young people, especially girls at the difficult age (between thirteen and eighteen), are very hard to persuade, if their earlier training has not been as wise as it should have been. Therefore permit me to advise much and earnest fellowship and prayer with the Father before making any efforts of this nature with them. A false move too often creates rebellion, frequently followed by disastrous results.

But to proceed. An invitation came from the chaplain of the Presidio of Monterey to visit army quarters, situated between the two towns. There I was taken through every department and afterwards invited to address a large body of stalwart young soldiers. You may be sure that, as I did so, my mother heart tenderly went forth to them, as I thought of my own precious son, who was now on the high seas and whom I had the privilege of seeing so seldom, and then only for short visits.

After luncheon with the chaplain and his wife we visited the hospital. I was, as usual, accompanied by my autoharp, and so was able to give a little cheer to the many lonely, suffering ones as well as to speak briefly about the Great Physician and also pray for them. It was all very sad, yet so precious. I would that I could, in the name of Jesus, have temporarily mothered one and all of them. They appeared to be so appreciative, and to be suffering as much from homesickness as from the many other ailments.

Every church threw its doors open to me, the interest grew, God blest my every step, and I (by faith) saw our hopes soon realized. About this time a letter forwarded from Santa Cruz, postmarked San Jose, reached me, telling of the return of the president and also the vice-president of the board of rescue home managers, and urging my return for a conference with them in regard to much renovation and also enlargement of their borders, for the present home was now altogether inadequate to its necessities.

Earnest prayer failed to bring me light on this matter. I could only await God's time. Then came a loving letter from my dear Lucy, stating that her mother had fully recovered and reminding me of my promise to spend my birthday with her and her dear ones. There being no reason why I should not accept, I bade farewell to many newly-found friends, and in a few hours I was being warmly embraced, also overwhelmed with kindness and gratitude, by my spiritual daughter and her refined, delicate-looking mother.

Imagine, if you can, how I, for several days, fared. It was most embarrassing, but very, very precious to my soul, especially so when one day Lucy followed her Savior's example in baptism in the presence of her family, her mother, and me. Placing her wet arms about my neck, she rejoiced my heart by saying, "O Mother Roberts, I've just had a wonderful vision of Jesus, and I want to say this to you: Much as I love my mother and dear ones, I would rather continue with you in the work if you'll take me; will you, dear?" "Will I? I should say I will," I answered, and gladly, humbly, thanked and praised God for the blessed privilege. So not long afterwards we took our departure for Los Angeles, our next field of labor, and, permit me to add, at this time a difficult one. There was an agitation on foot for the closing of all the questionable resorts, and this meant much strenuous, problematical work on the part of the agitators. Amongst these I make mention of the, late Rev. Sidney Kendall, a noted writer and rescue worker, a person who proved to be one of our very valuable friends and advisers during our sojourn in that great and beautiful city (Author of the "Soundings of Hell," etc.)

Matters, through correspondence with the San Jose board, were now assuming such shape that indications were that we should soon return to that place. In the meanwhile we were much occupied, through the daytime largely, in making personal visits to the poor outcasts, who were in great stress of mind at this time. Consequently, many returned to their parental homes, others were taken care of or furnished with situations, but not nearly so many as we could have wished, and all for lack of finances. Oh, how I have wished that those who pray God's will to be done in their lives would only mean it and live up to their prayers, professions, and privileges. What a rich harvest the Master, at the final summing up, could then reap! but alas! not many live the prayer.

CHAPTER XXII
ANNA—WE LEAVE FOR SAN JOSE

One evening, during the temporary absence of Lucy (on a few days' visit with friends), Sister Taylor, matron of the Door of Hope, home for girls, and I were invited by Brother Trotter of the Rescue Mission, then situated on Main Street near St. Elmo Hotel, to take charge of the meeting. When the invitation to seek the Savior was given, the altar filled with many mothers' boys, both young and old, and in all sorts of condition—semi-intoxicated, ragged, dirty, etc. (Reader, I have seen this sight scores of times in similar places.)

Several workers joined us on the platform in aiding the seekers. As I was kneeling with my autoharp lying across my lap and my eyes closed, I inadvertently opened them. Out at the open door, about forty feet away, stood a throng of observers, amongst them a girl. Never did I so long to leave the platform, but I feared that an interruption might mean disastrous results to both workers and seekers. Soon the meeting gloriously closed, the doors were shut, and we were hurrying home. As I walked up the street with Sister Taylor and presently stood waiting with her for her approaching car, my lodging being in close proximity, I told her of my seeing that girl by the door and of my longing to have obeyed the impulse to go and speak to the stranger. Sister Taylor comforted me with the assurance of God's never-failing response to the prayer of faith for even the unknown, and urged me to pray for the girl. I replied that it would have been infinitely more satisfactory to have dealt with her face to face.

Suddenly some one gently touched me on the shoulder. Turning about, I beheld a tall, pretty, but weary-looking young woman. It was the girl whom I had noticed in that open doorway.

"May I speak to you a moment?" she asked.

"Yes, dear, gladly! I was wishing I might only meet you, for I saw you looking into the mission just now. Come with me to my room," and I placed my arm through hers.

"No, no!" she replied, "you wouldn't want my kind to visit you there."

"Indeed, I would, and do, dear child, so come along. Good night, Sister Taylor. Remember us in your prayers." ...

It was nearly two o'clock in the morning, and Anna had told me her story—her sad, sad story. Girls, you ought to hear it; so presently I'm going to relate it for your benefit, but first I want you to know that before we left my room, she had surrendered her future to her loving Savior. Before we were off of our knees, she, with the tears in her eyes, suddenly exclaimed:

"Oh! I quite forgot, I quite forgot. Let's go quickly. Poor Flora, my chum, is awful sick, and I came out to hunt her friend and take her some medicine." We hurried away.

There lay a dark-haired girl moaning and gaping for breath. She managed to inquire:

"Who's this, Anna? Who've you brought with you?"

Soon I was reassuring the poor sufferer, whilst endeavoring to make her more comfortable.

"Dear, have you a mother?" I inquired.

"Yes, only two blocks from here; but she doesn't know I'm anywhere near her. She never comes near such a neighborhood as this. Don't tell her. please don't. It would break her heart."

"Very well, my child; I won't."

But she hadn't told Anna not to tell; so I excused myself, called Anna out of the room, and whispered:

"Get me a certain medicine; and if you know where her mother lives, go there, gently break this news, and tell her that if she still loves her child to come immediately with blankets, pillows, and a hack; to be very, very gentle and quiet with her; to talk as little as possible. And we will help to take her home; then she must send quickly for a doctor."

Before five o'clock poor, forgiven, suffering Flora was in bed in her mother's home, where we shall leave her for the present, in order that we may hear Anna's story.

She said: "I'm not seventeen years old till next month, and I'm the oldest of five children—three girls and two boys. My father is a mechanic, but sometimes he's out of work, and then didn't he used to scold! Just as though we were to blame! Poor Mother! I've often pitied her for marrying my father, who was naturally cross and ill-tempered even when things didn't go wrong. Half the time mother daren't say her soul was her own, and, besides, she was naturally one of those meek, timid kind that would put up with anything for the sake of peace.

"Winter before last when he was out of a job for quite a while and mother was having a hard time of it trying to keep us warm and fed, I heard of a place in the next town, just a car-ride away, where I could work for my board and get my fifty cents a day and car-fare if I wanted to go home at night. It was to work in a nice, genteel restaurant; so I coaxed mother to let me take it, which she did. I didn't ask father.

"No, he wasn't what you'd call a drinking man, though he liked a glass of beer once in a while.

"I soon caught on now to do my work well; sometimes used to get tips, but not often, 'cause I had the family and ladies' department to wait on. There was one swell-looking lady used to eat there, and used to come to my table whenever she could. We weren't allowed to chat with the customers, though sometimes we did, if the boss wasn't looking. One day she told me she was very much taken with me, asked if I had a mother and father, and several other questions. So I told her just how it was with us and how I happened to take a situation until father got back to work. Then she asked where I lived. I told her, but that now I was only going home once a week in the afternoon for a little while, it being too dark and cold to get up so early to take my car, and that, besides, I had to work late sometimes, so the boss gave me one dollar and fifty cents extra a week to pay my room rent. She asked if I liked my room.

"'Well, nothing extra. One can't expect much of a place for one dollar and fifty cents a week, can they?'

"She said no, certainly not; but as she had taken a fancy to me, and had a nice house with a nice little spare room in it, if I liked it better than where I was stopping, she would rent it to me, and for me to come and see it that afternoon; which I did. Of course I took it. It was fine! Worth double. She said she did it to encourage me, and for me not to say a word to any one about it, as it might make the other girls jealous; besides, she didn't keep lady roomers. So I promised, and I kept my word.

"Some way, I can't just tell how, I got acquainted with one of her roomers. He soon began to say nice things and make love to me, and we got so well acquainted that he'd leave his door open when I was off duty of an afternoon and would call me in for a chat. But one day—oh! I hate to tell it—he closed the door, and by and by who should walk in on us but Madam herself. I was scared half to death, she raged so, said I'd lose my job, threatened to tell my father, and ordered me to leave her house. By and by she cooled down, and as I'd been crying till I was a sight, said I needn't go back to the restaurant, she'd take care of me, because, after all, she was sorry for me, and as things were so bad for me at home, she'd see what she could do for another situation for me, so for me to stay in and keep quiet.

"The next day she said she'd just fortunately received a letter from a friend of hers in Council Bluffs, Iowa, who wanted a girl like me right away. I wanted awful bad to go and say good-by to Mother and the children, but I was too ashamed, so I did as she advised. I just wrote a little note to tell them I had got a fine situation out of town, and would soon send full particulars and my address; but I never did, no not from that day to this. I couldn't. You know I couldn't, and you know why."

"Yes, dear child, I know. You fell into the awful clutches of that procuress and her accomplices. Poor, poor Anna! There are thousands of cases similar to yours, my poor child. Of course you did not know. They all say that. But go on with your story, Anna."

"I was awful homesick, Mother Roberts, and my conscience was hurting me; my, how it was hurting! There was I decked out in gay cheap silks and laces, drinking, and smoking cigarettes, and carrying on and doing things to please people that I just hated; but I had to; there was no getting out of it. All the time I was longing to go home or to send money to my mother, though I didn't want to send any that came out of that house. No, indeed. Besides, I had to give it nearly all to Madam. One day I told her I was going back home and for her to give me my money. She told me she didn't owe me any, that I owed her.

"'What for?' I asked.

"'For your clothes, jewelry, board, lodging, and the good will of my house,' she said.

"'I thought you gave all that to me,' I said.

"Mother Roberts, you ought to have heard her laugh. It makes me shudder when I think of it, it was so cruel and fiendish! Presently she added:

"'You can't leave till you've paid your debts. I'll have you arrested if you do.'

"'How much do I owe you?' I asked.

"'Pretty near six hundred dollars,' she said.

"I nearly fainted with fright, but what was I to do? *I was afraid to die, or else I'd have ended it then and there....*

"That night I told a friend of mine, a railroad employee, and he said for me to keep a 'stiff upper lip,' and he'd get me out of there next trip; so I kept my own counsel, and Madam concluded I'd decided to stay where I was and make the best of it. She didn't know I was counting the hours for three days, until my friend got back.

"When he came, he advised me to play drunk, and to go out with him to dinner. He said I need never go back; he'd take me with him on his train when it went out that night.

"'What about my debt?' I asked him.

"'Debt nothing!' he said. 'She can't have you arrested. She can't collect one cent of a debt like *that*. Don't take any clothes, for fear she'll suspect.'

"Pretty soon I staggered down the stairs, but I wasn't drunk; no, indeed.

"'Where are you going, Anna?' she inquired.

"'Out to dinner with — —. Any objection?' I asked.

"'No, only be in in time for business.'

"Oh, thank God! I never laid my eyes on her again, nor she on me from that day to this. But I don't want you to get the idea that that escape from her ended my troubles. By no manner of means. Listen!" And then she told me of experiences too dreadful for publication—experiences in Ogden and Salt Lake, Utah; Reno, Nevada. Now she was in Los Angeles—farther away from mother and home than ever; as unhappy, as homesick, as miserable a girl as ever trod the earth. When she happened to be passing the mission door, some one was singing, "Just as I am without one plea." After that door had closed for the night, she followed Sister Taylor and me, trying to summon up courage enough to approach me, fearing that if she did not I should soon get on a car and her opportunity of ever meeting me would be lost.

At the time of our meeting, Anna was well-nigh homeless, friendless, penniless, and, worst of all, Christless. In less than four hours, praise God! she had her greatest needs supplied, and, best of all, she had found her Savior.

In memory of this, one of the songs appearing in this book was written— "The Value of a Song." It was a particular favorite with our family in the rescue home, some girl often remarking, "Doesn't it just seem to fit my case, Mother Roberts?" Then she would get me to relate the story of Anna or of some other poor unfortunate. Alas! their name is "Legion."

THE VALUE OF A SONG

Words and Music by Mrs. Florence Roberts

1. A poor girl was wand'ring alone on the street Of a great busy city, thro' dust and thro' heat, With despair in her heart as she walked to and fro, When she heard a sweet voice singing softly and low:

CHORUS

Just as I am, without one plea, But that they blood was shed for me, And that thou bidd'st me come to Thee, O Lamb of God, I come, I come!

2. As she noted the words of this beautiful song, Her thoughts wandered back to the days that were gone; And in fancy she hears her dear mother once more Sweetly singing the song she now hears thro' that door.

CHORUS

3. "O God, I have sinned, I will do so no more, If thou wilt forgive and a sinner restore; For the sake of my Savior, for mercy I pray: Lord, give me a home with some Christian to stay."

CHORUS

4. "Thou knowest my weakness, my sorrow, my sin, Now grant me, dear Lord, a new life to begin." And soon came the answer to this earnest prayer,—A pardon, a home, and motherly care.

CHORUS

CHAPTER XXIII
NORTHWARD BOUND—THE OUTCOME

More correspondence, also the return of Lucy, decided our length of sojourn at Los Angeles. After prayerful consideration, we, with Anna, soon took our departure for San Jose, where we were warmly welcomed by a now former matron (Callie's dear Sister Griffith). At this time the family consisted of fifteen girls and two workers. Imagine our crowded condition!

The following day the entire board of managers convened, specially to meet me. After prayer and the reading of Scripture, there was an earnest discussion regarding the need of an evangelistic and field worker. Because of my being constantly referred to as the person for such office, I requested permission to retire for brief prayer, also to give them more freedom.

Going to the matron's room, I bowed before the Lord, earnestly petitioned to know the mind of his Spirit, and sought a test. The test was this: If it was his will that I accept this office, the board should, on my return for further conference, give satisfactory answers to the following questions: "Are you willing to incorporate?" "Are you willing to change the name of the home?" and "Are you willing to purchase desirable property?"

When I was once more in their midst, the president, in the name of the board, honored me with the above-mentioned call, stating in detail its necessities. Responding with words of appreciation, I propounded the three questions named.

Answer No. 1: "Yes, quite willing, but unable to do so, for lack of funds. An empty treasury."

Answer No. 2: "Can you suggest a better name?"

"Yes, a God-given one," I answered. Then I stated the objection of many who disliked being styled, "One of the Rescue Home girls." I suggested "Beth-Adriel," meaning "House of the flock of God." All being delighted with this name, it was adopted.

Answer No. 3: "Yes, if you will accept the office of field representative."

In the name of the Lord I accepted; then agreed to pay for incorporation (a matter that was immediately attended to) and to place the remainder of the money in my possession, minus five dollars, into the Beth-Adriel treasury. (This sum amounted to over three hundred dollars.)

Before the board adjourned, Lucy, at my request, was appointed assistant matron, and a most efficient one she proved, until illness compelled her resignation several months later.

All the details of the preliminaries being duly attended to, I now proceeded to fill official engagements, the first of which the following press notice announced:

Mrs. Florence Roberts, a singing evangelise and noted speaker, will sing and speak in the Presbyterian church of Los Gatos, Sunday evening. Mrs. Roberts is the field secretary of the non-sectarian industrial home for women in San Jose; the same is now being incorporated under the name of Beth-Adriel.

The Lord graciously encouraged me with a large and deeply interested congregation, who contributed liberally toward the fund. (This was in November, 1903, four months from the time of my leaving San Francisco for Redwood City with sixty cents in my purse. Traveling and other expenses came out of the fund. Praise, oh! praise the blessed Redeemer forever!)

The following notice is copied from the *San Jose Mercury*, May 7, 1904:

LAND FOR BETH-ADRIEL HOME

The California Non-sectarian Home for Women.

Three years ago last September a number of Christian men and women established a home at 673 East St. John Street for unfortunate women and girls. The work still continues at the same place. Last autumn it was incorporated, but to adequately carry out the intentions of the home, there has always been felt the need of a permanent building, planned with reference to the work.

Through the generosity of parties interested, there is a little sum on hand toward the purchase of land.

The board desires to secure a piece of land from two to five acres, where the inmates of the home can raise chickens also cultivate flowers, plants, etc., giving them a percentage on their efforts to encourage them.

The opportunity is now given to some philanthropic party to either donate or sell on easy terms land, as above described, on or near any one of the car lines.

Immediately following our first Christmas in Beth-Adriel I was taken suddenly and dangerously ill, so that my life was despaired of. Many were the prayers for my restoration. How devoted were my dear young friends, especially Lucy and Anna! Praise God! I was unable to resume my duties until April, 1904. Then I responded to a call from Boulder Creek, a lovely town in Santa Cruz mountains; next I went to Watsonville and vicinity; and after that I returned home for a rest, for I was not yet very strong. I arrived at home June first.

Being impressed that my next field of labor was to be in a city in the extreme northern part of California, I, after a week of loving intercourse with my precious girls, sailed for Eureka, Humboldt County, arriving there on June 8, 1904. As usual, the local papers immediately announced my coming, one saying, through the interviewing reporter, that I had $1,200 toward purchasing property.

Two days later I was the guest of Rev. and Mrs. Franklin Baker, whose home became my headquarters during my stay of over two months' duration. I was now in an excellent field of labor amongst the fallen. Moreover, I fulfilled pulpit engagements in practically every church and organization in Humboldt County.

From noon until about 5 P.M. each day (with very few exceptions) I was engaged in house-to-house work in the undesirable districts. After word had been passed around that I was sincerely the friend of the fallen, many a poor wandering girl listened with profound respect to God's loving message in word and song. Even most of the landladies of these houses of sin and shame invited me in, when convenient. Frequently have I been humbly asked to join them at their repasts. Never did I refuse. (Reader, our Savior ate with publicans and sinners; are we, professed Christians, better than he? God forbid!) What golden opportunity to converse whilst we ate! How the best, the very best, would then rise to the surface! On one of these occasions B— — F— —, soon to quit forever this mode of living, said:

"Mother Roberts, I've a friend close by. She's taken to drinking heavily lately; otherwise she's refined and accomplished. Can you spare time to see her today?"

"Most assuredly, B— —. Can you accompany me?"

She gladly, hurriedly changed her attire, and soon appeared, heavily veiled.

"Why are you veiled, B— —?" I asked.

"I don't suppose you will want to be seen walking on the street with me, Mother Roberts," she replied.

With my own hands I removed the veil whilst the tears of tender, humble appreciation and love, gathered and flowed down her cheeks. We were soon at J— —'s place, where B— — knocked at a side door, because of the noise of carousal in the front of the house. A beautiful but greatly intoxicated young woman opened the door and began upbraiding B— — for bringing me. But B— — marched right in, pulling me after her.

"We'll go into your bedroom if no one's there, J— —," she said, and forthwith proceeded to do so.

"B— —, you shouldn't have done this. I'm drunk. I don't want a lady like this one to see me in such a beastly state. You shouldn't have done it, B— —," said poor J— —.

Such a noise of rowdyism was proceeding from the front room that presently she said: "I'll stop that!" and to me, "Please excuse me a moment."

There was a hush and then sounds of several footsteps. She threw her door wide open, marched them all in, turned the key in the lock, and put the key in her pocket. What did this mean? I soon found out.

"Talk to them, too. They all need it as much as I," she said.

They surely did. All told, there were nine, not including B— — and me. Four were mere lads, who were so ashamed that they tried to hide their features by pulling their hats as far over their faces as possible. I sang a song; they called for another, and still another. During the singing of the third one, J— —, with her beautiful hair streaming about her face and shoulders suddenly threw herself lengthwise on the floor, crying out, and calling on God for mercy. Mary Magdalene, prostrate at the Master's feet, was being reenacted once more. I quickly knelt, put my arms around her, and prayed and prayed and prayed. Before I finished, every boy and girl in that bedroom was kneeling.

Some of them I again met, though never in such a place. As for J— —, she immediately disappeared, and I have never heard of her since. B— — went East and became a trained nurse, one who spiritually administers to the patients in her charge.

CHAPTER XXIV
THE SUICIDE OF L——. ITS AFTER-EFFECT

After much effort and following repeated calls with "not at home" responses, I at last was able to meet one Miss Blank. Seated in her private reception room, I listened respectfully to her recital of vindication because of her present position, and then told her the nature of my errand.

The door was partially open. A beautiful, very beautiful blonde girl attired in pale blue stepped partly in, saying as she did so, "May I come in. Miss Blank?" "No, not just now," was the answer. "I'm engaged for the next few minutes." At her request I sang.

I sang a song entitled "My Mother's Voice." I was sitting where I had a view of a portion of the stairway, and, as I sang, I saw a little blue slipper and part of a dress. That girl sat there listening.

I soon left. Before doing so I asked if I might call again, and received permission.

The following Sunday evening, after I had addressed a large audience in the Presbyterian church and just as the meeting closed, two ladies hastened forward and thus excitedly addressed the pastor (Reverend S——) and me:

"Oh! we thought the meeting would never end. Do you know a girl shot herself just now in Miss Blank's house? She may be living yet. Hurry! You may be able to get there in time to save her soul before she dies." I ran, without even my hat, the pastor quickly following. When we rang the bell, Miss Blank came to the door and, throwing herself into my arms, exclaimed:

"Oh! if I had only let her in! if I had only let her in! Mrs. Roberts, it's the girl who asked to come in the other day when you were calling on me."

"Is she living yet? Quick! let me see her. This is the Rev. Mr. S—— who accompanies me," I said.

"Too late! Mrs. Roberts, too late! She died in awful agony about twenty minutes ago. Those two men in the hall whom you saw as you came in are the coroner and the doctor. Oh! my God! my God! Pray, please pray for her soul," wailed poor Miss Blank.

"Miss Blank, she's gone, never to return. We want to pray for your precious soul," pleaded Brother S— —.

"No, no, oh! no," wept Miss Blank, and nothing we could say or do would induce her to kneel with us. She only clung the closer to me, and wept and mourned piteously.

It was early morning before we left.

All that was mortal of beautiful unfortunate L— — had been removed to the morgue, and, the name and address of her parents having been discovered, the following telegram had been sent: "Daughter L— — died suddenly. What disposition of remains?" As quickly as possible came this reply: "Embalm. Leave for Eureka immediately."

(Father's name.)

On Monday afternoon I was once more with Miss Blank, now sufficiently calmed to relate this:

"L— — was taken with a spell of despondency Saturday. [I was there Friday afternoon.] It wasn't like her, for she usually was the life of the house. She didn't get up all day Sunday. I went up after dinner to try to jolly her up, and soon left her, as I thought, more cheerful. Presently we all were startled by the firing of a pistol, followed by some one screaming: 'Oh! my God, my God! what have I done? Help me, please, for God's sake help me!' But she was soon past all earthly aid. All of us were paralyzed with fear, as you may readily understand." Then she wept, as few weep, whilst I also in tears sought to comfort her and to point her to the merciful Savior, but she would have none of him. All I could do was to wait patiently and pray.

I went to the undertaker's to view the remains. He and his wife remarked that they had handled many a corpse, but none so beautiful as this one. But I was grieving for the lost soul. Where, oh! where was it now? Where, where were the others going?

The steamer arrived, and on it not alone the father but also the mother of beautiful L— —. No one had expected the mother. To me was assigned the painful task of breaking the news to her. I believe I was the most burdened woman on earth at that hour and time. Rev. S— — introduced me to the stricken father in the hotel office, who presently took us up to their room. To my dying day I shall see that scene. After the introduction to the mother, the father and Brother S— — retired to another room. I was standing there alone with the mother, who leaned against the dressing-case, her hands behind her back, gripping the woodwork. She was a magnificent, majestic-looking lady; the father also was a tall fine-looking man. It was easy to discover whence the daughter had inherited her beauty.

"Who are you?" she gasped.

I explained.

"Tell me, did you know my darling girl?" she inquired.

"No, dear lady, not in life, although I had seen her," I replied.

"Where? where had you seen her?" she next interrogated.

"In the house where she boarded," I answered.

"Was her husband with her?" she inquired.

"No, not that I heard of," was my reply

Next came that dreadful, dreadful question. She shrieked it:

"Tell me, madam, was—it—all—right—with—my—baby—girl?"...

My tongue clove to the roof of my mouth. I tried to answer. Not one word could I utter. The mother with the exclamation. "O my God!" went down in a heap on the floor and I with her. For a long time the silence remained unbroken. She was the first to speak:

"It is so kind of you to come; so kind to help me in my terrible trouble. God will reward you. I never can. Now, dear, I must have particulars, if its kills me. To help get them, I must tell you this: My L— — was my youngest, my petted, spoilt, baby girl. Her every wish was gratified from the time she drew her first breath. Nothing was too good for her, and no expense spared. We sent her to Europe to complete her education. Did you ever hear her sing?"...

Erelong this soul-stricken mother lay in her bed sleeping as only the grief-exhausted can sleep; then I left for a much-needed rest. After a few hours I returned. When I left her late that night, she had sent for poor terrified Miss Blank.

When I came down-stairs the following morning, Mrs. Baker told me that some one was anxious to talk with me over the telephone—some one who would not give her name, only her number. Going to the telephone, I soon recognized Miss Blank's voice.

"Good morning, Mrs. Roberts," she begin. "I've been very anxious to get you, but would not have your rest disturbed, as I was sure you must be worn out. I've been talking to L— —'s poor mother all night long, and she has agreed to a funeral service which we can attend. Neither she nor her husband will be present; *only our kind*. We want to know if you will conduct it for us."

"Where, Miss Blank?" I inquired.

"In the undertaker's chapel tomorrow afternoon at three o'clock. They are going to take her remains back to her old home on Monday's steamer. Do say you will, Mrs. Roberts, *please.*"

I consented, provided I should be allowed to give a message to the living. She gladly acquiesced.

With difficulty I made my way through the crowd that blocked the street in front of the undertaker's the following afternoon. None were admitted but L——'s associates. There she lay, apparently sleeping sweetly, but this was only the beautiful, fast-decaying mortal form. The remains were surrounded by fragrant tributes of exquisite floral pieces, and girls dressed in black robes, heavily veiled, and weeping bitterly. With great effort I at last spoke and sang. I do not remember if I had a text; I do know that *the message came to the living straight from the throne of grace.* Even until recently some one has occasionally reminded me that she was present on that occasion and that it brought about her reformation. The father and mother departed with their precious burden the following morning. They came early on board, in order to avoid curious eyes. I spent the time with the mother in their stateroom until they sailed. When that casket was lowered into the hold of the steamer, I so obstructed the doorway that she could not look past me.

Before our final parting the poor mother gave a farewell message for other mothers. It was this:

"Mrs. Roberts, I was too indulgent, too weak, with my little girl. All she had to do was to tease until she got her own way even though I knew it would prove to be detrimental to her good. If I resisted or advised ever so little, she would overrule every time.

"When she returned from Europe, she sang in our church choir and proved to be a great attraction. She and the tenor singer, —— ——, were betrothed, and with our consent. He was a schoolmate of hers. For some trifling offense on his part, she became angry and unfortunately showed a relentless spirit; consequently, the breach widened.

"Poor darling! She was so impetuous, so impulsive. I have never quite recovered from the shock I received when she suddenly announced her marriage to an utter stranger—an educated young scoundrel, as we soon learned to our sorrow. Papa and I decided to make the best of it now the deed was done; so he took him into his employ in order that our baby girl might be near us. He robbed us in less than six weeks of several hundred dollars; then Papa told daughter that she was welcome to her home as long as she lived, but that he must go; that she would be compelled to choose. I know she did not want to; but, oh! she was so proud, and she would not give in. She chose her husband, and *that was the last I saw of her until*—Oh! I can not, can not bear it. Mrs. Roberts! It is killing me!"

"Miss Blank knows him. She had more than once ordered him out of her house for abusing L— — and living off her dreadful earnings...."

When the steamer was far away, almost out of sight, Brother S— — at last turned to me and asked whether I had seen L— —'s dairy, now in her father's possession. "No," I replied; "I had no idea she had kept one." Then, as we walked home, he repeated some recent entries in it. I give them to you as best my memory serves me:

(Date) "Just as I feared: Bert has been grafting again and has lost his job...."

(Date) "We're going to Spokane. My! but I'm homesick; I'd like to give in, but I won't! I won't!..."

(Date) "Bert has secured a job at last. Better than nothing—clerking in the soda fountain department of — —'s drug store. Hope he'll quit grafting."

(Date) "I've a good position now in — — — —'s cloak and suit house. Afraid I can't keep it long, my health is so poor lately...."

(Date) "Bert and I had words tonight. He's quit. I suppose he had to."

(Date) "There's a very pleasant lady in the next bed to mine [sanitarium]. I'm going back with her when she goes home, and until Bert is on his feet again...."

(Date) "How much has happened since I last wrote in my diary! I've some fine clothes and jewelry. Bert is sporting a suit of fine clothes and diamond pin, but—I can't write any more."

(Date) "Miss Blank says Bert will have to keep away. I'm glad of it. How I hate him!..."

(Much later) "A lady called yesterday. Wish I might have talked with her. Sang about mother I wish, oh, how I wish—what nonsense I'm writing...."

(Next morning) "I'm so wretched, so very wretched.... Oh! mama, mama, mama! If you could only read between the lines—"

And that was all. No name was signed. But—we can all of us read between the lines, yes all of us.

CHAPTER XXV
GOOD NEWS FROM HOME—MISS LORAINE

Letters from different members of Beth-Adriel board were now constantly reaching me. They contained interesting accounts of the doings at home and also much concerning various properties, none of which, from all accounts, appealed to my fancy. Reader, I was hard to please. I wanted something better than had as yet been described. Somehow I felt God had it for us. Sure-enough, as I discovered on my return home in August.

A letter from the vice-president described a property of ten acres of orchard and grounds, all under cultivation; a commodious dwelling, partly furnished; outhouses, etc., situated just outside of the city limits. It was not for sale; but as the owner, who resided on the premises, was a Christian man, it was thought that he might, for such a purpose, be induced to sell. It was deemed best, before approaching him to await my return. You will be pleased to hear more concerning this later. Just now I want to tell you about Miss Loraine.

There was one house in Eureka into which I had never been admitted. One day whilst I was visiting another, the landlady asked:

"Have you ever called on Miss Loraine?"

"I have been there more than once," I answered, "but as yet I have been unsuccessful in gaining admittance."

"Would you still go if you could? I can get you in. I am a personal friend of hers," said Miss — —.

"Thank you, I shall be very glad to have you make the necessary arrangements," I replied, upon which she went to her telephone, took down the receiver, and held the following conversation:

"Hello! is that you, H— —? Good morning...."

"Quite well, thank you. How are you?"... "I called you up to tell you of a lady who is calling on me, and who would like very much to meet you. We all call her 'Mother' Roberts."

"No, she isn't a crank."...

"Now, look here, H— —, you'll have to see her. You ought to know better than refuse me."

"Well, when will you be at home? At five o'clock? Wait a minute."

Putting her hand over the mouthpiece and turning to me, she asked: "Can you call at five this evening?"

I could; so she made arrangements, hung up the receiver, and then wrote a note of introduction, wording it thus:

Dear H— —

This will introduce my friend, Mother Roberts. She is all O. K. Hoping you will have a pleasant time together,

Yours as ever, — — — —

This I presented with my card at Miss Loraine's door at exactly five o'clock. A Japanese page dressed in uniform ushered me into a conventional but well-furnished reception-room. There sat a young woman in a handsome silk negligee, who invited me to be seated, remarking that Miss Loraine was out, but would soon return, and that she was to entertain me in the interval. In a few minutes there came up the steps and then entered the room three splendid-looking young women, richly attired. The one in black silk, Miss Loraine, received me with all the manners of a lady of birth and good breeding, and soon asked me if I would come with her to her private quarters, so that we could converse undisturbed. I followed her up-stairs into a Dresden-draped bedroom, where ensued the following conversation:

"Mrs. Roberts, I feel I owe you an apology for not sooner receiving you. To be candid with you, my door is closed to all who have not made previous engagements; then, too, I shrink from the embarrassment of meeting any ladies from the better walks of life," etc.

Whilst endeavoring to reassure her, I happened to look at a silver-framed photograph of a handsome, white-haired old gentleman. Quickly remarking this, she reverently handed it to me, saying:

"I notice you are attracted to this. Would you think there was anything out of the common in any of these features?"

Upon my replying in the negative, she added:

"This is the photograph of my dearly loved father. He is stone blind."

I expressed my astonishment, for there was no indication in the picture.

After a pause she said, "Mrs. Roberts, will you please do me a favor?"

"If it lies in my power," I replied.

"It does," was her rejoinder. "Will you honor me by dining with me this evening, half an hour hence?"

For one second I hesitated, but on interpreting her expression I instantly replied, "With pleasure," for like a flash came a mental vision of the King of kings dining with Simon the leper (Mark 11:3-9). Then she absented herself for a few minutes, doubtless to make necessary arrangements.

"I feel disposed, if you care to listen." she said on her return, "to give you a synopsis of my life."

I assured her of a great desire to hear it and, if possible, to prove more than simply a hearer. Briefly, it was this:

She was an only child of rich parents. She was reared in a luxurious home, where card-playing, theater-going, dancing, and all other high society amusements were continually indulged in. When she was entering her teens and most needed a mother's care, her mother died, and her father placed her in a fashionable boarding-school. She remained there until she was seventeen, when he sent her, under the chaperonage of friends, on a trip to Europe.

Whilst she was in Rome, she received from her father a cable message reading, "Come home on next steamer." Upon arriving in New York, she soon learned from her father's lips of his total failure in business (he was a stock broker) and also of the fast approaching affliction—blindness. Property of every description was swept away. She soon secured a position as nursery governess, but erelong she realized that she was unqualified, never having been coached for any but high social life.

The gentleman (?) whom she had expected to marry some day proved untrue as soon as her riches fled.

Just at a time when her employer had gently informed her of her inability to fill her position of governess satisfactorily and of her (the employer's) intention of dismissing her, the tempter, in the form of an unprincipled but well-to-do man about to make a trip to the Pacific Coast, crossed her path and ensnared her. Under promise of marriage, she agreed to go with him. After telling her now blind father, who was being provided for out of her earnings, that she had secured a position for better pay, but that it would take her away from New York for a time, she bade him a tearful farewell.

Before long the rich reprobate deserted her, but he was merciful enough not to leave her penniless. With a considerable sum at her disposal, and for advisers one or two whose morals were at a low ebb, she came North and furnished the house in which I was now sitting.

She was in constant correspondence with her father, who supposed that she was married and that the fifty dollars or more (never less) which he monthly received came from his wealthy son-in-law. And now hear her own words:

"Mrs. Roberts, I believe you will give me an honest answer to my earnest question. Would it be possible for me to secure any honorable position whereby I might continue to send my dear father fifty dollars a month, as well as live respectably myself?"

Reader, what answer would you, had you been in my place, have made? I was in an awkward position—in the presence of one who had never attended any but a fashionable church and hence—who knew little or nothing of God and his Son, one who had never been taught anything which in the event of accidents or business failures would prove practical. She was indeed and in truth to be pitied. My reply was a question:

"Could you not have kept a respectable lodging-house, my dear Miss Loraine?"

"Perhaps, had I been advised by the right kind of people, but I met the wrong ones," she replied. "As long as my dear father lives," she added, "I must send him this sum for rent and ordinary comforts. The moment word reaches me of his demise, I will forever cease living such a life. I will quietly disappear to some remote corner of the globe."

Then she showed me a letter just received, one beginning, "My dear Son and Daughter." How my heart ached as I silently prayed to know what to do!

"What about the inmates of your house. Miss Loraine? How do you procure them?"

"Pardon me, but I can not explain that. I will say, though, each of them has a sad story. They are, as you will presently infer from what you see, refined, more or less talented girls; but they will soon drift downward. The life is too rapid, and nature will not long stand the strain and abuse. I never interfere if a girl shows an inclination to quit; on the contrary, I gladly help her."

Here a gong sounded, announcing dinner. She preceded me to the dining-room. When we entered, I saw five handsome young women, whose ages varied (I should judge) from eighteen to twenty-six. They were all attired in quiet dress, surely in honor of the occasion, which courtesy I greatly appreciated. Permission being granted, I invoked a blessing. The meal was served in courses, and we were waited upon by the Japanese page. I ate very sparingly, in fact, made only a pretence of eating, for God's message lay so heavily on my heart that I had to deliver it. They listened with rapt attention, and all but one shed tears. How stolid she appeared to be! yet she was possibly the one many months later most impressed. I met her again. She was home then in her father's house once more, but was not yet a Christian.

As for Miss Loraine, I never saw her again, but about a year later I learned that her father had died and that she had taken her departure for parts unknown. I can only pray and trust that she will, if living, turn to the ever-merciful Savior.

CHAPTER XXVI
LUCY'S LETTER—THE SCHOOL TEACHER

On July 29, I received several letters, one of which is well worth copying:

Beth-Adriel, San Jose, July 27, 1904.

Mrs. Florence Roberts, Dear Mother:

I wrote you a letter several days ago, but have had no answer to it as yet, but thought I would write again, as it seems so long since I saw or heard from you.

I wrote and told you all about my trip to San Francisco, and what a good time I had [on that occasion she visited the jail where she was once a prisoner and where she was converted on or about Feb. 14, 1903], but I presume you have been very busy, or you would have answered.

Well, I can praise God for some wonderful victories, and I do praise him every day. Just last night I was talking to our matron [Mother Weatherwax] and saying how perfectly wonderful his strength was; for it is his strength, and not mine, that has kept me up and is still keeping—me up from day to day.

The home is full now.... We have one case of clear-cut answer to prayer, where it just took real faith to hold on. But isn't it just like our dear, good heavenly Father to do and answer just the impossible. It was a case of abduction and attempted seduction of a lovely Christian girl, the daughter of a Free Methodist minister, into a terrible house of ill-fame, one of those notorious road-houses, and it was such a filthy, vile place, that the chief of police [Carroll] would not let Mother W— — and another lady go with the officers and the lady's husband after the girl. Thank God, He gave us the law on our side, and we have the girl here safe and well and doing fine; and I can say the same for all of the rest of us girls.

The girl referred to had come from her Eastern home to southern California for her health. As her means were limited, she sought employment, and one day answered an attractive advertisement for a housekeeper for an invalid lady. A favorable reply, urging her to come at once, quickly came, stating that in the event of her paying her fare it would be refunded on her arrival, also that she would be met at the San Jose depot by a lady wearing a bunch of red roses on her left breast.

When she arrived, she was welcomed and taken in a hack to the awful place of which Lucy wrote. She managed to write a note with a match stem, wrapped the paper round a small piece of rock which she found in the room where she was imprisoned, and prayerfully threw them through the grating: toward a man who was watering his horses at the trough and who evidently knew the nature of this notorious resort. Praise God, the stone did not miss its mark. The man was wise enough to notify the authorities, and that place was compelled to go out of business in short order.

I have not been able to go to church for three weeks now, but God is here at home with me, and I am learning more of him every day. My verse for today was Ezek. 34:12, and I think it is so beautiful, especially about the dark and cloudy days.

We went to Alum Rock [a beautiful resort adjacent to San Jose] three weeks ago Thursday, and I got so badly poisoned [poison-oak] that there was not an inch of my body that was not covered and my eyes were swollen shut for two days. I was sick in bed with it all day the Fourth and here alone; but not alone, for if ever I had a happy day, it was that. Lots of times I feel discouraged to think I can not remember the Scriptures that I read, but it was just marvelous the way they would roll over my mind on those two or three days that I could not see even to read. I believe God just wanted me to see when my eyes, hands, tongue and feet were quiet how active my mind was.

My head and throat are still very bad, and I go to the doctor about three times a week, but still have those terrible ulcers gathering and breaking in my head. I am so thin that I can not wear the black dress you made me at all. Mother W— — says she is afraid something will give way in my head one of these days. She wants me to go home for a rest, but if I did, then Mama [her own mother] wouldn't come here for a rest, and I want her to have a rest, and then, too, I would have to ask them to send me money to go home on. [Lucy's services were gratuitous.]

Just the other day I was reading how much Delia did for the Lord in her short Christian life [Before conversion known as the "Blue Bird" of Mulberry Bend of New York], and it has made me feel bad; for here I have been saved over a year, and what have I done? It is said that she had over six hundred souls in three months, and I can not claim one that I know of. I know that I have tried to be what God would have me be, if ever a girl did try. [Indeed, indeed you have, dear child, and God smiles on you for it.]

There is one thing sure. I have prayed a great deal for you lately for ever since two weeks ago Tuesday night, which was our prayer-meeting night of course, I had a real hard fight with Satan, and he had tried to get the better of my better self, and Miss Sisson came and told of your being at a house to see the landlady and then of your going back in a few days to preach the funeral services over the dead body of one of the girls [suicide]. Oh, how it helped me to see what I had been spared from and how much I had to praise God for! and it also showed me how many prayers you needed to help you in your work, and so I have held you up more than ever before His throne, and maybe if I can not reap myself, I can pray for those that are in the field.

God has been so good that all through my sickness I have missed but two days' work, that is, there were but two days that I was not able to get the meals (all of them). It is perfectly wonderful, the strength, willingness, and determination He will give us if we but want it.

Sometimes lately when my head has been so bad, I have thought, what if I should be taken now. It would be grand to go home; but I have talked with Mother W— — so much lately, and I do not feel I could go till I have done something for Him who did so much for me. Pray for me, Mother, that I may get better and do something. I want to go and tell Mattie [a former companion in sin] and the girls, that what God has done for me he will do for them.

I'll tell you what Doctor A— — says is the matter with me. She examined me, tested my blood, and said it was not in the system from disease of myself, but that sometime, when my throat was sore, I inhaled the germs from some sick person, that the throat was just in the condition for them to germinate, and now my throat and ear are eaten out terribly. [Cigarette-smoking the probable cause] She hasn't said she couldn't cure me, but that it will take a year's solid and continuous treatment, without any neglectfulness whatsoever.

Oh! isn't it true that if we sow to the flesh, we must reap corruption. I know that I did, and am willing to suffer the pain and endure if I can only tell others—yes—warn them. But I know that I can not do it away from here until I can do it better here, so I want more courage to do it better here.

Mania doesn't know much about my throat, only what Mother W— — wrote her that tune.

Oh! this is an awfully long letter, so I must close it. I am nervous and can't write well.

Pray for us, as we pray for you. Everybody sends you their love, and God bless you.

Your daughter in faith, Lucy — —.

How I loved to receive her appreciative, newsy letters! but oh, how they saddened me as I more than ever realized the truth of that statement that "whatsoever we sow, that shall we also reap," Gal. 6:7.

But one more incident and story before we leave Eureka.

One day, on one of my house-to-house visits, and following considerable disappointment, for so few were at home, or else the inmates did not want to receive me, I at last received a response from a frail-looking woman of about twenty-four years of age, who said, "I should very much like to have a heart-to-heart talk with you, but this is no place for it. Can you come to my private room in the — — — — lodging-house. Go to room No. —, first floor at 1:30 tomorrow, where we can converse undisturbed."

At the appointed time I was kindly received, and soon I was listening to her troubles; but before rehearsing them she called my attention to a framed diploma on her wall, a teacher's certificate.

"Have you taught school?" I inquired.

She simply answered, "Yes."

"Are you not taking great chances by having that where strangers can see it?" I asked.

"No," she replied; "I do my own work, and have a patent lock, so that none but my husband and me have access to this room."

I was still more at sea. Over the head of her bed hung a picture which I never shall forget. Let me endeavor to describe it:

The beautiful nude form of a young woman lay on a couch. Horror was depicted upon her countenance, and she was frantically but vainly struggling to free herself from the great boa-constrictor which had coiled his ugly thick body about her. Standing beside her and looking on with a dreadful expression of devilish satisfaction was a representation of Satan, whilst coming in at the open door reeled a young man in a woeful state of intoxication.

The old, old dreadful story! When, oh! when will they ever profit by this only too true picture, being really enacted every day, every hour, by some mother's wandering girl?

Would that I might be able to tell you that this ex-school-teacher yielded to our Lord and Savior, but alas! that boa-constrictor had too firm a grip on her. Listen to her story:

"Less than four years ago, I was a happy young woman, living with my parents in the South, in a modest but very happy home, and surrounded by loving friends.

"My downfall dates from a picnic. I was exceedingly fond of dancing, with no ill effect from indulging in what hitherto I had regarded as a most innocent pastime, but that day I was introduced to one who peculiarly affected me. Why, I used to laugh to scorn, and express contempt for, any one who could be so very weak as to succumb to evil influences through the dance, never dreaming that my day of doom would come.

"How I loved him! and how I hugged my secret! At least, so I thought; but he read me, read me like a book. He was a traveling man, and showed me many excellent letters. I told my parents, who felt interested, and the next thing I was enjoying his company in our home, where he made himself very agreeable to the old people. Soon I was attending several social functions, some at his invitation, particularly where there was dancing, for I loved to feel his arms about me, his breath on my cheek.

"A day came when, for love of him, I bartered my soul. The remorse which soon followed was so deep that I took what little money I had, stole away from home, and my relatives haven't seen or heard from me since, although I hear of them through a trusted friend, who has promised not to further bruise the old folks' hearts by letting them know of my downfall or whereabouts. I'm dead to them forever; dead to them forever!"

"I was the supposed wife of my first love for over a year. How I begged him to marry me! but he only laughed and asked if I wanted to have him arrested for bigamy. Then he left me.

"My baby was born dead. Thank God for that! and now as soon as able, I must move on.

"Some of these girls on the downward path are so kind-hearted, Mrs. Roberts."

"Yes, Saidie, I know it well," I said. "I've been their friend for several years, and I know many of them and their good traits and deeds; but pardon me for interrupting." "I drifted from place to place," she continued; "now I'm here—here facing an awful future. No God, no home, sick in body and soul, not fit to live and certainly not fit to die."

"How happened it that you met the man you called your husband, Saidie?" I asked.

"Just as nine-tenths of them do," she replied. "We take up with some one who is seemingly kind. It's an awful mistake. *They profit at our expense every day*. They take our earnings of sin, and are often brutal besides," she sobbed.

"But does not the vagrancy law protect you?" I asked.

"No; not so long as they can prove they are working," she answered. "He is a bar-tender."

"Saidie, I want you to leave this life," I pleaded. Come with me, dear. I will treat you as though you were in deed and in truth my own daughter.

"Listen, I will even go further; you shall travel with me. I need an amanuensis and secretary. I am overworked, dear. Say you will, and I will make all the necessary arrangements."

How I begged her to consent! I wanted to take her then and there, but, *unfortunately, no one I knew would harbor, even temporarily, such a girl, until I was ready to leave—not one*. I could linger no longer that day, excepting for short earnest prayer, in which she took no part. We agreed to meet the following day at noon in a certain restaurant, where we could enjoy privacy. She kept the appointment, but something—I could only conjecture—something had cooled her ardor. I apparently made very little headway with the Master's message. She was silent, obdurate, and she soon left. The next day I followed her up, only to learn from the scrub-woman that Saidie was intoxicated. Again I called; for I was to take the next steamer, and felt I must make one more effort in her behalf. I was told that she had received bad news, that she was drinking deeper than ever to drown her misery, and that it would be worse than useless to see her. After returning to San Jose, I wrote a renewal of my offer, but received no reply. In all probability poor Saidie, *another victim of the dance*, now lies in one of the nameless graves.

CHAPTER XXVII
SAN QUENTIN—WE SECURE
A LOVELY PROPERTY

On or about August 18, 1904, I was in San Francisco. Thence I went to San Quentin, State's prison, where I was graciously given an opportunity of addressing over one thousand prisoners and also of having many individual heart-to-heart talks, the latter a favor which has been granted me for many years. At this time there was no admission into the women's quarters; under the new and present administration I have been allowed this valuable privilege. To see the faces light up and to hear the hearty expressions from warden, officers, and prisoners was always well worth a special trip at any time; consequently, I looked forward with pleasure, though sad at heart, to visiting our penitentiaries whenever opportunity afforded. Sometimes my efforts seemed barren of results, but only in eternity may we learn of the good accomplished through faithful seed-sowing.

On this particular occasion I had requested of Captain Ellis (captain of the guard) an interview with a young girl, sentenced for two years (I think) for robbery. Before leaving me, she told me of an old woman, a life prisoner, who had not seen the outside of the women's quarters in over twenty years, and asked me if I would not please give her the next call. Captain Ellis having consented, I was soon shaking hands with a very neat, white-haired life prisoner. In a few moments she asked me if I would have any objection to her gazing out of the window at the beautiful bay and scenery, it having been so very many years since she had enjoyed that pleasure.

You can never know the impression made on me by this humble request; my only regret may be readily surmised. How I do praise God that he put it into the heart and mind of the present matron, Mrs. Genevieve Gardner-Smith, to appeal to kind-hearted Warden Hoyle and the board of prison directors for a special concession in behalf of all the well-behaved women prisoners. She asked for a monthly holiday, to consist of a two-and-a-half hours' walk within the grounds on God's beautiful green hills, so that these poor women might briefly feast to their heart's content on the lovely landscape and view of San Francisco's unsurpassable bay. A motion being made and passed, one of the many new and excellent concessions is this one of a Sunday walk on the hills once a month in charge of the matron, after the male prisoners are locked in for the day. The first time this occurred, some of these poor women knelt on mother earth and bathed it with their tears. Ah! reader, are you not, with me, daily demonstrating the fact, that *only godly wisdom, coupled with love, can win?*

My visit was all too short. I had to hasten to San Jose, where the board of Beth-Adriel managers were awaiting my arrival to inspect some properties. Please, if you can, imagine the welcome home from my dear Lucy, Anna, and the rest of the family. A warm attachment soon developed between the new matron, Mother Weatherwax, and me. She held the matronal office until health no longer permitted. (Our readers will probably have observed the tendency toward illness on the part of the workers. In this branch of home missionary work there is a great need of strong physique and nerves; otherwise there will be frequent prostration from the constant strain on the system.)

The first joyous greetings over, next in order was inspection of property. After many trips for this purpose I at last saw a place which delighted my heart; but—would the owner part with it? It was the one spoken of previously—the one consisting of ten acres, a commodious house, etc. Some of the members of the board knew the owner, Mr. R. D. Norton. We were all in the spirit of prayer whilst they laid the matter before him. He asked for time to consider, the ultimate result of which was his decision to sell it for such a purpose. Oh, how we thanked and praised our kind heavenly Father! The purchase price was $10,000—$2,000 to be paid by October 9, the remainder on time at six per cent interest. Above all expenses, there was now in our treasury $1,300. We gladly agreed to accept the proposed terms and to wait on the Lord for enough means to make up the deficit.

On October 8 while I, with the other members of the board, was in Judge Rhode's court negotiating for the mortgage, word was sent over the telephone that Mrs. Mary Hayes-Chynoweth, now deceased, would like to have me come to her residence, Edenvale, a most beautiful spot adjacent to San Jose. There was barely time to make the train, but the Lord was on my side. It being a few minutes late, I caught it, and was shortly in earnest conversation with this charitably disposed elderly lady. She asked me many questions and introduced me to her daughters-in-law, Mrs. J. O. and Mrs.

E. A. Hayes, who listened with marked attention to my recitals. Presently Mrs. Chynoweth said, "Mrs. Roberts, I am going to request you to excuse me briefly. I wish to pray with regard to this matter; my daughters will be pleased to entertain you during my absence."

In about a half hour she called both of them for private conference, leaving me with some of the grandchildren. Soon I was invited into the next room. With a smile, this dear lady said, "I feel that God wishes me to give you $500." Before I had a chance to speak, the Mmes. Hayes said, "We will add $100 apiece." Reader, I was too happy to reply immediately; and when I did, I could but poorly express my gratitude, first to God, then to them.

In answer to prayer we had our $2,000—first payment—according to agreement. Hallelujah! A $10,000 home for my dear prison friends, in one year, three months, and six days from the day Lucy and I arrived in Redwood City, strangers, with two telescope baskets containing all our earthly possessions, sixty cents, and a little God-given faith. Hallelujah! Did I regret the past toil, privations, and disappointments? Never, never; but soon went on my way rejoicing, to secure future support and payments.

During my absence of little less than one month (for I was to return for the dedicatory exercises of the new Beth-Adriel, to take place Tuesday, November 22, 1904) sad news reached me. My poor Lucy was taken so alarmingly ill as to necessitate her immediate removal to her own home. Although I have often heard from her, I have never since had the privilege of meeting her face to face. Her fond dreams of seeing the beautiful new home she had so greatly aided in procuring, were never, so far as I know, realized. If she is still living, I hope she may have the pleasure and satisfaction of reading this book and of knowing how dearly I loved her and how much I appreciated her every effort. This I know, that she sufficiently recovered to resume work for the Master; but on account of the removal of her people, I temporarily lost track of this trophy for the Master's crown. God forever bless her wherever she is.

The night previous to our removal from the little old home on St. John Street, I was lying on my couch in the parlor, sleepless for very joy, and reading God's blessed Word. I happened to look up. On the wall hung a motto bearing these words:

> God has his best for those
> Who dare to stand his tests;
> His second choice for those
> Who will not have his best.

"Lord!" I said, "I want your best."

"My child," came my soul-answer, "It is for you; but there are hard roads still to travel, hard battles to fight and win, privations, disappointments, losses, much more. 'Can thine heart endure, or can thine hands be strong, in the days that I shall deal with thee?' Ezek. 22:14."

"Lord, thou knowest," I answered.

Then came a desire to write. I took up tablet and pencil, always ready to my hand on the little stand by my couch, and spent the rest of the night writing the verses that you will find in our next chapter.

CHAPTER XXVIII
GOD'S BEST

_Child, did I hear you say you want my best?
With nothing less—will you be satisfied?
You add you'll follow where I choose to lead,
Though all forsake, e'en to be crucified.

You ask you know not what ... Well, let it be
As you desire ... And now, a little test:
Your social standing I shall first require;
A humble place must bring to you—my best.

It hurts? ... Of course it hurts—the snubs, the slights,
From those whose favor you delighted in,
When they were told you'd found "The Priceless Pearl"
And willingly renounced this world for Him.

The step you've taken, they pronounce insane!
Wilt go a little further on this road?...
Your reputation. How you shrink! Too much to pay?
Child, I do only take you, at your word._

_Beloved one, still more I now desire;
Your worldly comforts — e'en your home which you enjoy.
Can't part with them? Step out, my child, and try;
I promise you I'll substitute — my joy.

You do not understand? But soon you shall:
I'm going to trust you in a hard, hard place;
Therefore destruction of your idols I must make,
To help you run —and win- this glorious race.

Come! take your place within these rescue homes,
Where I have brought some priceless gems of earth,
To cleanse, to cut, then polish for my crown:
Your services I need to enhance their worth.

The world has long rejected them with scorn,
These human gems from out the mire and dust;
A lapidary I would make of you,
Whilst I some precious gems with you entrust.

Your patience and forbearance will be taxed
Beyond endurance! And you've none, you say.
Then I must teach these lessons to you, child;
You promised to go with me all the way._

The trials are too great! Nay, say not so.
Privations too! and disappointments sore!
And just as the gem begins to scintillate,
My search-light doth disclose some dreadful flaw.

And you must start anew the task again....
Cheer up, dear child. I never will forsake.
Come, dry those tears and rest a while with me.
I soon will rectify your very sad mistake.

Think not you are the only one who fails,
For all have failed. Not all have tried again;
Thus have they missed my best, for which they prayed.
Courage. Be brave. The attempt was not in vain.

Now then, that gem with such a dreadful flaw,
Bring it to me.... Ah yes! I now will prove
Too soon the surface you did undertake
To polish—e'er the ugly flaw's removed.

Plunge it anew into the precious blood of Jesus,
Thus anew—the work's begun....
You're wining? My beloved, obedient child,
Not many live the prayer, "Thy will be done."

I'm going to prove this precious gem by fire;
'Tis next in order. This, to consume the dross.
It's size will be reduced. Nay, do not fear;
Perfect and flawless gems must suffer loss.

For further process, see these varied wheels
For grinding, till the blemished spot we reach.
Not too much haste! Be careful. Watch and pray;
Soon then you'll learn each lesson as I teach.

You wish to know the names of all these wheels?
These two are Joy and Peace, and this, Long-suffering.
This one is Gentleness, then Goodness next.
Now to the front the wheel of Faith I bring.

And are these all? Not quite. The Meekness wheel
So gently polishes. Then Temperance comes in
To aid in handling gems with special care:
Thus give the final touch of polishing.
(The nine fruits of the Holy Spirit. Gal. 5:22-26.)

You ask what motive power propels these wheels.
Dear child, your teacher is the God above.
He tells you. Surely you have learned his name;
His motive power is Love, and only Love,

Press on, press on. The secret now you know;
The willing, the obedient stand the test.
Supported by my love, your eye on me,
Surely I have—for you—my very best.

CHAPTER XXIX
DEDICATION OF BETH-ADRIEL

We now busied ourselves putting our new home in order. It was a blessed, blessed day, that day on which the dedicatory exercises took place (Nov. 22, 1904). They were participated in by an immense gathering of representative men and women, and account of which you may, if you so desire, read in the San Jose and San Francisco dailies of that evening and succeeding morning. Amongst others who delivered addresses was my now personal friend, Mrs. Mary Hayes-Chynoweth, the report of whose speech it gives me pleasure to quote:

She expressed her thankfulness at being present and seeing so many interested in a line in which she had been working over fifty years. She emphasized the necessity of having the spiritual life of God in the heart to live a Christ-like life. She spoke trenchantly of the need of purity, not only on the part of young girls, but young men and old men, too. She bespoke the help of all for those engaged in this work.

Young men need much attention, too. If they had more, there would be less need to work for women. If the heart is pure, no temptation outside can have the power to overcome. If every man were in that condition, there would be no temptation for girls. Let all work together, men and women, nor one think or claim to be better than the other, etc.

The pastors of all the denominations were present, some making brief addresses, and a most excellent program was enjoyed by all.

For some time my work, with the exception of taking an occasional trip after some dear child, lay in the immediate suburban towns, or in San Jose proper, so that I was able to spend Thanksgiving, Christmas, and New-Year with our now large family. In February, 1905, I again started out on a protracted trip, through central California, making brief stops to address audiences in Mountain View, Palo Alto, San Mateo, and, before going further, Redwood City. There was no trouble now to obtain a church in the latter town in which to plead the cause so dear to my heart. The only trouble was that the building could not admit the overflow of people. Thence I went to San Francisco. There I was warmly received by dear Sister Kauffman, whose hospitality I accepted whilst I was filling church engagements and visiting once more the county jail No. 3. Numberless were the questions propounded by the inmates. Many had gone, but alas! many more had filled their places. The work promised to be endless.

It was early in May when I returned to San Jose. No sooner had I arrived than the chief of police telephoned me to come to his office at my earliest convenience. This was by no means uncommon. Frequently Chief Carroll had some one whom he preferred should have the benefits of Beth-Adriel rather than be sentenced to a term in jail.

I hurried to town and was soon in conference with him concerning a young woman that had arrived in San Jose that morning with a youth, who was caught in the act of trying to secure lodging for her in a disreputable house. Evidently it was her first incarceration behind iron bars. When we approached her cell, we could hear her screaming and crying with both fear and distress. Upon seeing me, she ceased temporarily. I put my arm about her in tender pity and tried to say words of comfort. The Chief had informed me that she had applied to the health officer for medicine as soon as placed in a cell, her physical condition being by no means good, in consequence of the sinful life she had been living. I prevailed upon him to have her committed to Beth-Adriel, where she was taken late that afternoon.

At the time we had a new matron, of whom I had heard through correspondence with the board, but had only just met. My impression of her was by no means satisfactory, nor was I wrong in my estimate, for she telephoned to my lodgings to say that, on account of this poor girl's physical condition, I should have to remove her *immediately*. On receiving this word, I made application and obtained a pass from one of the supervisors for her admission into the county hospital, and then went to Beth-Adriel to convey her thither. Poor, poor child! That matron had barely allowed her to sleep under the roof, and at daylight had ordered her out on to the back porch and there had given her her breakfast in discarded dishes. In fact, the matron treated her as though she had leprosy or smallpox. By the grace of God I kept silence, but resolved what should be done when the board convened the following week.

I left Martie at the hospital, only to receive word before the day was over that I had made another mistake, that they did not take cases like hers. "What is a county hospital for?" I inquired of the one who was talking to me over the telephone. Answer: "Mrs. Roberts, were we to take in those kind of cases [venereal] there wouldn't be a building in California large enough to receive them. We're sorry, but *she must* be removed from here." However, as it was late, they isolated her for me until the morning. In the meanwhile I again conferred with the chief of police, and also I received a severe reproof from the supervisor for not informing him of the nature of poor Martie's complaint.

Upon our discovering that she came from Oakland, Alameda County, I was requested to remove her early the following morning to that place. Poor wronged child! She was perfectly pliant in my hands. I felt as though I could not be tender enough. On the train she told me her story.

Her father and another man were hung by a vigilance committee in northern California for highway robbery and murder. The shock and horror of this cost her mother her life. Martie was an orphan as soon as she came into the world. Her grandmother cared for her two years, and then she died. On her death the baby was placed in the Salvation Army home for homeless children at Beulah. At the age-limit (fourteen) she was hired out as domestic for a lady about to become a mother, who, as soon as able again to resume her household duties, discharged the girl. Then Martie began to drift. No one really cared for the poor wronged child. For about a year she procured one temporary situation after another in inferior places, visited cheap vaudeville shows and dances, and made the acquaintance of undesirable people, amongst whom was the young man now awaiting trial for vagrancy in San Jose.

Upon reaching Oakland, I at once repaired with my charge to the office of the chief of police. He referred me to the mayor, who, in turn, referred me to the supervisors. Not knowing any of the latter, I threw myself on the kind mercies of the chief, who, after much difficulty, succeeded in locating one; and late in the afternoon I procured a pass for Martie into a certain ward of the county infirmary of Alameda County.

Rest assured I did my utmost in the short while at my command to convey the Master's message of love and pardon for her and "whosoever will"; promised to write, also soon to visit her; and then, my heart heavily weighted, bade the poor, wronged girl farewell. It was indeed and in truth farewell. I never again laid eyes on her, for she disappeared within two days, and not until I read two years ago of her death by carbolic acid, did I learn the ultimate fate of this another victim of pre- and post-natal conditions.

In consequence of this and other similar cases that were being refused the home, I realized that we must have a sanitarium on our grounds as soon as the bulk of the debt had been wiped out.

On returning, I had a heated discussion with our board, only succeeding in gaining the reputation of being rather ill-tempered and hard to please. But oh! dear reader, I was not. I was only zealous, so zealous for the cause. God knows. Nevertheless, I refused to work until they promised to be on the lookout for a more efficient matron; consequently, the next time I met with them, an elderly couple, husband and wife, were in charge. I perceived, however, that the work was drifting from its original purposes and fast becoming that for which it was not incorporated—a maternity home. This tendency was hardly perceptible at first, but ere-long I discovered to my keen sorrow that apparently much of my labor had been in vain. What to do or what course to take I did not know. I prayed earnestly and continued to work, though with less fervor than at the first. How could I? During my absence such new rules and regulations were being adopted as made it no easy matter for any needy girl to become an inmate of Beth-Adriel.

Feeling, after constant prayer, that my loving Lord would have me exercise patience and forbearance until the annual board meeting in January (it was now November). I refrained from further interference or discussion, and again put a distance between them and me, though I kept in constant communication with several of the family.

CHAPTER XXX
THE JUVENILE COURT COMMISSION—HENRY

Whilst I was in one of the Coast towns, the mail one day brought me the following notification, which, rest assured, was at the time as the "balm of Gilead," leading me to believe that God, who never makes any mistakes, was going to take me into more definite work for the unfortunate children.

Office of County Clerk, Santa Clara County, California. San Jose, Dec. 13, 1905.

Mrs. Florence Roberts, San Jose, Cal.

Dear Madam: You will please take notice that pursuant to an order made this 13th day of December, 1905, by the Honorable M. H. Hyland, Judge of the Superior Court, in and for the county of Santa Clara, State of California, in Dep't 2 thereof and duly entered into the minutes of said Court, that you have been appointed a member of the Probation Committee of the Juvenile Court, and you are hereby directed to appear in said Court on Monday, December 18, at 10 o'clock, A M. Very respectfully, Henry A. Pfister, Clerk. By J. C. Kennedy, Deputy.

This changed the nature of my plans, though at first not interfering to any great extent with the work already in hand.

As never before I began to get insight concerning the disadvantages under which many a wronged child was, and is laboring, and oh! how I thank and bless God that there is now protection and help for many through the officers and the instrumentality of the Juvenile Courts. This subject, however, will furnish material for another book; therefore it will be but lightly touched upon at this time, for I want to have you again visit with me San Quentin and on this occasion become acquainted with Henry. I first heard of him through Captain Randolph, captain of the yard, and next through Captain Sullivan; then I obtained permission from Captain Ellis to interview this young man.

He was sentenced from ——- County to serve twenty-five years for homicide. Over seven years had now expired, and seven, I assure you, seems like twenty-seven, even more, to every one of these poor prisoners. He was a very bright young man, aged about twenty-five years, and he had the record of never having yet lost a single credit since his incarceration. I listened with intense interest whilst he told me this:

"I don't suppose I differed much from other boys in my school days, was just as full of fun and mischief as any of them, but there was no real harm in me that I knew of. My father is a miner, a prospector, always on the lookout for, and locating, claims. Mother was always a hardworking little woman, and raised a large family. We had a neighbor who didn't like us, neither did he like my dog, which, just as any dog will, intruded on his premises once too often; so he shot and killed him, remarking with an oath as he did so, that there'd be more than one dead dog if we didn't make ourselves scarce—anyhow, words to that effect. The killing of my pet made me very mad. I am, unfortunately, very quick tempered, though I soon cooled down. I felt as thought I could have killed him then and there for his dirty meanness, but pretty soon father and mother succeeded in quieting me.

"We had no more trouble or communication with these neighbors for some time; then one day, when I was playing ball with some of the neighbor boys with some potatoes, he happened to pass and one of the potatoes struck him. It didn't hurt him a bit, but he ripped out an awful oath at me, and called me and my mother by a name that no man with a spark of spunk in him would stand for a minute. He threatened me at the same time. I hurried home, changed my clothes, and told my father I was going over to the county seat (near by) to have him bound over to keep the peace, as I was afraid he would carry out his threat. Before I left the house I took down father's gun. 'Henry, what are you doing? You put that gun right back where you got it,' he said. 'I'll not do it,' I replied. 'He's threatened to kill me. I'll need it for protection,' and on I walked, too quickly for him to overtake me.

"As I was passing ——'s warehouse on the county road, this neighbor walked into it out of his yard, and just as I came opposite the door he stuck his head out and put his hand into his hip pocket. Before he got a chance to shoot, I had shot him through the fleshy part of his right hip. He lived several days. I feel sure he needn't have died, if given proper care.

"I laid a long time in jail before the trial. My people were too poor to get me all the defense I needed. Unfortunately, my lawyer, though a brilliant man, was a drunkard. Father impoverished the whole family to raise money to clear me, all to no effect. I am here for twenty-five years, when I ought to be out trying to help make them comfortable in their old age. I hear they are very, very poor. Oh, how I wish I could help them!…"

He told me where they lived, and I resolved, God willing, to take a trip, in the interests of Beth-Adriel, in that direction, and told him I would try to see them, though making no promises toward aiding him in gaining his freedom, for as yet I had only his word as to the truth of this story.

It was a whole day's journey, and, being very tired on reaching my destination, I did not look them up until morning. I can yet see that very clean, poverty-stricken room. I sat on the only chair it contained, the little mother sat on the bed, the father on an old trunk. The father hadn't "struck it rich" yet. Prospectors are always hopeful, sometimes realizing their hopes, but not often. The mother, whenever able, worked in the fruit. In some way they managed to eke out a bare but honest living. They could not have been much poorer.

We discussed Henry's case pro and con. Evidently he had not overdrawn the truth. Before the day was over we were in consultation with a friendly disposed attorney, who drew up petition papers. Before these were out of the printer's hands, I had held conferences with several people and clergymen, and had also made engagements in the interest of Beth-Adriel. The Lord was touching hearts and money was being added to its treasury. Soon I was doing double duty, aided by Henry's father. He went on his bicycle from place to place in the county where this homicide had been committed, whilst I took the stage or the train as the case might require, speaking in his behalf as well as securing funds for the home. Finally we reached the county seat. There I learned from many—even officials—that Henry's sentence was unjust; but, owing to their political positions, I could obtain very few of their signatures. The judge who had sentenced Henry told me that he could not sign, he being then the attorney for the widow of the dead man.

A very severe cold, threatening me with pneumonia caused me to leave hurriedly for home, where for several days I was well-nigh prostrate. There were many earnest prayers for my speedy recovery. These the dear Lord heard and answered, so that before long the work so suddenly laid down was, through his loving kindness and grace, resumed.

Henry's father sent by express the package of signatures he had procured, and I felt the witness of the Spirit that we now had sufficient. The next move, as I thought, was to present them at Sacramento to the Governor. He received me most kindly, talked at length on rescue work, Henry's case and other cases, etc., but informed me that he would have no jurisdiction to act until the matter had been duly presented after receiving the written approval of the board of prison directors. At their next monthly meeting I was present; but, owing to stress of other matters, Henry's case could not at this time command their attention, nor for three successive meetings.

Then occurred an adjournment until July. Henry wrote that he could not conscientiously ask me to come again, but the still, small voice bade me try once more. Oh, praise the dear Lord for answering many prayers in his behalf! Henry was granted his parole. The news was telephoned to me early in the morning. I hurried down to Captain Ellis' office to offer Henry my congratulations, but, above all, to direct his mind toward the Author of his freedom. What a blessed opportunity to honor the Master! and he promised to try to serve him thereafter.

Then he whispered something to the Captain, who replied, "Certainly, you have my permission." Excusing himself, he hurried into the inner yard. Presently he returned with an oblong box. Handing it to me, he said: "Mother Roberts, I have long observed that your little autoharp was wearing out. This one, my companion in my lonely hours, must now take its place. I know the use you will make of it. I wish, how I wish, you might be able to appreciate with what pleasure I make this slight token of my eternal gratitude!"

I had not dreamed of my prayer for a new instrument being answered in this manner, I having never learned that Henry was musical or possessed any such thing. It was a much finer one than mine. Had I been presented with a gold mine, I could not have felt better pleased. From that day to this autoharp, No. 2, and I have been inseparable.

But I must proceed. Before taking up other matters, I will add this: Henry made good for two years, received pardon from Governor Gillett, married his faithful little sweetheart, and named his first little daughter after me. A few days ago I received a letter telling of the birth of another little daughter. He took up a claim, and he is now farming his own homestead.

Many were, and no doubt still are, his trials and temptations. Not always was there victory, but I am sure as he reads this that the tears will come. He will probably retire to some quiet spot, fall on his knees in gratitude to God, who pardons our sins even though they be "red like crimson," and then ask him to guide him in the way he should go and to help him to bring up his dear little family in the fear and admonition of the Lord. May God forever bless Henry, his faithful companion, and his dear children, is my earnest prayer.

CHAPTER XXXI
THE ANNUAL BOARD MEETING—
DOLLIE'S STORY

I believe the spirit of prayer rested mightily on every one of us present at that very important business meeting, yet I doubt if any member realized its vital importance more than I myself. Like David of old, I inquired of the Lord as to whether to continue with them or start anew? The token asked was a unanimous reelection to the office he had called me to fill. It was by ballot, and was unanimous. I was satisfied, and for another year cheerfully continued to fill the office of field secretary and evangelist.

I now visited Sonoma, Mendocino, and other counties in that locality. A kindly reception awaited me everywhere, and no wonder—I petitioned the Lord to go before me. He answers such a petition out of Isa. 45:2: "I will go before thee, and make the crooked places straight: I will break in pieces the gates of brass, and cut in sunder the bars of iron."

One day whilst I was making calls amongst the unfortunate, I was met at a certain door by a neat, intelligent-looking young woman, attired as though for a journey. A glance through the open doorway revealed the presence of three others; they, however, were in house dress peculiar to their mode of existence. One of these spoke, "O Dollie, invite the lady in. It's going to be lonesome without you." She, none too graciously, extended the invitation. If I had any pride left, I stifled it for the sake of these poor lost souls, sitting around in their tawdry finery, smoking cigarettes. My heart went out in tender pity for them as I attempted to introduce our loving Savior.

"Hold on," said Dollie, at the same time looking at a beautiful gold watch on her breast, "I think I will have time before the train comes [the depot was but a block away] to tell you my story...."

"When I was fourteen years old, I had the misfortune to lose my dear mother, who died in childbirth. Father was a very hard-working man, a mechanic. He broke up housekeeping for two reasons: First, because mother had been very indulgent, so that I didn't know the first thing about domestic duties, so wouldn't have been able to even get him a decent breakfast. Next, because everything spoke to him of mother, whom he fairly idolized. I used to see him evenings when he came home from work to the place where we boarded. Seldom in the mornings. Guess I was too lazy to get up in time for anything but a hasty breakfast, then hurry off to school.

"We used to have Friday evening dances in our neighborhood, which I attended with my classmates. My but I loved to dance! It got so that Friday evening wasn't enough, so many a time found me with some of them at a hall down-town enjoying the public dance. The school-dance was always private. It didn't take long for some one to turn my silly head and make me believe he was dead in love with me. What did a little fifteen-year-old fool like me know, with no mother to teach her, and no woman to take a real interest? That wretch could fill me with, and make me believe, the biggest lies you ever imagined, and I drank it all in as though it were gospel truth. To this day I sometimes wonder if all men are liars.

"I'm not going to mince matters. I fell; and pretty soon *everybody was helping to grease the hill I was sliding down. In consequence, I soon reached the bottom.*"

"Some one told father; but I denied everything, yet I was so afraid he would make the statements be proven, that in my fright I ran away, and I have never seen him since. He's dead now. Poor father! I expert that, with his other sorrows, this trouble finished him.

"Two years later found me in just such a place as you have discovered me today. One afternoon, a sweet-faced Salvation Army lassie called. She talked as only you people can talk. I was but seventeen, still tender-hearted (wish I was yet); so it was not difficult to yield to her earnest persuasions to kneel beside her while she prayed. There was another girl in the room at the time, but she had a caller, so got up and went out. I learnt my first prayer from that Salvation Army girl. It was 'Our Father.' I used to see it framed on a wall in a house where my mother visited, but never did I understand it till that day. Then she asked me to talk to God in my own way. I felt sorry for what I'd done, and the life I was leading, and said so; so when she explained how God would forgive me, I believed her and told her I'd quit if she'd take me away, and she did. I left with her about dusk. She took me to her lodgings and for several days I shared her bed and board, until she got me a situation to do light housework at fifteen dollars a month. Light indeed! It was the heaviest, washing included; but I did as she suggested—prayed to God to help me as I worked, and he did. They were Jewish people and so did their own cooking; otherwise I couldn't have kept my job.

"Never shall I forget the joy of receiving my first month's wages. As I looked at that little sum in my calloused hand, I said, 'Dollie, it's the first honest money you ever earned; doesn't it make you feel good?'

"Before long my Salvation Army friend was called away to another field of labor. I promised to write to her, and to this day I am sorry that through my own carelessness I lost track of her. But I always did hate to write letters, so it's all my own fault.

"A girl told me of a nice place out near Golden Gate Park; only two in family, and twenty-five dollars a month. I called on the lady and she hired me. My but she had a dainty flat! One peculiarity I couldn't help noticing. She was always afraid some one was deceiving or going to deceive her, and would often make the remark, 'No one ever gets the second chance with me, no indeed.' And I used to say to myself, '*I wonder what she would do if she found out who Dollie was?*' She was a Christian. No, I'll take that back. She called herself one, and was the secretary of the ladies' aid of her church. Sometimes we had teas for them, and then she would take them all over the house and brag on my work and me. I knew how to cook pretty well by this time. She taught me. There was nothing I did not do to try and please her.

"One day I heard the hall door bang. Some one was coming up-stairs in a great hurry. Next she threw open the kitchen door, and I shall never forget the ugly face of her as she said, while I ran in my bedroom with fright and shut the door, 'Dollie! I want you to pack right up and leave this house, you — — —! How dare you impose yourself on me?' Oh! I ran and groveled at her feet; I begged; I cried; I besought her not to turn me away. I told her that I had repented and that God had forgiven my sins and that *if she was a Christian she'd help me*. That only seemed to make her madder than ever. 'Pack up your things and get out. Here's your money. I won't put up with deceit from any one.'

"I went into my room, and in my rage and despair tore my clothes off the hooks, emptied the bureau drawers, jammed everything any which way into my trunk, and in my anger went out, called the nearest express man, ordered my baggage to my old address, where the Salvation Army lassie first found me, told all the girls down the row what the Christians were like, and then plunged deeper than ever into a life of sin. *My heart, once so tender, is hardened forever.* Save your tears for some one who is worthy. You can never touch me. I wish to God you could. I must go; but you're welcome to remain and talk to the others, if you think it will do any good. Good-by, lady. Good-by, girls. I'll be back in less than a week"—and she was gone; but oh! could I, could these girls, ever get over this recital and its impression.

As soon as I could find my voice, I begged, implored them, not to let that story further influence them on the downward course. I pictured the judgment-day with that woman who turned Dollie away being interrogated by the King of kings, and the terrible doom awaiting all who did not repent and forsake sin; but, apparently making no impression, I soon left, unable to proceed further with the work that day because of the great burden with which this poor girl's story had weighted me.

I lay on my bed shortly afterwards, meditating upon the probable results had this mistress been loyal to her Lord, whom she professed to love and follow. I tried to picture her as saying:

"Dollie, a distressing story has reached me. It concerns your former life, but I know you must have repented, or you would not be doing hard, honest work for your living. Surely there are many you know and would like to help lead better lives. It is in my heart to assist them, Dollie. Let us together look some of them up. I realize that few, comparatively speaking, attempt this line of work. They think it is too humiliating, degrading, demoralizing, but it is what our Savior did whilst on earth, and I have vowed to follow him."

What think you, dear reader, would have been the outcome? How many trophies for the Savior's crown would have been hers? How many outcasts would have been turned from the error of their ways, and, having found their Redeemer, would have instructed their former companions in sin? It may never be revealed how many souls were lost through this professed Christian's shameful unfaithfulness.

Christ, when teaching occasion to avoid offense, uttered these words: "It is impossible but that offenses will come: but woe unto him through whom they come. It were better for him that a millstone were hanged about his neck, and he cast into the sea, than that he should offend one of these little ones." Luke 17:1, 2

Have you, my reader, helped "grease the hill" that "one of these little ones" was sliding down, so that she soon reached the bottom? or are you helping and cheering them on the upward way until they reach the goal? May God help and bless.

CHAPTER XXXII
LOST SHEEP—THE EX-PRISONER'S
wHOME—HOSPITAL SCENES

Who does not love that beautiful, most pathetic song entitled "The Ninety and Nine"? but how many have literally helped to emulate the Great Shepherd's example? Methinks I hear now, as I often have heard, great throngs singing:

> It may not be on the mountain height
>   Or over the stormy sea,
> It may not be at the battle front,
>   My Lord will have need of me,
> But if by a still, small voice he calls
>   To paths that I do not know.
> I'll answer, dear Lord, with my hand in thine,
>   "I'll go where you want me to go"

Our Lord takes every one of us at our word, whether we are singing it, praying it, or testifying to it. He does, indeed. *He takes us at our word.* How many of us make excuses? Because of this, how many souls are going to be lost? Oh! the pity of it, the everlasting pity of it!...

In my possession are several photos. Most of them have been handed to me by the weeping mothers of lost, stray lambs; some have come through the mail; all contain the one cry: "Dear Mother Roberts, ... Won't you please try to find my poor little girl? She may be in prison, or in the slums, or perhaps sick and dying in some hospital." And then follows a minute description of every feature, height, weight, peculiarities of character, etc. Many times the parents admit their own weak traits and failures. Poor, poor mothers! poor fathers! Not very often do we find them for you, sometimes where we would rather not; but you said that, no matter what their condition, I should tell them that you still loved them and that you would gladly welcome them home. We've found them sometimes when too far gone ever to come back to their earthly home, and but just barely in time to be rescued from eternal ruin.

Not always is the wanderer a girl, either. Sometimes a broken-hearted parent is looking for a lost boy, and solicits our help. I've met a few of them in the penitentiary, who have all but sworn me to secrecy.

"I'll be out soon," they've said. "No need to grieve the old folks at home by letting them know I've been in trouble."

"But, my boy," I've replied, "how are you going to account for your long absence and explain where you have been?"

"I'll fix it some way. Say I've been traveling or off in the mines. Anyhow, I'll fix it so they shan't find out."

"But don't you know, dear boy, you are going to live in constant dread if you do that? The Bible says, 'Be sure your sins will find you out,' and also that 'nothing that maketh a lie shall enter the kingdom of heaven,' I can not write a lie to your parents, and they've written to me, asking me to try to find you. Besides, you'll need money to take you home. It is not so easy as you think to step out of here and obtain immediate employment. Even if you do, some one will be constantly crossing your path and demanding you to pay him 'hush money' to keep his mouth shut."

Then I have recommended them to the care of Mr. Charles Montgomery, president of the board of prison commissioners, who, through great self-denial, toil, and energy, succeeded in establishing, little more than two years ago, a beautiful home and mission for discharged prisoners. It is located in San Francisco. To it they may go and be well provided for until employment is procured for them. Truly this is a most blessed work for the Master. This home is the outcome of a plan long cherished by Brother Montgomery, who for nearly fifty years has labored for the reformation and welfare of convicts and ex-convicts. It is now situated at 110 Silver Street, near Third Street, and is well worth a visit from those who have the interest of these men at heart. It was opened June 9, 1909, and it has been doing an immense amount of good, helping many a discharged prisoner to be once more a desirable citizen and a man of honor. I would also add that it is a work of faith.

Will you come with me to one of our county hospitals this afternoon?

Soon we are kindly greeted by the matron, and almost the next words she utters after welcoming us are: "I'm especially glad to see you today, Mother Roberts, because in Ward X a girl who is dying has been asking if I knew where you were. You're none too soon. She can't last much longer, poor thing!" and she leads us to the bedside of the dying girl. I recognize her as Ruby — —, with whom I have more than once earnestly pleaded to forsake the wretched life she was living, warning her of the ultimate results of such a course. How changed she is as she lies there scarcely breathing!

She opens her dying eyes at the sound of our footsteps. "Ruby dear, do you know me?" A barely perceptible nod. "I'm so glad Jesus sent us to you today, dear child. Won't you take him for your Savior right now?" In as few words as possible she is told of the dying thief on the cross. As she can not speak, we ask her to pray with her mind, whilst we kneel with her hand in ours, calling on Jesus for mercy, for pardon in this the "eleventh hour." The tears which she is too weak to wipe away are wetting her pillow, but we observe a look of peace stealing over her countenance. Soon we leave, believing that some day we shall meet her among that great throng of the blood-washed.

Following a mothers' meeting one day in a Northern town a care-worn-looking woman invited me home with her. Here she related another heartrending story of a lost girl, an only child, for whom she had toiled day and night at the wash-tub, so as to send her to school dressed as finely as the other girls. "I have had to work very hard as long as I can remember," the poor mother said, "and when I married, I made up my mind that if I ever had a daughter I would not teach her domestic duties, for fear she also would have to be a drudge all of her life." So she raised a lady (?). The girl grew to be very independent and disrespectful to her breadwinner, her mother, who was a deserted wife. At the age of sixteen Elsie, without even a note of farewell, left her comfortable little home and heart-broken mother, never to return. She had intimated her going, but the mother had attached no importance to these remarks, but she recalled them after her daughter's departure. Furthermore, Elsie carried away nearly every dollar of her mother's meager, hard-earned savings.

After a long look at a photograph I perceived that, because of a peculiar mark on the cheek, not removed by the retoucher, perhaps overlooked, I could readily recognize Elsie. Therefore, when visiting the slums, jails, and hospitals I kept a lookout for her as well as for others, and also notified some coworkers.

One day whilst visiting the old city and county hospital (where Mary's baby was born), I passed a cot where lay an apparently old woman; she looked to be fifty and appeared to be in the last stages of some dreadful form of tuberculosis. *That identical mark was on her cheek*, but surely this could not be twenty-three-year-old Elsie. Surely not. So I passed on to the next cot. The impression to return to the former one was so strong that it was acted upon. Stepping over to her, I softly said, "Don't be frightened, dear, but is your name Elsie?" The next moment I was quickly calling the nurse, for I feared the shock had killed the woman. The nurse came and administered some restorative and then advised me not to excite the patient further, for she was dying; but the girl had sufficiently recovered to be able to ask questions.

"Who told you?" she whispered.

"It won't hurt you if I tell you?" I asked.

"No; please."

"Elsie, it was your dear mother, who has never ceased to love you and to look for you all these years, and has kept the home so pretty and comfortable, waiting for you to come back."

"Where is mother? Don't, oh! don't tell me she is here."

"No, dear, she is at home. It is nearly a year since she asked me to try to find you."

"Elsie do you love Jesus?" I continued. "Have you asked him to forgive you?"

"It's too late, I've been too bad."

"We have all sinned, Elsie. 'All have come short of the glory of God.' May I pray for you?"

"Yes, if you think he'll hear."

After my prayer she offered one—so short but oh! so contrite, so very, very contrite.

I called again the next day. She could barely speak even in a whisper, but she managed to let me know that she had had a beautiful dream and that after her death I was to write her mother that Elsie's last words to me were, "Tell mother I'll meet her in heaven," but not to let her know when and where her daughter died. She passed away that night. The letter to the mother was very brief, and no address given, so that there was no opportunity of subsequent correspondence. Three months later news came to me that the poor, loving, well-meaning, though mistaken mother had gone to join her dearly loved, lost and found Elsie in that "land that is fairer than day."

CHAPTER XXXIII
A WONDERFUL LEADING—HOW GIRLS
ARE LURED TO THE DANCE-HALLS

Early in March, 1906, I returned to a board meeting at Beth-Adriel, following which I began speculating as to my next move, for as yet I had no direct leadings. Before retiring I prayed earnestly to know the mind of the Spirit. It was in the neighborhood of 2 A.M. when I awakened with the impression to "Go to B—-." As I knew it would be an expensive trip, I decided to ask the ticket-agent whether he would grant a stop-over privilege on my half-rate ticket. Learning that he would, I decided to take every advantage of this and eventually, say within six weeks, to reach B—-. That afternoon, whilst on the train, I suddenly remembered that I had ordered my trunk checked to B—-, and again I felt that strong impression to *go right through.* So when the conductor called for tickets, I forfeited all stop-over privileges.

I arrived there about 2 A.M., and at once went to the leading hotel. About ten o'clock the following morning I was asking the gentlemanly clerk a question similar to the one I had asked the Redwood City depot-agent. It quite disconcerted him for a moment; but, upon learning my object, he referred me to a Salvation Army woman, whom I immediately looked up and fortunately found at home. She was pleased to receive one on such an errand, and agreed to accompany me to the dance-hall and slum district that night.

My next errand was room-hunting. Very seldom do I remain more than one night in a hotel in a strange town, for almost invariably many doors are soon opened to the non-salaried workers in the Master's vineyard. Then the next thing is to walk around in order to get my bearings and familiarize myself with the town, the churches, the press, the pastors, etc As soon as possible I call upon the pastors and make engagements to fill pulpits. This privilege, however, is granted only after the ministers have, to their satisfaction, examined my credentials and indorsements.

At seven o'clock that evening I was again with Mrs. Wilson, now attired in her regulation uniform, and at half-past eight we stood in one of the popular dance-halls. Here dancing, drinking, smoking, and gambling were being indulged in by black, white, tan, and mulatto of both sexes. Barring a few exceptions, I have never seen such an array of the inferior type of nationalities. The place was crowded; for this was Saturday night and also St. Patrick's Day.

While Mrs. Wilson was at the bar asking if I might sing and speak, a slender, fair-haired girl suddenly seized my left hand and quickly whispered: "Lady, we are trapped. Quick! your number. Where do you live? Act as though you weren't speaking to me. The proprietor may be watching. I'll be there at ten in the morning." I immediately gave my street and number, and she skipped away, just as Mrs. Wilson returned to tell me that she had not succeeded. This refusal was only what we had expected. After distributing a few tracts we were requested to desist; so we concluded to go elsewhere. *That sight was sickening.* And that refined-looking girl— who was she? What did she mean? We shall soon learn.

Other places which we visited that night were equally as bad, in fact, indescribably so, and they were numerous. However, we did what we could; but only once could I make use of the autoharp, and then only to sing to the poor souls coming out of the first dance-hall, for we held a brief street-meeting. I observed that not one girl or woman put her head out of the door; afterwards I learned that a fine of $2.50 was imposed for every offense of this nature between the hours of 7:30 P. M. and 3:30 A.M.

Upon returning from my breakfast the following morning, I was informed by my landlady that two young women were awaiting my return. After the greeting both commenced to talk so excitedly that I requested one to be the spokesman for the other. They appeared to be nearly of an age, about sixteen and seventeen, and were sisters. As nearly as I can remember, this was their story:

"We were attending high school several miles from our home. When we returned home at the time of the spring term, we learned that father's crops had failed and that mother was almost disabled from rheumatism. What little reserve fund they had was almost used up for medicines and necessities; so after a discussion of the matter they agreed to let us go to the city (San Francisco) to work, provided we should promise not to separate. This would leave our fourteen-year-old sister to help mother, and the two boys to assist father.

"A few days later we, alter kneeling in prayer with our mother, started on our journey. In a few hours we were asking the matron at the Oakland ferry-depot for a respectable lodging-house. She directed us, and from there we obtained situations as waitresses in a first-class private hotel on Bush Street, where we remained and gave satisfaction for some time; but one afternoon we were foolish enough to yield to the persuasions of some of our girl companions to take a car ride to the Park and Cliff House. I suppose we were enjoying ourselves so much that we did not realize how quickly the time was slipping away until some one remarked, "O girls, look at the clock!" It was within fifteen minutes of the hour when dinner must be served. We all ran for our car. When we arrived at the hotel, the landlady had put a new crew in our places. She would listen to no excuses, but told all four of us to go to the office for what wages were due us. Ours wasn't much, for we had been sending most of it home right along; so we were soon reduced to our last dollar.

"One of the girls who had worked with us told us to go to a certain employment agency (situated then on Ellis Street). The man behind the counter seemed to have lots of situations, but only one where we could work together, and as *neither one of us knew how to cook,* we couldn't take it. It was for cook and second girl in a private family. 'Hold on,' he said, as we were about to leave and try some other agency; 'would you be willing to leave town? If so, I have a nice place for two waitresses in a resort patronized by none but the best people of the neighborhood.' We told him we couldn't afford to take it unless some one would advance our office fees and our fares. 'I'll see to that,' he replied. 'Can you be ready to leave right away?' There was nothing to prevent, as our trunks were packed with the expectation of obtaining immediate employment; so all we had to do was to go quickly to our room with an expressman, then take a car to the depot, where the agent would meet us, check our trunks, put us aboard our train, and leave us, with our tickets, bound for B——.

"My! how we did hurry through! The girls who roomed with us had gone out; so as our weekly rent was paid in advance, we didn't see even the landlady when we left our lodgings. We reached the Oakland Mole, took our train, and after a long day's journey arrived at our destination in the early morning hours. We were met by some woman, who brought us in a hack to the place where my sister spoke to you last night—only she did not take us into the dance-hall, but somewhere up-stairs, into a comfortable bedroom. In a few minutes she came with a nice meal on a tray, told us to eat, to put the tray outside the door after we had finished eating, and then to go to bed and sleep as long as we wanted to, as she knew we were tired; then she left us.

"It seemed to be pretty noisy in the neighborhood, but we were too weary to care, so were soon asleep. When we went to leave that room in the morning, we found we were locked in. Sister hammered on the door, and soon the woman came. She told us she had done it to keep the other lodgers from disturbing us; but before evening we knew that something was wrong, for she never lost sight of us for a moment. Then she told us there was going to be a dance that night, and asked us to look our best.

"About half-past seven we went with her downstairs and then along a passage-way into that hall where you found us last night. Sister and I looked around for a minute, and then both of us said to the woman, 'What kind of a place is this?' There was a long bar, and two or three young men were cleaning glasses and wiping bottles, and there were lots of girls in fancy dresses standing around, chatting and some smoking cigarettes, also a few men, young and old. We were [reader, I will give you their exact expression] scared stiff. The woman, after introducing us to a fine-looking young man, said to him, 'These are the young girls sent by — —, the Ellis Street employment agent.' Then she took us into the dance-hall a few feet away. She told us that the young man was the proprietor of the place and that he would be a good friend, as would she, if we wouldn't 'do any kicking.' About 8:30 the crowd began to come in earnest, and by 9:30, and from that on, men and girls drank, danced, and cut up until closing-time.

"Mother Roberts, I can only liken our first night in that awful saloon and dance-hall to a bad nightmare.

"The woman didn't require us to dance unless we wanted to, until the second night; then she said that *we must*, or else we would be fined, and that as we already owed our fares, also other debts for incidental expenses, the sooner we made the best of the situation the better it would be for us. She called some girls to come and tell us how much they enjoyed the life they were now leading, and how much money they were making in percentage on the drinks that were sold across the bar to the men and them. They said we needn't drink whiskey if we didn't want to, as we would need to keep our heads if we were going to make all we could out of the men in getting them drunk."

"Why didn't you appeal to the authorities, girls?" I inquired.

"Mother Roberts, *they only laughed at us. We tried. It was no use. They seemingly stood in with the proprietor.* Millie went to the post-office, accompanied by one of the girls, an old hand, the second day after we arrived, to see if any mail had been forwarded, and on the way back stepped into the — — Hotel to inquire if they had any vacancies for two waitresses? The clerk asked, 'What address?' She was too ashamed to tell him where we really were; so told him to drop a card into the post-office general delivery as soon as he had situations for two. About three days afterward she got a post-card saying there was one vacancy; but we couldn't take it, as we were more determined than ever not to separate."

When I told them how it happened that I came, those two poor girls cried with joy and thankfulness. And now to act quickly. We all knelt in prayer. They agreed to stay in my room whilst I went out to notify Mrs. Wilson and the pastors. Never in all my life did I work faster, and in an hour I had these sisters safely housed with Mrs. W—, as she would not be suspected of secreting them. At two o'clock the pastors met me in one of the church studies. They decided to call immediately for a mass meeting of women on the following afternoon, to be addressed by me. Notices to this effect were gladly inserted by editors of the daily papers. *The whole community was astir.*

In the meanwhile the dive-proprietors were searching for the girls. No one suspected Mrs. Wilson or me. In fact, those dive-keepers had not regarded me as any more than an ordinary visitor that night of my introduction to their dance-halls, and had not noticed the girl speaking to me.

Before they left B——, the following article came out as an editorial in one of the leading daily papers. It appeared on the morning of March 23, 1906.

HOW GIRLS ARE LURED TO DANCE-HALLS

The general interest in the efforts to better the conditions of the fallen women, make timely a rough outline of the methods by which girls are lured into the haunts of vice, and kept there until they have lost all power or desire to escape and win their way back to decency and respectability. It is not pretended that this line is accurate, or that it fits any particular case, but the information on which it is based is gained from what are believed to be reliable sources, and it is not likely to be misleading: if applied in a general way.

HOW GIRLS ARE LURED

In the first place, of course, no girl that has not made some misstep or committed some indiscretion, could be enticed to a dance-hall or kept there for a moment if it were possible to get her inside its doors. But in every city or village in the country there are persons in the guise of men [yes, and women also] who are actively interested in helping girls to make the first misstep. These scouts and envoys of infamy are at the public dances; they waylay waitresses and working girls who are struggling to keep themselves on wages that are insufficient for their actual needs of food and clothing.

They get into the confidence of these girls, and sometimes when they are "down on their luck" or when they have committed some act that makes them ashamed to look their family or their employers in the face, these men come in the name of friendship and promise to find the overworked and underpaid girl, or the indiscreet girl, a place where she can earn money fast and earn it easily.

THE DANCE-HALL LIFE

As a usual thing the girls are taken to some place in another town where they are not acquainted. This suits the girl, because she does not want to meet her acquaintances, and it suits the man, because it gives him greater security in his evil transaction. The girl is nearly always penniless at this stage, and the man advances the money for the railroad ticket and the necessary food. The first act that lures the girl to the dance-hall is disguised as an act of friendship, and the first bond that is placed on her to keep her there is the bond of gratitude and obligation. In addition to that, where would she go if she did not like her first glimpse of the dance-hall, an ignorant, friendless girl in a strange town?

THE "RULES" OF THE HOUSE

One of the first things in which the recruit to the dance-hall is instructed is the rules of the house. She must be on the floor, ready to dance at seven o'clock, and they must remain on duty until 3 A.M., or so long as the patrons of the house continue to come and buy drinks. Between these hours they have thirty minutes for supper. If they are a minute late or stay a minute over the time allowed for supper, if they step out on the sidewalk during their hours of duty, if they get drunk, or if they commit other stated offenses, they are subject to a fine by the manager of the house, and the fines range from two dollars and a half up.

In the beginning of her career the new recruit usually gets fines charged against her faster than her credits mount up on the manager's book. But there are other rules, one of the chief of which is to make the men who come into the dance-hall buy as many drinks as possible, and if a man comes in who has money, to see that he spends it all before he departs. The girl is coached in the art of getting the money from the men, and in some of the worst dives they are told that if they get hold of a man who has money, and who does not seem inclined to give it all up, to give the bar-tender a wink when the refractory customer calls for his drinks, and the bar-tender will "slip him something" that will make him more amenable.

THE PERCENTAGE SYSTEM

The way girls make money for themselves is through percentages on the liquor which the men they dance with buy. After every dance the dancers line up at the bar and drink. The drinks for a man and his partner are twenty-five cents, and the girl's percentage is ten cents. If a man is liberal and will buy wine at one dollar a bottle the girl's percentage is forty cents. If he is still more liberal and will buy wine at five dollars per bottle, the girl gets two dollars and a half. The percentages are punched on a little card which the girl carries, and they are added up in the morning.

The money which the percentages represent, however, is not all paid over to the girl in the morning. She is given what cash the manager thinks is necessary to keep her through the day, and the remaining is credited against the railroad fare that has been advanced, and against the fines that may have accumulated. If a girl does not like the place and wants to leave, she is shown her account and informed that there is a balance due the house, and that it will be necessary to hold her clothes and other effects.

BECOMES SCHOOLED IN VICE

In the meantime the girl is being schooled in vice and crime. She learns that it is more expeditious sometimes to take a man's money out of his pockets than to wait for him to spend it twenty-five cents at a time, buying drinks. No matter whether the house profits by these thefts or not, they form another bond to tie the girl to a life of shame; for some one must always know of them, and if the girl is untractable she is threatened with criminal prosecution. If she commits no crime, she can still be charged with vagrancy, and it too often happens that police officers, knowingly or unknowingly, are made the instruments of persecution and the means for whipping these unfortunate women into submission to any wrong.

Dancing all night every night, drinking after every dance, living in the fumes of liquor and tobacco, and in constant jangle of profanity and obscenity, how long is required to snuff out every spark of womanliness that a girl may bring with her to such a haunt?

DOG-LIKE DEVOTION TO MALE ASSOCIATES

And yet there is one trait of her sex that is not snuffed out. It is the distinguishing trait of womankind and one of the finest traits that the human race can boast of—the trait of constancy and devotion.

The lower the fallen woman sinks, the more wrongs and iniquities that are placed upon her, the stronger it sometimes seems this devotion and constancy becomes. Nine-tenths of all the women of the tenderloin, it is stated, have some man, or some animal called a man, about whom this affection, this dog-like devotion centers. No matter how much he may abuse her, no matter if he takes every cent of the earnings of her misery and shame, no matter if he beats and kicks her because she can not give him more, the girl in nearly every case, is faithful to "the kid" and the worst fate than can befall her is that "the kid" should "throw her down." [In other words, forsake her.]

And "the kid" always throws her down some time; for "the kid" is not encumbered with any such inconvenient traits as constancy and devotion.

Then there is carbolic acid, or a long debauch, and a sinking down of the system, and the horrible disease against which even the county hospitals, which are open to the criminals and outcasts of society, who never did a stroke of useful work in all their lives, close their doors. And then there is the dishonored grave, over which the friends and the relatives, maybe, are ashamed to weep.

DANCE-HALLS TABOOED

In the enlightened communities, where there is a healthy public sentiment, dance-halls are no longer tolerated. Their day is over in California, and in only a few places are they permitted to exist. In the places where they do exist the communities are still hanging on the ragged edge of frontier life, where there is little regard for the common decencies of life. Sacramento recently made a clean-up of its dives, and disreputable dance-halls were closed up.

It is recognized by those who are observant, that dance-halls are more degrading than any other form of dissipation. They are public institutions with their doors open to all who enter, and those with money to spend are made welcome. When the money is gone, their welcome is worn out, and if the person is saturated with liquor, he is kicked out ignominiously, only to return when he has more money to spend.

THE RECRUITING STATIONS

In the large cities agents ply their trade of securing recruits for the dives in the interior. Girls on whose cheeks the blush of innocence still remains, are employed for various respectable positions, and sent to the interior. They are escorted to the trains, and even in some instances the proprietors of the dives see that they are on their way safely to their dens of infamy. A telegram is forwarded informing the resident manager, that more material for the dive is en route. The local manager meets the girls at the train with a hack and when they arrive at the place, almost invariably at night, they find their trunks have preceded them. They learn little of their surroundings in the late hours of the night, and when they do realize their positions, they feel altogether lost, without money or friends.

RECENT CASES SUBMITTED

The foregoing is not always the case. Some know the place of their destination, but some of them do not. Not long ago a Los Angeles girl answered an advertisement for work and was told a respectable position awaited her in R——. Just as she prepared to board the train for the mining town, she was taken in custody. On investigation it was learned that she was destined for a notorious dance-hall in R——, that even the respectable people of the town had not been able to close up.

About two weeks ago a woman was arrested in R—— and is awaiting trial in the United States court in Los Angeles for using the mails for immoral purposes. It is alleged that she was an agent for a dance-hall in R—— and had sought to obtain recruits for the dive.

Those in a position to know, state that the dance-halls are far more infamous than the real palaces of degradation. They are the stepping-stones to the other places, and lead on to destruction, preceded by misery and shame....

CHAPTER XXXIV
THE WOMEN OF B—— UP IN ARMS—THE
SISTERS TAKEN HOME—MORE ABOUT B——

MRS. FLORENCE ROBERTS STIRS HER AUDIENCE

Addressed Church Full of Women—Her Pathetic Stories listened to Attentively—Much Interest Manifested in the Cause—Raised Nearly Fifty Dollars to Take Two Girls Rescued from Dance-hall to Their Homes.

The above was the heading of an article which appeared in the local papers on the morning following the largest gathering of women ever congregated at one time in one of B——-s largest churches.

The morning before, escorted by the chief of police and two officers in plain clothes, I went to that dance-hall to demand the trunks of the sisters. The persons in charge claimed that they did not know where the girls' baggage was; that the proprietor was away; that they could not give the trunks up without his authority; and, furthermore, that there were debts of $22.50 booked against one sister and $21 against the other. Acting under legal advice, I gave them two hours, no more, to produce those trunks and their contents, also two itemized bills. I returned at the close of that time and found the keepers ready to accept the fares advanced (no bills produced) and to have the trunks immediately removed. When the sisters received their baggage, they declared that both locks had been broken and that each trunk had been robbed of many things; but the girls were so frightened and so anxious to get home, that they willingly stood the loss rather than be delayed through the arrest and the prosecution of the proprietors.

That night the two sisters and I went to the depot under an armed escort and started for their home, a day and a half's journey distant. I paid the porter to be on the lookout for any suspicious-acting travelers in our coach. Engagements for the following Sunday necessitated my immediate return to B——. On our arrival at their railroad destination I had barely time to catch my next train; therefore I had to leave explanation of the situation to the sisters, now with an aunt, the parents being on their ranch in the mountains, forty miles distant and accessible only by wagon. They bade me a most touching farewell, promising not to fail to correspond.

Truly, all through these strenuous experiences I was daily, hourly demonstrating to my soul's satisfaction God's wonderful leading, his strength, his wisdom, his great, great care, for no evil befell me, neither did any plague come nigh my dwelling (Psa. 91:10-12).

On my return to B—- on Saturday sufficient engagements to keep me in that vicinity at least three weeks and over were immediately made. After filling these I hoped, God willing, to take a rest in the beautiful homes of some of my Santa Cruz friends. There was an immense audience in the First Methodist church on Sunday evening, April 8, and a large collection was taken for the Beth-Adriel fund....

Before I left B—-, God gave a most blessed realization of his wonderful watch-care over those who are earnestly trying to serve him. On Monday, April 9, word reached me that I should be on my guard. The proprietor of the — — dance-hall had declared vengeance. I had accepted an invitation to dine with the chief of police and family that evening, but on account of this word of warning I deemed it wise to telephone to the sheriff's office and ask protection. An enemy must have received the message and responded. When I came out of the house to keep my dinner engagement, I had walked but a few yards when I received a sudden impression to look behind me. On a fenceless lawn, not three feet away, stood —- —- with his hand in his right hip pocket. Quick as a flash I pointed the forefinger of my right hand in his face, saying, "You dare not shoot." "Only your sex protects you, you —- —-- —-," he sneered. Never mind the vocabulary of awful adjectives and names he hurled at me, dear reader. I've never heard their equal before or since. There was no one in sight until his sister presently crossed the road. But God was protecting me, and I knew it. Then the man sneered about my calling up the sheriff's office for protection. I now knew he had a coworker there.

When at last there was a chance for me to speak, I quietly told him that he was soon going to an awful hell unless he quickly amended his ways, and that God was going to hold him and his kind everlastingly responsible for the ruination of many, many souls, and implored him to turn to this outraged God and plead for mercy and pardon before it was eternally too late. As they turned to recross the street, I added, "God wants to bless you." With an oath he hurled back at me," — — — — — — — —! I don't want God to bless me." Then I heard a fiendish laugh from behind a hedge; somebody clapped their hands in great glee, and a woman's voice shouted, "Good for you — —! Give it to her, the — — — — — — — — —! Why didn't you finish her while you were about it?" ...

The chief of police and his wife saw to it that I was protected the rest of my brief sojourn, but no one can ever know how much nearer that experience drew me to my loving Lord. More than one woman told me the next day that they were watching that encounter through their lace curtains, and that if he had laid even a finger on me they would have thrown up the windows and screamed for help, even have attempted personal aid. But there was no need of that; for hath our heavenly Father not said in Isa. 51:17, "No weapon that is formed against thee shall prosper; and every tongue that shall rise against thee in judgment, thou shalt condemn. This is the heritage of the servants of the Lord, and their righteousness is of me, saith the Lord"? And in Psa. 34:7 is this blessed assurance: "The angel of the Lord encampeth round about them that fear him, and delivereth them." Hallelujah! "In thee, O Lord, do I put my trust: let me never be put to confusion." Psa. 71:1.

Before I left B— —-, that town had a well-organized law and order league. The members chose me as their first honorary member. I doubt whether any of God's stewards had more friends and more enemies at that one time, in that one locality than did the writer of this. But I loved all and prayed God to bless their precious souls for Jesus' sake.

As usual, I was not leaving unaccompanied, so that instead of passing through San Jose, as I had expected, I chaperoned a young girl to the home, remaining there over night and reaching Santa Cruz the next evening.

CHAPTER XXXV
SANTA CRUZ—REBA'S LETTER—
THE EARTHQUAKE

"The Lord God is a sun and shield; the Lord will give grace and glory: no good thing will he withhold from them that walk uprightly." Psa. 84: 11. I was now enjoying a few days' sweet rest and fellowship in the home of my sanctified friends, Sister Bessie Green and her mother. Oh, how I enjoyed every moment! What a wonderful exchange of experiences and demonstrations of God's mighty love, power, and wisdom was ours! and what good times we had going about amongst certain ones in whom she was interested, visiting the mission, enjoying the lovely ocean-breeze, etc.! On Sunday, April 16, we went with a large band of consecrated young people to assist in a meeting of song and gospel cheer for the inmates of the almshouse and county hospital.

My visit was destined to be of short duration, for the next day there came among forwarded mail a letter reading somewhat as follows:

Dear Mother Roberts:

I am just as blue if not bluer than the paper I am writing on, and I'll tell you why, for you know all the circumstances of our recent trouble

When girls through no real fault of their own get into such an awful scrape as Millie and I were so unfortunate as to get into, but thank God, were rescued from, … what kind of Christians can they, must they be, who will do their utmost to help still further crush us by talking all over the town about what happened, and everybody putting their own construction on what they hear, then giving us the cold shoulder.

Millie is at home. She's sick from the awful effects of it yet, and I'm trying to earn an honest living, but it's no use. My so-called friends won't give me a chance. I've about made up my mind I might as well have the game as the name, so by the time you receive this, I shall probably be with Miss— — at her house in C— —, for I'm sure she will be kinder than the folks here. I don't suppose they've meant to harm us, but just because they love to talk they've settled it for us forever. I forgive them, but it's no use to try to be good any longer.

Don't think I forget you or your kindness, and I will always love you no matter what becomes of me. Gratefully yours,

Reba — —.

"Bessie! Bessie! what shall I do? what must I do?" I cried, wringing my hands and handing her the letter to read. Hurriedly reading it, she quickly said, "Let us pray." Immediately suiting the action to the word, she as briefly as possible asked the Lord for speedy help. It came—an instantaneous impression to telephone to the hotel at S— — where Reba had been employed. "Keep on, Bessie, keep on praying," I requested as I arose from my knees and hastened into the next room, took down the receiver, called for the long-distance operator, asked for my party, and emphatically declared it to be a matter of life and death requiring immediate service. Shortly I was talking to the landlady of the N— —- J— —- Hotel, who told me that Reba was still under her roof, but was expecting to leave for San Francisco on the next train.

"Please call her to the 'phone," I said, and very soon I heard Reba's voice.

"Hello; who wants me?" she said.

"Mother Roberts, Reba dear," I replied. "Stay where you are. I am coming on the next train"

"But I'm going on the next one to San Francisco I can't; my trunk is at the depot."

"Reba, you *must* wait till I come, dear. I've some good news for you."

"Very well; I'll wait. Fortunately, I haven't bought my ticket yet."

"Good-by," I gladly said. "Meet me."

There was barely time to make the next train; but, as usual, the Lord (bless his dear name forever!) favored me. I reached S— —- at 7:30 P.M. On our way to the Hotel Reba whispered, "Mother Roberts, will you occupy my room with me tonight? I want to have a long, long talk and it's the quietest part of the house, up on the third floor."

After supper we repaired to her neat little room, and following prayer, soon retired, but not to sleep. Dear Reba, with many tears, particularized the trying situation, as she lay with my arms about her. Shortly after midnight she sweetly slept. Not so with me. I heard every hour and half-hour strike, up to half-past four, on some clock near by. It seemed very close and warm, attributable, so I thought, to the smallness of this inside room.

I must have just fallen asleep when suddenly I was awakened by a terrible, terrible sensation, accompanied by fearful screams and crashing of glass and furniture. Reba was thrown out of bed, then back again, where I locked her fast in my arms, gasping the words, "God cares! God cares, Reba! 'We shall see him face to face and tell the story saved by grace,'" for at first I could only believe that the end of the world had come. This dreadful noise was followed by an awful stillness in our immediate vicinity, though we could hear, apparently from outdoors, mingled cries, screams, and groans of fright, distress, and pain.

Reba leaped out of bed, instantly grasped her clothing and mine, and was rushing from the room when I called out: "Come back! Come back and dress. We've had an earthquake and an awful one, but somehow I feel the worst of it is over." Never did we more quickly get into our clothing and step outside. The hallway and rooms were piled with debris. Plaster, laths, broken pictures, and furniture lay in shapeless confusion on every hand. We came to the staircase. Part was gone; every step was likewise covered with the ruins of broken ceiling and wall. Devastation was everywhere, everywhere. Trusting the Lord, I landed safely on that tottering staircase, Reba quickly following; and soon we were with the frightened population out on the streets, gazing, well-nigh speechless, at the awful ruins which lay on every side. Every one was wondering, with aching, troubled hearts, concerning their absent loved ones. How was it faring with them? How far had this earthquake extended? Could it possibly have been any worse in other places than in this one? Soon we discovered, as we hurried to the telegraph and telephone offices, that all communication with the outside world was absolutely cut off. All sorts of dreadful rumors were afloat; later many were verified; whilst some proved to have been more or less exaggerated.

In the afternoon word reached us that San Francisco was burning. My dear son, now in the employ of the Gorham Rubber Company was living there. I wondered if it had reached Haight Street: all I could do was to pray and wait, wait and pray. Many, I suppose, gave hunger no thought that day, for anxiety was well-nigh consuming us. The depot was crowded with people anxious to get aboard the first train that might arrive, but there was no promise or prospect of one that day. Reba and I put in our time between the telegraph-office and the depot; so did hundreds of others.

That night we had a shake-down at the home of her aunt, whose house had not been very badly damaged. I had so satisfactory a talk with her that Reba agreed to remain with her until she could get back to her mountain home.

Early the next morning I was again at the depot. About nine o'clock the agent privately notified me of the prospect of a train from the south in perhaps an hour, at the same time advising me to "hang around." I made a quick trip to where Reba was staying, bade her farewell, managed to purchase a few soda crackers and a piece of cheese (the stores which had not suffered severely were speedily cleaned out of all provisions), and returned to the depot to watch and wait.

At last! at last! praise God, at last! a train, a crowded train arrived. In a very few minutes, standing room was at a premium. After a long wait we began to move slowly, but we stopped after going a very few miles, for the road was practically being rebuilt. This was our experience the livelong day. In some places we sat by the roadside for hours, or watched the men rebuilding the track. When we came to one high trestle, only a few were permitted to cross at a time, it being not only severed from the main land at either end, but also very shaky. Here we parted from train No. 1.

At the other end of this trestle, we waited hours for the coming of a train from the direction of San Jose. This delay seemed interminable, for all of us were now out of provisions and in an intense state of suppressed anxiety and excitement. But finally a train slowly moved into view, and we all lustily cheered, once, twice, thrice, and again, as we gladly boarded it. Then we learned somewhat concerning the terrible destruction in other places all along the line, and also of the fearful holocaust in San Francisco.

What, oh! what was the fate of our dear ones there? Ah! dear reader, people who had never given much thought to God and their Savior were now imploring mercy and pardon, and making, oh! such promises of future loyalty and service, if he would but spare their loved ones. Alas! but few of these promises were kept. These people soon drifted back into the world and the former error of their ways.

CHAPTER XXXVI
RELIEF DUTY—SAN FRANCISCO—MISS B___

As this is not a history of the awful calamities of that trying time, they will be but lightly touched upon. Suffice it to say that when late that night our train slowly crept along the streets of San Jose and finally reached the station, the people thronged the streets. They heartily cheered and welcomed us. Upon learning that an "inquiry bureau" had been established right there, we soon packed it almost to suffocation, and oh! bless the Lord! I was one of the few to receive news. I got three unstamped, torn-out-of-note-book letters from my dear son, stating that the fire had not reached beyond Van Ness Avenue. He lived a little beyond. He was anxious for my safety. I at once sent similar short messages of assurance to the "inquiry bureau" of his residence district. Then I was passed through the line and taken to Beth-Adriel (martial law was in force), there to discover all of the family lodging under the beautiful walnut-trees. The house had suffered considerable damage, but, praise God! the inmates had escaped personal injury.

Relief duty at the depot was my next call. For two days and nights a large delegation of us remained on perpetual watch; for the refugee trains, crowded with sick, hungry, homeless, or penniless men, women, and children, were now arriving, at intervals of from fifteen to thirty minutes. Statistics show that San Jose, the first large city southwest of San Francisco, fed, clothed, and sheltered, temporarily, some permanently, in the neighborhood of thirty-seven thousand refugees. Moreover, its probation committee of the juvenile court handled the cases of over fifteen hundred destitute children. Busy times! I should say so! Only the wonderful power of God sustained us, for it was break-down work. At the close of the second day I was compelled to rest. After a good night's sleep I procured a furlough of forty-eight hours; for two more notes from San Francisco had reached me, and they described the great suffering, especially because of long waiting (sometimes all night) in the bread line.

San Jose generously supplied me with an immense telescope basket filled to its utmost capacity with canned goods, cooked meats, etc., so that it required the assistance of two to put it on the train, it was so heavy. On reaching the outskirts of San Francisco, I was informed that I could be taken no further than Twenty-fourth and Valencia Streets. There people seized every available rig, even to garbage wagons, paying exorbitant prices for conveyance to their points of destination. What was I now going to do? The eight hundredth block on Haight Street seemed miles away (I think it was about three and a half), and I had nobody to help me. Everybody was strictly for self. Bless God! he had not forsaken me, as I soon found out, when he gave me the strength to shoulder that stupendous burden. Oh, bless God! Every few steps I rested. I would rest and pray, go a little farther, and then rest and pray again. I kept this up until completely exhausted; then I sat on a broken-down step, minus the house, imploring the kind heavenly Father to send me help. Did ever he fail his own in the hour of need? Never, no never.

Coming over the hill several blocks distant, carefully guiding his horse through the debris, was a man in a wagon or buggy. Like a drowning person grasping at a straw, I frantically called and waved my hands. It took me some time to attract attention, but finally he turned in my direction. Hallelujah! As he neared me, I noticed the words, "Spring Valley Water Works," on the sideboard of his wagon. "Madam, can I assist you?" he inquired. Most certainly he could. And I humbly, tearfully, and wearily described the situation. To lift that heavy basket into the vehicle required our united effort. Never did I more appreciate help. The sun was at its zenith when I started; it was now setting. God bless that dear young man, whose name I have forgotten! I hope that he is living and that this book may fall into his hands, so that he may better than ever realize that our blessed Lord never forsakes those who truly love and trust him.

Reader, I leave you to imagine the joyous reunion of mother and son.

Perfect peace and good will was then temporarily reigning in that stricken city. Would to God it had continued! but alas! it was but for a few days. Once more the adversary of the souls of men reigns in its midst; the liquor devil reigns supreme; whilst the few faithful ones are still daily crying to the throne of grace, "How long, O Lord, how long?"

Before all this occurred and whilst I was in San Francisco one day seeking aid for Beth-Adriel, I called at the house of a Christian friend of mine. Presently, in the course of conversation, she informed me that her niece, who was an employee in one of the large department stores of San Francisco was at home sick with severe headache, and asked if I would care to see her. I gladly acquiesced. Then my friend took me into the next room, where lay the young lady with her head swathed in a wet towel and evidently suffering keenly. I expressed sympathy and at once offered to pray for her, to which she replied:

"I'll be so glad, though I fear I haven't much faith in its efficacy. Yes, pray for me, for I must get down to the store to report for duty at one o'clock. I *must*. Sick or not sick, I *must*."

After prayer I inquired, "Laura, dear, why must you be compelled to be on duty? Under existing circumstances they will surely make every allowance."

Instead of making immediate answer, she asked for her business dress and presently drew from its pocket a latch-key.

"Do you see this?" she inquired.

"Yes," I replied.

"Yes, but you do not know what it means. Let me tell you. This key is to be used to unlock the door of the down-town private apartments of one of our floor-walkers. I've had my place only a few weeks. Auntie is having a struggle to keep her lodging-house filled so as to meet her payments on the furniture, rent, etc. I am only getting small wages, not sufficient to support me, as yet; but if I can manage to qualify in a large reputable store like —- —-, I shall have no trouble in commanding a better salary before long—having become so well acquainted with my position as to then be a necessity."

"But what has all that to do with your possession of this key?" I interrogated.

"Wait, I am coming to that," she replied "About a week ago he (the floor-walker) said, among other things: 'I observe that you are quite ambitious. I intend, if you will allow me, to still further your interests. In order that I may do this, I must have your promise to respect the confidence I am about to repose in you.' Innocently I promised. 'First of all,' he went on to say, 'you have doubtless heard I am a married man and a father.' I had. He has a very delicate wife and two dear little girls. He then produced the key, *stating why he wanted my friendship.*"

"Why did you not immediately expose him to the firm?" I indignantly inquired.

"Mrs. Roberts," said Laura, "you don't know what you are talking about. My word would not be taken against his. I do not yet know what door this key unlocks. I am not to know until I consent to use it whenever he may request a private interview. Every chance he gets, he wants to know when I mean to yield. I am, for the sake of business experience, resorting to all sorts of strategy; then, when I qualify, I can afford to snap my fingers in the face of this profligate. *You've no idea how much the honor of business young ladies is menaced, Mrs. Roberts. I'm not by any means the only one. The trouble is, very few have the backbone to resist these propositions, which invariably come in one form or another to the working girls attractive of face or form, or of both.* They are, with scarcely an exception, poor; from infancy they have been well dressed, too well in fact; very few are qualified in domestic art, and those who are would almost rather do anything than be subjected to such humiliations as some people in social standing inflict upon their maids—maids who ofttimes both by birth and breeding are their equals if not superiors.

"I want to help Auntie. She is so good to me in giving me a home. If I can only keep up, I shall soon be able to repay her."

"I'm glad to tell you my head is much better, so that I shall be able to report for duty. I'll be all right so long as I trust in God and have people like you and Auntie pray for me."

I wanted to report this case to the proprietors of that store; but Laura was so distressed for fear of notoriety, ultimate results, also the deprivation of a living for that libertine's delicate wife and children, that I reluctantly desisted. This I know: In answer to many prayers, both her friends' and her own, she won out; but she never gave up that key, and to this day she does not know what door it unlocked or whether some other poor, silly girl received and made use of its duplicate.

In visiting among the outcasts, I have learned from the lips of many that the primary cause of their downfall was the inadequacy of their wages as saleswomen, stenographers, etc., for their direct necessities; temptations became too great; the ultimate results were, alas! inevitable.

CHAPTER XXXVII
THE HOME REPAIRED—MRS. S—'S EXPERIENCE

Thinking to appeal for the required means to repair our home, I, after prayerful consideration, journeyed to Portland, Oregon, for our State was now taxed to its utmost for finances. My sojourn was brief; for, besides being seized with sudden illness, I learned that a large sum of money (thirty-five thousand dollars, I think) intended for the erection of a Florence Crittenton home in their midst had now been generously donated and sent to the general fund in San Francisco, to be applied to just such charitable needs as I represented. In consequence, I decided that, as soon as I was able to travel, I should go back to San Francisco. Through the interposition of the Y.W.C.A., I was furnished with free transportation. Upon my return I learned that all available funds for that purpose had already been bespoken; but God, ever mindful of his own, had laid it upon the hearts of some people of means, in the interior, to pay all expenses for repairs, so that before many months Beth-Adriel was once more in good order. In its interest, many, many miles were traveled and thousands of people addressed, personally, also collectively.

Rarely did any service close but that one person or more had an unusual case of some unfortunate one, demanding immediate and special interest; for instance: Mrs. B——-, who personally knew me, approached me one day in a greatly agitated state of mind and confidentially imparted some dreadful knowledge concerning her son, aged fourteen, and a girl schoolmate of his, but a few months younger. Producing some notes, she permitted their perusal. They were from the girl to the boy, and were couched in the most licentious, unguarded language imaginable. I was unutterably shocked. "Mother Roberts," said Mrs. B——-, "I will deal with my son, but what about the girl who has written these and, as you read, has met H——- clandestinely? I can not go to her; will you?" The girl's mother was a lady of means and fashion, a member of one of the exclusive card-clubs of that town, and an inveterate player. Pearl was an only child. I admit I felt timid about approaching the mother, but—It had to be done and done quickly.

In glancing over the local paper, I had observed that her progressive whist-club was to be entertained at Mrs. ——'s lovely residence that afternoon. It was now 11 A.M. I must telephone, for I knew that I should not be received except by previous appointment. Soon I heard her voice:

"What is it, please; what do you wish?"

"A private interview immediately, of the utmost importance."

"Impossible. Every moment is engaged until I go out this afternoon."

"Can not help it. You *must* grant it. It concerns a member of your immediate family. It is of *vital import.*"

"Very well; you may come right away, but be brief. I will grant you only a few minutes."

"Thank you," and both receivers were hung up.

In response to my ring the maid ushered me into a lovely reception-room, where Mrs. S——-- soon appeared in a high state of nervous excitement.

"You have greatly upset me, Mrs. Roberts," she said. "Kindly be brief. To your point at once. I have much to do, also must dress before luncheon, for our card-party at Mrs. ——'s this afternoon."

"Mrs. S——-, you no doubt will be able to identify Pearl's handwriting." I replied.

"Most assuredly," she rejoined. "What of it?"

"Simply this: In my possession are three notes. They were written by your daughter to a boy companion in school. The boy's mother lent them to me. It is my painful duty to show them to you. First of all, permit me to assure you that this matter is perfectly safe with me," I said.

"Come into the next room where we can be undisturbed and unobserved," she requested. Then she rang the bell and said to the maid:

"I shall not be at home to any one who either 'phones or calls."

(Here let me say that having once been associated with Mrs. S—— socially, I was not a stranger.)

"Mrs. S——, doesn't Pearl sometimes ask permission to go home with a favorite girl companion, also at times remain with her over night, or else she with your daughter?" I asked after we had retired to the other room.

"Certainly," she answered, "and I may add, I am quite satisfied to have her do so, *for they can both be implicitly trusted.*"

"Mrs. S— —, please read these letters. I beg of you, prepare yourself for an awful shock...."

Presently the great beads of perspiration broke out on her forehead and dripped unheeded into her lap. After reading those notes she made mincemeat of them, and then lay back in her chair white and speechless. The silence was painful beyond description. Finally I broke the silence by saying:

"Mrs. S— —, permit me to assist you to your room, then 'phone Mrs. — — of your sudden illness, and also send for your daughter to come home immediately."

She gladly acquiesced. Before my departure she faintly acknowledged her realization of neglect of duty and confidence toward the precious soul entrusted to her keeping, and promised to deal gently with the erring child. Furthermore, she said that *she had played her last game of cards.*

Pearl and her mother became inseparable companions. To this day the daughter has no idea who informed on her, but this occurrence taught a never-to-be-forgotten lesson to more than one I hope and pray that the mothers who read this may profit by the story.

One with whom I am well acquainted has an only son. She also was a great lover of cards. When the boy was quite small, this mother in order to prevent his disturbing her and her friends in their social game, provided him with a tiny deck of cards. She often smiled approval at his and his little companion's attempts to imitate their elders. Time went on. He grew to manhood. Many an anxious evening she now spent alone; for seldom did he spend one with her, and he always had a plausible excuse in the morning.

He was employed by one of the leading firms of the city and stood an excellent chance of future promotion. One day, however, he came home, informed her of his discharge, refused to give the reason, but begged her to go to his employers and plead for his reinstatement. The grief-stricken mother was soon ushered into the manager's private office and there very kindly treated; but her pleadings were all in vain. Her son, she learned, had been discharged for card-playing and frequenting the pool room. He had been warned twice, but he had failed to take heed. The firm would make no exceptions.

On her return he eagerly interrogated her as to the results of the interview.

"When?" she asked, "when did you ever learn to play cards and pool?"

"Why, Mother, don't you remember?" he answered. *"You taught me yourself when I was a little shaver."*

"No, dear, not a real game," she sobbed.

"No matter if you didn't," he rejoined. "It didn't take me long to become fascinated and learn how from older boys and girls. Then, when it comes to playing, I hate to remind you, Mother, but I can not remember the time when you didn't play. I've seen you, time and again, work harder to earn a dinky vase or prize than at anything else under the sun. You can buy them anywhere for fifty cents or thereabouts, and without such hard work as I've seen you put in for a whole evening. *You can blame yourself, and you ought to, more than you blame me."*

Then he flung himself out of the room and went up-stairs to bed.

The next evening he returned from an unsuccessful day's tramp. His chances for further employment in that city were anything but encouraging. That evening as they sat by the fireside, Will's mother said:

"I've been thinking very, very seriously during your absence today, my dear. I've made a resolution, but with this proviso: if I never touch another card, will you promise me never to play again?"

"Mother, I should like to, but I'm afraid to make such a promise," he replied. "You don't know what a hold it has on me. But I will try, I surely will."

Will's mother worked hard to substitute other pastimes and to make his home life as interesting as she knew how. She gathered musical friends about her, encouraged him to cultivate his voice, and worked herself almost to a shadow in order to wean him from the hurtful habit for which she knew she was directly responsible. She succeeded, bless God! she succeeded. Later he married a very sweet young lady, and God blessed their union with three children. It is safe to say that, because of his experience, card-playing will never be tolerated in that happy little family, and my earnest prayer as I relate this is that my reader, if a card-player, may consider this: "If meat [card-playing] make my brother to offend, I will eat no flesh [no more play cards] while the world standeth, lest I make my brother to offend." I Cor. 8:13.

CHAPTER XXXVIII
THE ANNUAL BOARD MEETING-RESULTS

I have mentioned the fact that the nature of the work of Beth-Adriel had so changed that many applicants were, for certain reasons, debarred from the home. One day whilst I was calling upon one of the board members my soul was greatly grieved; for a girl who came and appealed for admission was refused—kindly but firmly refused, on the grounds that her physical condition would be detrimental to the welfare of the many mothers and babes with whom Beth-Adriel was now well filled; *and yet it had never been incorporated for a maternity home.*

What was I to do? God knew how hard I had Worked. The property was now more than half paid for. What was I to do?

As the holidays, which always caused a temporary cessation in fund-raising, were approaching, I busied myself in making little gifts for each member of the family. Whilst so doing I prayed unceasingly to know the mind of God's Spirit and to be definitely led of him.

Can I ever forget that first prayer-meeting of the new year, 1907? It being a wet night, there was nobody present besides the members of the family, the matron, and her husband, except Brother Norton, his son, and I. We had had the usual songs, prayers, and Scripture-reading, and we were now testifying. I had testified, as also had most of the family, when one of the young mothers suddenly said:

"Mrs. Roberts, I've something to ask you. When you persuaded me to come to this place, didn't you tell me I need give only my first name?"

"I did, Amelia," I answered.

"Didn't you say that no questions that might embarrass me would be asked?"

"I certainly did."

"Didn't you say no girl had to sign any papers here, and that if she had no money, the home was free to her?"

"Most assuredly."

"Then—you—lied."

Reader, that poor girl dealt me a blow that I can not say I have yet fully recovered from. Then I knew that modern Tobiah and Sanballat and Geshem (Neh. 2:9) had interfered and intercepted the building of God's work. I felt brokenhearted and could not be comforted. That night I spent in tears, nor could I pray as I desired to pray. The next evening as I was kneeling by my bedside, worn out with sorrow, I chanced to look up, and I found my gaze riveted on a little wall-motto containing these precious words: "*Rest in the Lord.*"

(It hangs here on my wall as I now write. It is a priceless possession.) Instantly I said, "I thank thee, O my Lord, I thank thee, for reassurance." Somewhat comforted, I then wrote the following verses:

> I was kneeling in prayer by my bedside,
>   Beseeching a comforting word,
> When I opened my eyes on this motto,
>   Simply telling me, "Rest in the Lord."

> It hangs where I ofttimes can see it,
>   This message direct from our God.
> As I ponder, my load seems to lighten,
>   I'm resolving to rest in my Lord.

> For, oh! I was troubled and weary,
>   And dark seemed the road that I trod;
> Of this I was telling my Savior,
>   When he showed me, "Rest thou in the Lord"

> I wonder why I should forget this
>   And weight myself down with a load;
> Why don't I depend more on Jesus,
>   Who loves me, and rest in my Lord?

> I'm persuaded this message from heaven,
>   Direct from his throne, will afford
> Perfect peace under trying conditions
>   To all who will "rest in the Lord."

> For, oh! if his yoke is upon us,
>   Our strength is renewed and restored;
> And the burdens, so heavy, are lightened
>   If we only will "rest in the Lord."

> I thank thee, dear heavenly Father,
>   When I prayed for thy comforting word,
> For directing my eyes to that motto
>   'Tis enough. I will rest in my Lord

Beth-Adriel cottage, 9:30 P.M., January 4, 1907.

It was enough. I was comforted, and I was determined, like Paul of old, that 'none of these things should move me.'

The annual meeting of the board for the election of officers for the ensuing year was about to take place. Before the board convened, I asked God for a test, promising him to abide by it even though he required me to give up this hard-earned home if necessary; then I quietly "rested in my Lord."

The day arrived. The rain poured in torrents all morning. I besought the Lord for a clear afternoon and also for the presence of every member. He answered my prayer. When it came to the reelection of officers, my election was *not unanimous.* As the test I had besought was that if the Master intended I should continue with them, he should cause my reelection to be unanimous, I read my resignation. Thus ended the annual board meeting of 1907. (My resignation was never legally accepted.)

With scarcely an exception, "they all forsook me and fled" (Mark 14:50). I walked out of Beth-Adriel unattended—one of the loneliest beings on earth, yet in the "secret of His presence." This created considerable newspaper notoriety; but though my resignation had cost me all, my conscience was "void of offense toward God" (Acts 24:16).

Soon I busied myself looking for other quarters. Even they were providential; for a friend met me in the post-office and proffered me her beautiful studio, then in disuse, for a merely nominal rent. There I rested and wrote for three months, intending that the proceeds of the book entitled "The Autobiography of an Autoharp" should start another home. But God willed otherwise, as you will presently learn.

Was the rescue work that I so dearly loved, at a standstill? Oh, no indeed. Not for one day was I idle; neither was Beth-Adriel. The name "Beth-Adriel" was soon dropped, and the place became one of the chain of Florence Crittenton homes. I have often sent there poor unfortunates that needed a refuge of that nature.

It was marvelous, the strength and the courage that the blessed Lord gave me during those trying days, even to the turning of my other cheek (Matt. 5:39).

Soon I received unanimous reendorsement and much encouragement from the pastors' union and other sources; but I was advised to try for a training-school and home for orphans at the limit age (fourteen) and also for juvenile court dependents and delinquents. As is my custom, I inquired of the Lord. I received so strong an impression regarding "an ounce of prevention," etc, that I said, "Yea, Lord, it is worth one hundred thousand pounds of cure." In a short time beautiful and practical plans were drawn up and presented to me by one of San Jose's best architects, Wesley W. Hastings. Before this took place, however, several very striking incidents occurred, in a few of which, I feel sure, you will be interested. One was a case of casting bread upon the waters and finding of it after many days (Eccl. 11:1).

Since my coming to San Jose it had been my habit to attend frequently the mission then situated on Fountain Alley. One night a poor, forlorn drunken man came to the altar and "got salvation." After rising from his knees, he said, "Lady, will you trust me with a quarter? I want to get a bath and bed and breakfast with it."

"You can not get all three for a quarter," I replied.

"Oh yes, I can," he said. "Down at the Salvation Army lodging-house for men."

One of the workers whispered, "Don't do it He'll only spend it for liquor."

He evidently surmised what the worker told me, for he quickly said:

"Don't be afraid to trust me. I promise you you shall never regret it."

I gave him what he had requested, and, in consequence, received rebukes from several of the other workers.

The next night he came in looking fairly neat, but surely clean. At the close of the meeting he returned the money, remarking that he had earned fifty cents that day mowing lawns and chopping wood. He continued to frequent the mission, a changed man. After moving to the studio I lost sight of him almost entirely, but often wondered what had become of him.

There came a time toward the close of my sojourn in San Jose when I was financially down to bedrock. Money and provisions were all gone. My rent, to be sure, was paid up to the first of the month (three weeks hence), but my cupboard was bare. A friend partook with me of my last meal. Little did she realize it, or she would never have stayed at my invitation. *I told only my heavenly Father.* After supper I went home with her, about three blocks distant. It was a beautiful moonlight night, and as I came up the garden walk on my return, I noticed a good-sized box resting on my steps, but simply thought the children must have been playing there and had failed to take it away after they had finished. I attempted to thrust it to one side, but discovered that it was too heavy. Looking more closely, I could read my name on a card. With considerable effort I lifted it into the room, pried off a portion of the cover, and was soon reading a note which said:

Dear Friend:

Please accept a slight token of appreciation from one who is

Your true friend.

From whom did this come? The crude handwriting was not at all familiar. I wondered, but in vain. Then I lifted up the paper cover. The box was filled with groceries. Not even butter and bread had been forgotten; also there were some fruit and vegetables. I fell on my knees, the tears falling fast as I humbly thanked God and prayed him to bless the donor. I had told no one. Who could have sent it? Inquiry the next day of several groceries failed to throw any light on the matter. I had to give it up, but oh, how I appreciated and enjoyed the contents of that box, which lasted me until my time at the studio expired.

I stored my few effects with a friendly furniture man. Whilst walking down Santa Clara Street near Market, I came face to face with Brother Louis, the converted drunkard. He certainly was looking his best. As he greeted me, he said:

"Mother Roberts, I was on my way to call on you."

"I've moved this very day, Brother," I replied, "but I'm so glad I met you. Where have you been?"

He had been working out of town. To honor God and also to help strengthen his faith, I related His care for me through all the trying times. I spoke about my being out of provisions and then finding them on my doorsteps, adding:

"To this day I haven't found out who sent them."

The expression that came over his countenance instantly betrayed him.

"Brother Louis," I said, "you sent that box."

"No, Mother Roberts, I didn't," he replied; "I brought it, and I'll tell you why. I read in the paper that when you quit Beth-Adriel you only had sixty dollars of your own. I calculated that couldn't last very long. I knew you wouldn't take money, and I wanted to express my gratitude in some way; so I decided groceries would not come amiss to one who was doing light housekeeping. I didn't knock on your door, because I thought you were in and what a surprise it would be when you opened it in the morning. I hope you aren't offended at what I did"

"Brother Louis, don't you realize that God used you to answer my prayer?" I rejoined. "He knew my needs, and laid it on your heart to supply them."

I do not know where he now is, but I earnestly pray that God may bless and prosper this kind-hearted man and finally receive him into glory.

Still farther down the street, near Second, I suddenly thought I heard some one calling my name. Again it was called, and I turned to find a Mr. Parkhurst, an old gentleman, endeavoring to overtake me. He wished to let me know that his wife, one of my valued friends, was very ill, and to inquire if I knew of any one who could come to their home and care for her a few days, at least until she was somewhat recovered. Instantly I felt that God was providing a temporary shelter for me; therefore I unhesitatingly replied:

"I myself will go, Mr. Parkhurst."

"What you! But are you not too busy?" he asked.

"Not just at present," I answered. "Besides, I gave up my studio this very day and therefore am quite free to go."

Their appreciation was such that a few days later I was invited to make this lovely home mine, or at least headquarters, which very kind offer was, in the name of our wonderful Provider, gratefully accepted.

CHAPTER XXXIX
A TRIP EAST—I ESCAPE FROM
A CONFIDENCE WOMAN

After I had enjoyed the freedom of the Parkhurst home for a few months I learned through friends that a young lady whom I had befriended at the time of the earthquake and who had become temporarily deranged was about to be sent to the East. The supervisors inquired whether it would suit my convenience to take the trip, and said if so they would defray expenses from and to California in order to have her safely chaperoned. I gladly consented; for, praise God! this would give me opportunity to pay a brief visit to my son and his bride, now making their home in Allegheny, Pa.

Following her safe arrival, I was on the way to Cincinnati in less than twenty-four hours. Thence I was to take train early the next morning. Having several hours to dispose of after securing a room in a hotel close to the station, I decided to see as many points of interest as possible in this fine city. Accordingly I was thus delightfully occupied until about four o'clock, when I heard some one speak of the Zoo. Upon inquiry I learned of the wonderful gardens so called. Soon, following directions, I boarded a car at Fountain Square, which conveyed me up a very steep incline. Returning in the neighborhood of six o'clock, I followed the example of several persons, who on the incline stepped out of the car on to the platform in order to enjoy the magnificent view.

A white-haired, elderly lady who had sat opposite to me on the return trip, now pleasantly remarked:

"Cincinnati is well worth a visit, is it not?"

Upon my replying in the affirmative, she rejoined:

"Doubtless you are a stranger. May I inquire from whence you come?"

"From California," I answered.

She clasped her hands together and exclaimed ecstatically:

"Dear, dear California! How happy I am to meet some one from there! Some of my most delightful, very happiest days were spent there."

We were now once more in the car and at the foot of the incline.

Presently she continued, "Are you going to remain for some time here? If so, I shall be delighted to contribute to your pleasure."

I then informed her of my prospective visit to my son and his wife.

Her next question was, "Pardon me, but have you any dinner engagement? If not, dine with me at — —'s restaurant, unless you have choice in the matter, in which case I gladly defer in your favor."

She had handed me her card, and of course common courtesy required that I reciprocate.

At the table I quietly (though not by request) returned thanks, and then followed this up with the message that the Master had, in answer to silent prayer, laid on my heart.

Her patronizing smile was rather disconcerting as she responded:

'My dear, I am much older and have had much more real experience than you. I've come in touch with every phase of humanity, and have at last reached the place where I have decided to get all I can out of life—all the fun, all the pleasure possible. *I once thought and felt as you do.* You'll get over it when you have had a few hard knocks to contend with. Take my advice. Enjoy yourself every day and hour, and as much as you can."

"I do," was my reply. "I would not exchange the experience of the past decade for all the former years of worldly dissipation and pleasure put together. They have all been unsatisfactory. This is quite the opposite, and, better still, it is the enjoyment of indescribable peace and delight. You are not going to be much longer in this world. Mrs. R— —, I beg of you to seek the Lord whilst he may still be found. It is not too late, but soon, yes, very soon it may be. Then where will you spend eternity?"

Her lips curled with a sinister, contemptuous sneer. Nevertheless she managed to smile as she resorted to repartee.

"You must come with me this evening," she said. "I intend to take possession of you for an hour or two, and give you a good time."

"You will please excuse me from anything of the kind," was my quick reply. "I have long ceased to enjoy worldly amusements."

Just then the waitress came with the cheque.

"One or two?" she inquired.

"Two," promptly replied Mrs. R— —

I politely wished her good evening as we stood at the desk, and was quickly walking away when she called after me.

"Wait a minute," she said, and took a firm hold of my arm and sleeve, so that it was impossible to free myself without attracting attention. We were now on the street. As she walked beside me, she said:

"You may not think so, but I intend to do you a favor. People in your line of work are never blest with overmuch of this world's goods, especially money. I'm going to take you with me across the bridge [into Kentucky] to the house of one of my friends and win a stake for you. You needn't touch a card unless you want to. Now don't be afraid to trust me, because — —"

Before she had hardly finished speaking, I suddenly tore away from her grasp, ran down the block to the corner, and boarded a passing car, not caring where it took me, so anxious was I to get away from this female gambler, this confidence woman.

Why did I not have her arrested? First, because I had already purchased my ticket for my journey to Pittsburg, and secondly, because her private conversation with me would not have warranted me in so doing. Moreover, I knew that the all-seeing eye of God was taking cognizance of her actions as well as of mine. He protected me, and you may rest assured that she and her kind will not go unpunished.

Why have I told you this? In order to show that it is not only the young girls and youth who are in danger, but also the more mature, even the rescue missionary. It therefore behooves us to be constantly in an attitude of watchfulness and prayer, for Satan goes about in all manner of garbs seeking whom he may devour. Nothing could better please him than to overpower or side-track one of the children of God, more particularly a missionary.

I took a long round-trip ride on that car, my heart overflowing with gratitude to the heavenly Father for having made the way of escape (1 Cor. 10:13). It was after nine o'clock before I reached my hotel. I wondered, as I retired, who would be the next to be victimized by that runner for a private gambling-house. I fell asleep with earnest prayer for the deliverance of whosoever it might chance to be, and for God to deal speedily with all such agents of the evil one.

CHAPTER XL
MY HOMEWARD JOURNEY—LAND FOR
THE TRAINING SCHOOL AND HOME

After a delightful five days' visit with my son and his bride I was soon back in California, both ready and eager to transact business for the Master's kingdom.

Anybody who has traveled on a tourist car can readily understand that, even though one may not be prying or curious, one is apt to learn more or less of its other occupants, particularly those in the adjoining sections; and be the porter ever so watchful, he can not cope with every suspicious situation.

Being a rescue missionary, I particularly yet secretly kept a watchful eye over a girl just graduated with honors from a school in the old country and now about to join some relatives at a point near San Francisco; for she was fast succumbing to the influence of a woman with whom some of the opposite sex seemed very familiar, considering the fact that the latter was as much a stranger to them (when first we started out) as she was to me. Besides, the pretty young graduate evidently was a very guileless, convent-raised girl. Matters assumed such a condition at the close of the third day of our journey that I felt it incumbent upon me to invite the latter into my section for the sake of some friendly advice. She appeared to take it all in good part and promised to act upon it. Had she done so, I should not now be relating that before the end of the next twenty-four hours I was subjected to most unkind, uncalled-for criticism from nearly all the occupants of that car, mostly young people. The schoolgirl was foolish enough to betray every word of our conversation to the older woman, whose actions that same night were such that the porter had to interfere. Notwithstanding the unkind treatment accorded me, I still continued privately to chaperon the girl until she reached her destination where she was, thank God, welcomed at the depot by her relatives.

That porter told me that he had constantly to be on the lookout for questionable characters of both sexes, who made it their business to travel back and forth continuously in search of victims to rob or aid them in plying their nefarious trades, but that some acted so sanctimoniously, as in this case, that they were rather hard to detect. I have no doubt that this adventuress obtained the young girl's address, so that the acquaintance could, a little later on, be renewed in order that some of this woman's accomplices, if not herself, could secure this another victim for the white slave traffic.

Moral: Parents and guardians, secure reliable chaperons for your young people to travel with, or else keep them at home pending such times as they can be accompanied by you or trusted friends.

A letter from a wealthy pioneer with whom I had had several interviews respecting land for a training school and home now sent me word that he had decided to donate six acres for that purpose, provided I should secure pledges to the amount of thirty thousand dollars for building purposes. The undertaking looked stupendous; nevertheless, what was to hinder if this were the plan of God?

At his invitation, I shortly went to inspect the land, then in grain. The tract was hardly as much as was requisite for horticultural purposes and a large home, but the situation was charming; so, without consulting any one as to the nature of the soil, I promised to do my utmost to earn a quit title to the land. I worked indefatigably for several months before being able to secure a promissory deed, but finally, after much effort and persuasion, I succeeded in obtaining the latter. Then I worked harder than ever. Two years were spent in this wise. Everything pointed to ultimate success. A board of representative business men was secured in order to meet legal requirements. By faith I now saw the beautiful, practical home for delinquent and dependent children looming up in the very near future.

One day whilst on my way southward I was telling an acquaintance of my hopes and also showing her the plans. Presently a gentleman sitting immediately back of us thus addressed me:

"Pardon me, madam, but I can not refrain from hearing part of your conversation, also seeing your plans." (With that he handed me his card.) "For over twenty-two years I was a resident of the place where you propose to build that home," he continued, "and I know every foot of its soil. Would it be asking too much of you to inquire just where those six acres are located?"

Upon his receiving the desired information, he said:

"I am very sorry to hear it. I regret to have to inform you that it is absolutely useless for horticultural purposes. It is worked out, having been in grain for at least forty years; besides, it is gravelly soil with clay bottom. I do not ask you to take my word for this. Inquire of — — — —- or any of the reputable business men. It is too bad that you should have had so much work for nothing."

Reader, endeavor if you can, to put yourself in my place at this moment. Through undescribable toil I had procured nearly ten thousand dollars in pledges, though, thank God, I had collected no money. So this distressing information almost stunned me. Thanking the gentleman, I promised, at his earnest solicitation, to satisfy myself beyond a doubt.

What he said was all too true. For a few days the effects of the confirmation of this stranger's statements almost prostrated me. I humbly thank God, however, that this experience was the means of His getting me into a place where He could have a chance to talk to me. He told me that zeal for His house had well-nigh eaten me up and that what was lacking was a need of more watchfulness and prayer on my part. Also, he assured me that notwithstanding another crushing disappointment, the home would be built, but not in the manner anticipated; that the silver and gold, "the cattle on a thousand hills," everything, everywhere was His. The wound eventually began to heal.

During this trying time, whilst I was one day conferring with Lieutenant-Governor Porter, a lady came into his office, to whom he immediately introduced me. Acknowledging the introduction with a very warm handshake and a sweet smile, Mrs. Tallman Chittenden, of Chittenden, Santa Cruz County, said: "Mrs. Roberts, for a long time I have heard or read of you. I so much desire to know you. Can you not return to my home with me today? My husband will be as pleased as I to have you for our guest." (They owned one of the most beautiful, picturesque estates in Santa Cruz County. The Southern Pacific passes through their magnificently cultivated grounds) Expressing my regrets, owing to having an urgent call from the probation officer of the juvenile court of Santa Cruz City, I promised to visit them on the return trip—a promise that I carried out on the following evening. Soon I was made to realize that God was adding two more to the list of true and tried friends; for after learning the nature of my recent disappointment and that I did not now have any settled abiding-place, Mr. and Mrs. Parkhurst having removed to Washington, they cordially invited me to consider their lovely home mine also indefinitely.

This kindness overwhelmed me with gratitude. Rest at last, real rest for the body as well as for the soul; but it was not for long. The calls accumulated thick and fast, and again I had to be up and doing. But even to this day (unless the place, which is for sale, has passed into other hands) I am at liberty any hour of the day or night to avail myself of the freedom and the home comforts of lovely Chittenden, where a most cordial greeting has ever been mine from the generous hostess and her friendly husband. Thus God is ever providing his chosen ones with what he has promised; for has not he said in Psa. 84:11, "The Lord is a sun and shield; the Lord will give grace and glory: no good thing will be withhold from them that walk uprightly"? He always knows best. He never closes one door but that he opens a better one. It pays to stand still, to be true to him.

CHAPTER XLI
CALL ON THE GOVERNOR
AND THEN GO SOUTH

Acting upon the suggestion of several sympathetic, interested friends, who realized, with me, the great necessity for "the ounce of prevention home and school" for many of the rising generation, I took a special trip to Sacramento in order to submit specifications and plans to Governor Gillett, then in office.

This was not our first meeting; therefore I was by no means a stranger to the Governor, who very kindly and cordially received me. Almost his first words were, "Time being at a premium with me, tell me what I can do for you." In as few words as possible the story of effort and apparent though not total failure was being poured into his attentive ears. Presently, to my great joy, he replied:

"Mrs. Roberts, this has been a pet project of mine for many, many years. All I have lacked was the time, means, and assistants to carry it into execution. Let me tell you something for your encouragement: right now I am considering certain offers of land for just such a purpose. No paltry six acres for it either, but three hundred or more. I hope soon to see this vitally important and absolutely necessary plan receive the approbation of our next legislative session, and an appropriation made for the purchase of a large tract of land, together with necessary and suitable buildings. I know you have been working very hard. Do not nurse disappointment any longer; instead join me feeling assured of the future welfare and maintenance of the delinquent and dependent children of our State."

Much more did he encourage me, but the above was the sum and substance. Lighter hearted than I had felt for many days, I now took more interest than ever in the rescue work. In response to a call I hurried to southern California, where, with others, I engaged in the Master's service in seeking and warning the lost, working from San Diego on up the coast.

Perhaps it would be advisable at this time to quote from the report made in the San Diego Sun of July 14, 1908.

LOW DANCE-HALLS, CURSE OF THE CITY

Mrs. Florence Roberts, known throughout the State as "Mother Roberts," who has been in this city for two weeks in the interests of fallen humanity has visited the red light district of this city. One conclusion that she draws is this: "The dance-hall is an abomination that must go. It is more degrading than any other form of dissipation. The future of the State is being ruined. The young—men are being degraded past redemption; the young women, especially working girls, are in danger."

Discussing her observations with a "Sun" reporter, Mrs. Roberts said: "I visited at least a dozen of the saloon dance-halls. The private houses would not admit me, not knowing who I was; but the saloons are of course public.

"As far as I can see, the traffic is not organized as it is in most places. Each saloon seems an individual institution.

"We went into place after place, dirty and squalid, most of them, and all very unattractive. The 'glittering place of vice' was not to be found; merely the girls, the low dance-music, and the catering to every bestial passion.

MEN ASHAMED

"Many of the men were young. Almost all were well dressed and respectable looking, and, thank God, many of them were ashamed when we came in, and pulled their hats down over their eyes. We saw, not only the common sailors, but the officers, the men who command the great ships, who plan and direct the battles of the world, parading their gold braid in these dens of vice, in the company of the lowest.

"The indecent postures, the short-skirted, low-necked dresses, the sensual dancing, and the frequent trips to the places behind the saloons, were nauseating and repulsive. But the heart-sorrow, the sometimes unconscious longing for something higher and better, showing through the paint and powder, the hard, sinister lines, the brazen, defiant eyes, touched my heart with the awful sorrow of it all, and I would give all I possess to be able to touch them and to help them.

"I said to one poor girl, 'Do you enjoy this life?'

"'Not on your life, lady,' she replied. 'We drift into it, and we can't see the way out.'

"Many are totally resigned to the life. One girl said to me indifferently, 'I don't expect ever to live any other life. I'm used to it, and it's good enough now.'

FORCED TO LEAVE

"In one place the barkeeper allowed me to sing to the girls, but just in the middle of my song, the proprietor came in and said something in a gruff voice to the barkeeper. The latter came over to me and apologetically said, 'Say, lady, the boss is giving me h— — for allowing this. I guess you'll have to quit.'

"Two of the girls were deeply touched by what I said to them. I spoke of the wrong influence of some kind of home life.

"'You're right, lady. That's so. It was that way with me. I was started wrong, and everybody helped to grease the hill I was sliding down, and I soon reached the bottom.'

"The girls are decoyed by some man friend, who has so compromised the girl that she feels she is being shunned, to the house of a 'kind woman who will protect her.' She is ruined. She begins smoking and drinking and soon unless she takes great care of herself, she is sent from a first-class house to a second class, then a third class, then lower and lower, until she ends in some vile dance-hall, compared to which the orthodox hell is a paradise. Five years altogether Is the average life in this business.

NO-SCREEN LAW

"One thing I found here that I have found nowhere else, and that is the rigid enforcement of the no-screen law. Everything was open. I shall speak of it in other places. And then the law forbidding the sale of spirituous liquors means so much to the girls, the poor, poor girls, who are so bitter against the whole world, and who are suspicious of every woman.

"A barkeeper asked me, lady, what are you doing in a place like this?'

"'I am here to do some good if I can. I am a mother.'

"'Well,' he replied, 'this is no place for decent people.'

"Just then a rough-looking customer spoke up, 'Don't you leave because he wants you to. Do all the good you can'

"I am afraid some of the girls thought I was there out of mere vulgar curiosity. No, indeed. I have seen the worst places in the State, I have visited the girls, talked with them, eaten with them, and praise God, have helped some of them to do better."

CHRISTIANITY

Mrs. Roberts has no use for so-called Christianity that forgets the virtue named charity. She tells a story of a young girl who was won from the tenderloin by a Salvation Army lassie.... [Here follows the story of Dollie, found between these pages.]

WORST RESORTS

"As I said before," continued Mrs. Roberts, "we visited all the houses, but were not admitted to all. They are very superstitious, and to admit visitors on Monday would 'hoodoo' the business for the rest of the week. None of the houses were attractive. We learned the name of only one, which, the girls tell me, is the worst in the whole district.

"There is one place, though, that I must mention. It is most attractive with lights, mirrors, and music. But I assure you it is the first step of its kind downward. [A first-class saloon.]

"This place has a most appropriate electric sign, a winding, twisting snake. 'There is one thing more I must tell you,' I said to a young, attractive-looking boy, 'What attracts you here?'

"'For the life of me I can't tell you, except that there's no other place where we fellows can enjoy ourselves.'

"What an opportunity for an immense, well-equipped reading-room, where the boys can have games, books, and all sorts of harmless amusements."

Mrs. Roberts will be here for some little time, and she expects to speak several times before she leaves. She spoke at the Central Christian church yesterday to a large audience.

Among other things at this meeting I mentioned this incident:

In one of the Northern towns, the chief of police, knowing I was in the town, sent for me to confer with him on a case of "strictest privacy." Wondering what was the matter, I hastened, and soon was hearing this:

"In one of the houses on — — Street, I have just learned from one of my men, who was told by a near-by saloon-keeper, of a young girl inmate who has been constantly in tears for the past two weeks, a new-comer aged about sixteen. I want some one to get her away from there. My political situation is such at the present time that it will never do for me to figure in this matter; at the same time I am aware if you are conspicuous in it, those doors will be closed upon you, and that will be unwise, seeing these landladies are more or less kindly disposed toward you.

"I understand this girl is from San Francisco, where she has a mother, who ought to be notified and the daughter at once sent home to her; but I'm in a quandary how to proceed so as not to incur ill-feeling with the politicians of that neighborhood. [He was a candidate for reelection.] What would you suggest?"

Quickly I replied: "If that landlady does not know your voice, 'phone, asking if she has any new girls at present? Then ask her to send the new one to the 'phone. If she does so, have a talk with the girl of a nature calculated to lead the landlady to infer you are friendly, and as soon as it is safe to do so, tell her, the new girl, that she is to come out presently as though to go to a restaurant for breakfast, that friends are going to rescue her from her awful predicament, but that she must be very cautious for fear of creating suspicion. Tell her to look on the corner of Fourth and L—— Streets for a lady wearing a small black bonnet trimmed with white and to follow her into the building where she sees her disappear. Tell her to act as though she were making arrangements for an evening engagement."

In less than half an hour that poor child was closeted with the chief and me in his private office. Soon, after reassuring her, he left us alone in order that I could freely interrogate, and this, after many tears, was the sum and substance of what she told:

"I've a very comfortable home, a dear mama and two little brothers. Perhaps I have a stepfather now, for mama was intending to marry again. He's a chef in —— Hotel."

"Is your papa long dead, dear?" I inquired.

"Papa isn't dead. Mama got a divorce from him a little while ago. He wouldn't support us —— and ——."

"Has your mama known this chef very long?" I asked.

"Oh, yes, quite a while. I never saw much of him though, 'cause Mama would rather I wasn't around when he called; so she often used to let me go to the nickelodeon or the dance with some of the girls I know, when she expected him to spend the evening."

"How did it happen you came here, my child?" was the next question.

"It was this way. I got acquainted with a fine-looking young lady, a swell dresser, too, at ——Hall. We took a 'shine' to each other on sight, and I asked her to call on me, 'cause I wanted Mama to meet her. Mama liked her, too. She told us she lived with her aunt, Miss Clark, on Post Street, who was quite nicely fixed. Said she must take me to see her soon.

"Well, we met often after that, *and Mama was pleased because I now had a companion old enough to take good care of me.* One day when I went home with Tessie, to take tea, her aunt said to her, 'I've just received a letter from Louise, and she wants to know when you are coming to make her a visit.'

Tessie said, 'Oh, I'd like to go next week. Mamie, I wonder if you couldn't come, too? Louise is my cousin; she's well off, and will give us a good time. You ask your mama and I'll write Louise.' Mama was willing. Tessie's aunt soon got another letter saying Cousin Louise would be pleased to have me come, so we made arrangements. I was to meet Tessie at the boat Monday morning at ten o'clock. Mama wasn't very well, so I went down alone on the car with my suitcase. We'd bought our tickets Saturday, and for fear of accidents Tessie gave me mine for safekeeping.

"I went on board the boat and waited and waited, but up to the last minute Tessie didn't come, but a messenger boy did—with a note saying her aunt was sick, but for me to go and she'd come on the next boat. Louise would be dressed—and described how I would know her, for she was to meet us. Tessie never came, neither did her cousin. This woman I'm with is named Louise, but she says she doesn't know Tessie. I don't know what to make of it, do you?"

Then she told me exactly what kind of life she had been forced to lead for over two weeks, and that when she first came the landlady dictated a letter which she (Mamie) wrote to her mother.

"As big a lie as ever was told," said Mamie; "but I had to do as Miss Louise said, and she mailed it. I haven't written Mama since, 'cause I didn't want to spoil her pleasure. Guess she's safely married now, 'cause she expected to be."

"My dear child," I said, "will you give me your San Francisco address, your mother's name and initials? You are going home on the next steamer. I am going to have her meet you at the wharf. I know the stewardess, who is a good woman. She will not let you out of her sight until she hands you over to your mother."

Poor, frail, pretty, little, sixteen-year-old Mamie wept with joy. The next morning, long before it was time to sail, she was safely hidden away on board the steamer. The mother, in response to the telegram, was on hand when the ship reached the San Francisco wharf, and unless she is different from other women of that caliber, she can not, I think, ever forget that registered letter, in which some good wholesome advice was given and such motherhood as she represented was so scathingly denounced as to upset her honeymoon. Furthermore, I did not hesitate to inform her that her little daughter was both physically and morally ruined and that God would hold her (the mother) and her alone responsible. Was that all? No. The right persons were put on the track of Tessie and her aunt. Unfortunately, however, they were never, on account of some technicality, made to suffer, aside from having to take their immediate departure. However, the just God is taking cognizance of all these things. Nothing escapes him. "Vengeance is mine; I will repay, saith the Lord."

Dear reader, I generally leave my audience with a heavy load on my heart. Why? Because, as other public workers and speakers, I find few, very few, comparatively speaking, who heed the warnings which observation and practical experience have prompted me to give out. Once as I was walking out of a church, two ladies directly behind me were conversing on the address just finished. One said to the other, "Weren't you immensely interested in those dreadful word-pictures from real life?" "Yes," replied the other, "but that work is very unpopular, and requires peculiarly adapted people, entirely different from you and me." I silently thanked God for so richly endowing a few of us with sufficiently peculiar qualities to seek for wonderful, priceless jewels among the fallen who, through lack of proper home training and companionship, have taken the downward course. Many of these outcasts, if sought and cared for, will some day occupy an exalted place in the Master's kingdom.

CHAPTER XLII
LOS ANGELES DANCE-HALLS
AND OTHER PLACES

Well, you may call them first-class if you like; I call them first-class stepping-stones to an everlasting hell. Furthermore, I will prove my statement.

On July 24 of that year (1908) I was again in Los Angeles. As usual, I was interviewed, this time by a *Times* editor. Among other things I made mention of the fact that many mothers did not know what their children were doing after school-hours, and stated that such women had better play less whist and give their children more attention. And oh! the terrifying iniquities of society. Do you know, the worst enemy a girl who has fallen into error has is her own sex. Women simply will not have anything to do with her, and that is what keeps the world back. The cause? Selfishness, of course.

"Yes, I believe there are too many marriages of convenience. And oh! the dreadful race suicide that I know is going on around me on every hand. It sounds the doom of the American race. We are indeed on the downward path."

"Why do not our mothers bring up their girls in a full knowledge of this world and its snares for young and faltering feet, instead of letting them run the streets and meet unknown men?"

"It is because the mothers themselves are too often unfit for the divine duties of motherhood. They are lacking in a knowledge of what makes for the best life. I have seen so much of it that I am going to try to arouse the mothers of Los Angeles at a special meeting."

The different dailies kept tab of "Mother Roberts" for some time. To be a target, a cynosure, is an indescribable cross to the Christian; but some one must be willing, else how is the world to comprehend the situation?

Among other things said in the mothers' meeting were these:

"Too many mothers will not, because of their false modesty, give proper instruction to their children. Yes, parents fearfully misrepresent conditions to their boys and girls, even resorting to absolute falsehood. Of course the children soon learn the facts, and instead of the parents and children making confidants of each other, both practise deception. When girls find out these things, they often slip away to their downfall.

"When I was sixteen years of age, I saw in a paper an advertisement stating that an elderly lady wanted a young lady as companion and amanuensis. The advertisement read very smoothly and I answered it. The woman, who was seemingly a prepossessing, lonely old woman, inspected my recommendations and at once engaged me on trial. I shortly returned to her, taking with me some of my choicest worldly possessions; but before I had been with her twenty-four hours, some of her strange actions so alarmed me that on the following morning I made the excuse at the breakfast table of wanting to go to my boarding-place for expected mail, promising to return within half an hour. After I had told the family of my experiences and suspicions, the mother would not allow me to return even for my effects, which I have not seen from that day to this. *It turned out that I was only one of about forty girls who had been engaged by that diabolical woman to fill 'positions as companions.'* I am very thankful that 'the way of escape' had been made for me, and though feeling badly about losing my belongings, I agreed with my friends that it were better to avoid notoriety than to create a disturbance.

"At the time of this occurrence (it was in San Francisco) I had but recently arrived from England, the land of my birth and breeding, under the protection of elderly people, who consigned me to the care of relatives in California. As with thousands of other girls, my education on certain lines had been badly neglected. I was, alas! too unsophisticated.

"In after-years, when I became a Christian in spirit as well as in name, I thanked God for this early experience, which has enabled me to sympathize with those who, much of the time, are more sinned against than guilty of sinning, and who so often are enticed away by the various methods devised by unprincipled beings called men and women.

SATAN LURKS IN THE WALTZ

"Yes; I have watched them dance in many places, even in Los Angeles. Is it degrading, demoralizing? You know as well as I that there is nothing uplifting, nothing of a good moral tendency, about the dance, especially the waltz; and I saw nothing else offered than the waltz, or round dances closely resembling it, in either of the places I attended last evening.

"My heart sorely ached as I observed mothers with their little girls, five to twelve years old, allowing, aye, even encouraging them to get up and waltz on the same floor with questionable characters. Evidently there is little or no need of introductions. Both sexes anxiously observe who are the best dancers, and soon these, though perhaps total strangers, are spinning, sliding, or gliding about together, in many instances in a close embrace, breast to breast, and cheek to cheek. But they 'must dance.' they 'love it so.' And the music! The most sensual, the most alluring, as subtle as a wily serpent, and just as harmful.

"There were church-members there; mothers chaperoning their young daughters; mothers who profess to be following in the footsteps of the Redeemer; mothers who have promised to bring up their little ones in the way Jesus would have them.

"In a few instances I even saw fathers waltzing with their own little girls on the great crowded dance-hall floor as late as nearly midnight. 'What!' you say, 'surely no father would think of such a thing.' Perhaps not; perhaps I am presuming. Perhaps it was the mother's escort to the ball in each instance. I don't know. This I do know: Those little children last night were *eager, hungry, craving, tireless dancers.* O merciful God! The pity of it, the pity of it!

"I observed some of the young men. The contour of some of their heads peculiarly interested me. To be sure, you could not tell what the girls' heads were like because of so many etceteras bulging out all over; but as I looked at many of the young men's heads, I was not long in deciding that *those who danced the most gracefully evidently had the bulk of their brains in their heels.*

"At the first place I visited, one young fellow walked up to a pretty pompadoured, short-skirted miss who stood close to me and who had waltzed with several strangers, and asked her to dance. She refused him. Why? He smelt too strong of whiskey and was unsteady in his gait, but she did not give him that as her reason, and because of his persistence she soon said to her companions (some other young girls), 'Come on, let's go down to— —; there isn't enough fun here.' It was no sooner said than done. I also left for this other place, where I found hundreds of couples dancing, and many refined, pretty-looking young girls sitting or standing around, waiting for any strange young man to invite them on to the floor and hug them (oh yes, better call things by their proper names)—hug them to alluring waltz-time.

EVEN ON THE LORD'S DAY

"There is hour after hour of this, day after day, night after night; yes, even on the one day set apart for the worship of our Redeemer and Creator, and this in the so-called respectable dance-hall. At the entrance is a prominent sign—'Dancing every night including Sunday.' 'No bowery dancing allowed.' Tell me why that sign if the dance is strictly respectable?

"A young gentleman made this comment to me: 'You won't find one girl in a hundred today, who is not fond of the dance.'

"'Why?' I inquired.

"'Considering their training, it isn't to be wondered at,' he answered.

"'What training?' I questioned.

"'Because their mothers loved it before them, and the girls do not hesitate to say so.'

"Another young man said: 'I can take advantage of the situation, if so inclined, every time. Invariably any girl who dances will drink, and any one that drinks will go still farther.'

"One girl said: 'It isn't what occurs at the actual dance, but any girl that dances often has to fight for her virtue, almost her life, after the dance—on her way home. Often her escort takes her only part of the way. Yet, "like moths that court the candle," even though we know that death and ruin are in the wake, still we will dance.'

"Whoever heard of any man worth the having, seeking for a wife and the future mother of his children in a ballroom?

WARNING TO GIRLS

"Let me quote another young man: 'If the pure-minded girls with whom we sometimes are dancing knew our thoughts, they would never put a foot on the ballroom floor again, as they value their lives; but lots of young girls don't know this, and their mothers who sometimes chaperon them, don't suspect us. I consider the dance-hall even worse than the saloon. I'm a dancer myself, but I won't pay serious address to any girl who dances.'

"Have matters assumed such shape that we can not furnish the majority of the present generation, pleasures so pure, refining, and alluring that the dance and other vices may not be relegated to oblivion? This question should stir the innermost recesses of the souls of all who are interested in the welfare of the young people of today, be they young or old, rich or poor.

The next generation is cursed already, frightfully cursed, unless unusual sacrifice will now be made. There is no time to lose, especially on the part of those who love the title, 'Soldier of the Cross.'

"'Put on the whole armor of God.' Go where he wants you to go. Do what he wants you to do. Be what he wants you to be, in thought, in word, in deed, even though it may mean to part with your very life. God is yearning for a few more Calebs and Joshuas and Daniels. What use to pray 'Thy Kingdom Come,' if you patronize or countenance places where, under no consideration, could you invite the One you profess to love and serve."

CHAPTER XLIII
WOMAN EMPLOYED AT DANCE-
HALL TELLS OF MANY PITFALLS

Whilst contending against the dance-hall evil, I received a note asking for an immediate interview. The writer, who signed her own name, stated that she had been an employee in ——'s Dance-hall (rated as one of the exclusive and first-class places) and that she believed that, under the existing circumstances, my granting her an audience, would still further aid the cause, as she could throw much light on the subject.

Soon she was at my rooms, also a reporter, and the following is, in part, what she had to say:

"I am utterly disgusted with dance-halls, and am determined to do all I can against them. Mr. C—— [her husband] and I came here from New York in reduced financial circumstances, and I applied for and obtained a position at ——'s Dance-hall.

"For reasons best known to ourselves, we posed as brother and sister, pretending my husband was in the East. I worked there only fourteen days, or until my husband secured a permanent position, but I left the place with a complete knowledge of the disreputable work done there under the guise of a respectable dance-hall. I do not wish to be mean in my assertions, but the facts will bear me up in what I actually saw and heard during the two weeks I was engaged at ——'s Dance-hall.

"I was on the reception committee to introduce the lonesome boys to the charming girls for the dances. It would take me two hours to state the disgusting features I saw there.

"The manager at one time asked me to drink whiskey with him. I told him that I was not in the habit of indulging and that if I should get drunk he would have to take care of me, to which he said, 'I can do that all right.'

"One night a young man became dead drunk in the dance-hall, in full view of the dancers, making a disgusting show of himself, all of which apparently passed unnoticed by the manager. The friends of the young man took him out of the hall.

"One time I saw a young girl dancing with a young man who was trying to hide a whiskey bottle, with which she and her partner appeared to be mixed. All this was supposed to be in plain sight of the manager.

"A young girl on duty selling tickets asked me to bring her an empty glass from the soda fountain. A young man took it and filled it nearly full with brandy and passed it to the girl. She slyly wrapped her handkerchief around it to hide the brandy, and drank it as if drinking a glass of water. This was seen by several by-standers.

"It makes me shudder to think of what I saw and heard in that hall. One young girl unused to the ways of the world was taken out of the hall in a ruined condition, and after an unlawful surgical operation had been performed, she was sent to a well-known hospital. She was the victim of a prominent lawyer of Los Angeles.

"One night last week the manager spoke through a megaphone, during the intermission of the dance, asking everybody to sign a petition he had prepared *stating that the place was properly run, and to sign it in order that he could continue the dance-hall business.* I know of one man who signed a fictitious name to the petition, with the remark that others were doing the same," etc.

She told much more, some of which was not fit to print, but surely that is sufficient from her.

I was able one night to show a reporter that no erroneous statements had been made. On the contrary, he was shocked as he noted the wily depravity. His attention was attracted to a good-looking young man who had slipped one of the reception committee young women a piece of money. Together we watched the outcome. She made for a pretty, graceful young girl just leaving the dance-ring and whispered audibly, "There's a swell young fellow wants to have the honor of dancing with you." Before the girl had time to think or answer, he was right on hand, saying, "May I have the pleasure of the next waltz? My name is Jones." Then the introducer manufactured a name for the pretty young girl, the music started up, and the next moment she was gliding over the perfect dancing-floor in the embrace of this strange fellow. Is that all? Not by any means. He invited her to an innocent dish of ice-cream. (If a girl does not accept such an invitation, but she usually does, the would-be seducer knows she is a gold mine if he can ever secure her, and he works to that end.) She accepted. We watched our opportunity, and, between dances, when no one was taking notice, we whispered the word of warning. For a moment she looked alarmed, but did she heed? Evidently not. Possibly she resented the well-meant advice, and, in consequence, soon paid the fearful price for so doing.

Upon getting out once more into the fresh air, we could not fail to observe the many automobiles in waiting. Wherefore? Listen! Shortly before this visit when I was accompanied by the *Times* reporter, I was a temporary guest in one of Los Angeles' representative families, the mother of whom was one of my tried and true friends. She had two noble, handsome sons. One of them came home one day in a high state of indignation. After he had related to his mother an incident that had just occurred, she besought him to repeat it for my benefit.

While he was resting in the park bounded by Fifth, Sixth, Olive, and Hill Streets, a middle-aged man of good dress and appearance seated himself on the same bench and, disregarding conventionalities, began to make himself agreeable, first commenting on the weather and then gradually leading up to the subject in which he was most interested. Presently he inquired if my young friend was occupied in business, and received the reply, "No; not at present, but I am on the lookout for something that will be worth while." As one word always leads to another, the stranger soon inquired if the young man could dance. Receiving an affirmative answer, he remarked:

"Good! I notice you are a swell dresser also, and a pleasant conversationalist; in fact, have all the requirements if I'm not mistaken."

"What requirements?" asked my young friend.

"Say, young man," the stranger answered, "I can put you wise to something that will bring you the quickest returns for the least labor you ever struck, but *'mums the word.'*"

"Fire ahead," replied my young friend; "'mums the word.'"

"First, I note that you are agreeable, educated, well dressed, and a dancer, all of which takes with the majority of girls, at least the girls we have to reach. Next, I need you in the ballrooms. Perhaps you may occasionally require an automobile. To be sure, that is expensive, but..."

"What is he driving at?" silently wondered my young friend. "Guess I will hear him through. Here's something out of the ordinary."

"Girls will be girls," the man continued. "It's dead easy to win some, harder with others; but there's big money in it for each new supply you can furnish."

"Furnish for what?" inquired my young friend.

"The necessary evil, my boy, the necessary evil, of course," was the startling answer.

Trembling with indignation, my young friend quickly arose and unhesitatingly shouted:

"Police! Police!"

The procurer disappeared so suddenly that no one of the small crowd which quickly gathered knew what was the matter until too late to arrest the scoundrel.

Is that stranger the only procurer? Common sense answers, "No!" My reader, there are thousands. Therefore if nothing else, no other reason —and they are many—should cause young ladies to refrain from a practise which means compromise or ruin, often eternal damnation, surely this illustration should be sufficient.

Permit me to mention another reason, one I am also able to verify, for it came from one shipwrecked at the age of twenty-two, and now passed into eternity, but then lying in one of the wards of the county hospital. To be brief, he was a dancer. Honor, however, forbade his making any improper advances to his girl partners, but the effects of their close proximity were fatal. All the evil of his nature was stirred, and it would not be suppressed. He yielded; visited places whose thresholds he would never otherwise have crossed; then followed depravity, disease, and an untimely death. Who was responsible for this? *The unharmed girls with whom he danced.* Surely a word to the wise is sufficient. If dancing causes my brother to err, I will dance no longer.

CHAPTER XLIV
SARAH

Whilst doing a house-to-house work in one of our large coast towns, also filling various pulpits whenever opportunity permitted, I was on one occasion cordially invited to enter the lodging of a girl, who, when I was seated, quickly turned the key in the lock, remarking as she did so: "You're just the kind of a person I have been hoping this long time to meet. Excuse me for locking you in, but I don't want to be disturbed while you are here, where I'm truly ashamed to have you find me. I want to tell you my situation and see if you can not immediately get me out of this awful predicament."

Calling attention to the fact that there was no odor of liquor, no signs of cigarettes about, and stating that in consequence she was unpopular with the habitues of the other lodgings in the immediate vicinity, she inquired:

"Do I look like a hardened sinner?"

"You certainly do not," was my reply.

"Oh! I'm so relieved," she rejoined, "so relieved to hear you say so, because I want to get away from this life, and I am sure you can help me."

"All that is in my power, dear girl," I assured her. "Now tell me your story."

"I've a little brother and sister," she began. "My father, when I was seventeen years of age, ran off with another woman and deserted poor Mother, who took it so hard that she lived only two years. This left me to provide for the children. I had to get some help from the county for the funeral expenses, and it wasn't easy to make a good appearance and provide properly for the little ones on what I was earning."

"What were you doing for a living, dear?" I asked.

"I was working in a laundry, from early morning till, many times, late at night. I got a dollar a day and for over-time was paid extra." (If I remember correctly, she said ten cents an hour.)

"Was that sufficient to provide food, clothing, and shelter for all three of you?" I inquired.

"No, mam, though I managed somehow. I boarded them with an old friend of mother's, who was very kind, and I felt she was never paid enough for her trouble, so you may be sure I was constantly on the lookout for a better-paying job. At last I thought I had struck one, but for a while it would take me away from them, for it was away off in Nevada.

"I answered an ad in the morning paper for a situation in a hotel. The man and woman wanted me right away, as they were leaving on the evening train, and would take me with them, also two others. So I quickly made all my arrangements. Two days later we were there, and it took me no time to see that our principal work would be to wait on tables in the saloon and gambling-hall. *I had no money, and was in debt. What could I do but make the best of it? and it is surprising how soon one can.*"

"Yes, my child. I've frequently heard others make the same sad remark—but proceed with your story."

"I was making quite a bit, besides sending money home to keep the children, when something happened which made me so despondent [she did not say what it was] that one day I quit my job, and one of the girls said, 'Go down to — —, Sarah. You'll be able to get plenty of honest work there, at good wages.' So I left; and, believe me, I hadn't struck — — before some one on the train recognized me as one of the girls who had worked in the — — Hotel. It was all up with me now. In my despair I took this den, for which I pay one dollar and fifty cents a day. I loathe, I hate the business. I am ready and willing to go into anybody's kitchen and work, and work hard and well, for I know how. Do you think you could get any one to hire me?"

As she had been brought up by a God-fearing mother, we knelt together in that vile den, where we both prayed. With the tears streaming down her cheeks, she prayed her mother's God and her God to forgive her for having been so weak as to yield to the devil, all because she wanted more money so as to be able to provide better for the little brother and sister, and implored Him to give her employment where she could have them near her until they were old enough to do for themselves.

Now listen to how God answered that prayer. On the next evening (Sunday), whilst I was addressing a large audience in the Congregational church, I related this girl's experience and then requested honest work for her, emphasizing thus: "She claims to be capable; she looks it; therefore she can earn good wages. Whoever is in need of such a girl, please privately inform me at the close of this service." In less than an hour, that girl could have had her choice of five situations in responsible families. I chose one for her, and for aught I know to the contrary, she may be there still. (Reader, it is impossible to keep track of different ones, there are so many.) She gave such excellent satisfaction that erelong her little brother and sister were provided a good home in her immediate neighborhood, and scarcely any one is the wiser for her unfortunate error.

Thus the rescue worker occasionally sees happy results of the travail of soul for the lost ones; but would to God there were many more Christian employers like the one Sarah found, who treat her so kindly, as well as give her what she is capable of earning, that she makes extra effort to prove her appreciation and gratitude. "But," you say, "there are not many like Sarah." True; also there are not many Christians like Sarah's employers. In fact, they are very, very rare. Many a time have I wearied myself in vain in an endeavor to procure honest employment for some young girl who has been convicted and imprisoned a short time for her first offense and who has told me of her capabilities and begged me to procure employment pending her release, so that she would not have to return to her undesirable home and surroundings, with their accompanying temptations.

"We dare say she means well enough now, but we could not think of hiring her until some one has first tested and proved her trustworthy. Besides, there are other members of our family; they must be taken into consideration," is the frequent excuse. Thus the responsibility is shifted, and, sick and sad at heart, we go away to inform the poor girl who wants honest work that our efforts have proved futile. We then implore her to make her home in one of the refuges until she can once more become established, only to hear her say: "That would hoodoo me for sure. You know as well as I do that scarcely any wages are offered to a girl who is hired out of a rescue home, even if she is quite capable." Reader, it is shamefully true. Oh! why will professed Christians take so mean an advantage of the situation and expect girls who have made some mistake, but *have the courage to live it down*, to go to work at menial employment for little or nothing? Under such circumstances, what inducement have they who, if encouraged, would do better?

May the dear Lord as never before give us an introspective vision of ourselves as he sees us. This will surely clothe us with the mantle of Christ-like charity, in the event of our determination to live up to our profession and numberless privileges.

CHAPTER XLV
THE WOMEN PRISONERS OF SAN QUENTIN

The present kind wardens (Hoyle and Reilly) of the two penitentiaries of California have granted me many more opportunities to enjoy heart-to-heart talks with the prisoners than I am able to relate. In but one of these places (San Quentin) are the women incarcerated. In this department let me endeavor to awaken your interest.

It is situated in a remote corner, inside the prison walls, and is accessible only through the passage-way underneath the central building seen in the illustration on next page. It is built two stories high around a hollow cemented square, with windows looking into the same. It affords no view, excepting barely the tops of the hills, the sky, and the matron's house. Truly these poor women are shut in. Not so with the men, as will be seen in the same picture. It shows a portion of the beautiful garden into which many a cell door opens. One corner of these quarters may be seen on the right, the women's being inside of the building near the tree on the left. Frequently have I, attended by the matron, Mrs. G. G. Smith, a very warm friend of mine, come through that iron gateway in the wall, always to be greeted with smiles and warm words, of welcome by my less fortunate sisters. These meetings were, without doubt, profitable to all concerned. I enjoyed their orchestra (some are very musical), and they enjoyed the songs to my autoharp accompaniment.

As I have previously mentioned, the present matron, after much intercession and with the warden's aid, succeeded, a few months following her accession to the matronal office, in prevailing upon the board of prison directors to grant the women prisoners a monthly walk on God's beautiful green hills. In order to prove their appreciation of her kindness, the women banded together to give her an entertainment on the first anniversary of her matronship. To this day they believe the affair to have been a complete surprise, though she was aware of their preparations from the beginning.

The day broke warm and beautiful. Immediately after dinner Matron Smith was escorted to a seat of honor in the yard and the program was opened by an excellent address of welcome (of which *I* have an exact copy) by E——, whose offense was—well, we won't say what nor how long her term of imprisonment. She is a bright young woman, as the following well-worded and *touching* speech amply verifies:

Trusting in your graciousness, and with your approval, we, the inmates of the female department of this institution, have taken the liberty of arranging a program for an entertainment to be given in the honor of, and to celebrate this, your official natal day.

Just a year ago today you came to us. To you it means just the passing of time in a sphere of action hitherto unknown to you; but to us a year filled with memories of all things good—easier times, warmer clothing, and privileges until then unknown.

We have enjoyed, through your kind intercession, and the courtesy of our noble Warden, the delight of walking forth into the outer world, even if only for a short time; of seeing once more green fields and hills clothed in nature's gown of green and flowers; of viewing the waters of the bay and inhaling the salt sea air; and of being entertained in your own sweet way, in your own sweet home. At last, but not least, to have the intense satisfaction of gazing at the outside of our prison wall, anticipating the time when we will always be outside of that old wall. And in our daily life together, you, in the discharge of your duties, have been a kind and gentle matron, listening always with patience to our tales of woe. And through all the past year you have been to us our guide, friend, and comrade. We one and all pray that life will give you health, happiness, and prosperity, and all of heaven's good gifts.

Then followed an enjoyable program.

Who could not be touched by such tender sentiment from those whom the world at large regard as well-nigh, if not quite, hopeless cases. Because of this and also because of the receipt of a recent letter (Sept. 14, 1911), I humbly and heartily thank God that I am able to prove that kindness, coupled with good judgment, is very effectual.

Enclosed in this lengthy, newsy letter from the matron are some excellent up-to-date photos of the San Quentin prison, two of which you will find between these covers, and also a clipping from one of San Francisco's daily papers, as follows:

2,000 LEAVE PRISON WALLS

WARDEN HOYLE GIVES SAN QUENTIN
CHARGES AN UNUSUAL PRIVILEGE

Nearly two thousand convicts at San Quentin prison walked outside the walls on Admission Day and spent more than three hours in God's out-of-doors, while they rooted for rival hall teams playing on a diamond beneath the blue Marin County skies.

No extra guards or precautions marked the first time in the history of a California State prison that convicts have been permitted to leave the walls.

JOKE AND LAUGH

In orderly procession the men filed out from the prison yard between the great stone gate-posts, laughing and joking like schoolboys in their joy at seeing once more an unobstructed sweep of smiling, open country.

From three o'clock until six fifteen every man in the institution except the sick and incorrigibles, stood or sat on the ground or perched on adjoining sheds while the "Whites" and "Blacks" played ball that would do credit to a fast bush league.

Over at one side sat a row of condemned prisoners, watching their last ball game and forgetting for a few blessed moments that the shadow of the scaffold hung over them.

WOMAN FANS, TOO

From other seats, the women prisoners saw the game.

For four innings neither side scored. Then the "Blacks" pitcher lost his control, and the two thousand frenzied rooters cheered as man after man slid home. The score at the close stood 7 to 2 in favor of the "Whites."

"It's only part of the new policy of trusting the prisoners and treating them like human beings," said Warden Hoyle today. Hoyle is the man who is responsible for the innovation. "We have no fear for a break for liberty, and the men showed that they appreciate decent treatment. I can't say that we will take the men outside every holiday, but the experiment was a success and will be tried again."

What the glimpse of a world outside the prison walls meant for the prisoners can be appreciated by readers of "The Bulletin" who have read Donald Lowrie's narrative of life within the prison walls.

The Admission Day game marked a new epoch in the history of California prisons.

What an innovation compared with former policies! Surely practical demonstration of these experiments in other parts of the country will have a tendency to reduce criminality. If not, pray tell me what will? Time and again have I heard prisoners and others comment upon the impractical Christianity portrayed, with seldom any exception. They weary of being only preached to. The actions of such men as Warden Hoyle and of such women as Matron Smith will probably have more to do with helping these convicted ones to lead upright lives in the future than will all the preaching of celebrated divines from now to doomsday, and I, a Christian, do not hesitate for one moment to say so frankly. In the name of the dear Lord, let us endeavor to practise what we preach, and thus win numberless blessings from the throne of grace for ourselves and others.

CHAPTER XLVI
VALLEJO, MARE ISLAND, AND ALCATRAZ

"I am sure you will enjoy a trip with me to Vallejo and Uncle Sam's great navy yard, adjacent to it. It is only about an hour's ride from San Francisco and is accessible both by train and boat," I said to my friend, Mrs. Walter C. Show, of Santa Barbara, whose guest I then was, in her lovely villa in that beautiful city by the sea. She had been giving me most interesting accounts of her entertainment of the marines and the cadets at the time when the fleet lay at anchor in the bay. As I was soon due in San Francisco, she accompanied me. Before starting we notified friends; consequently, warm welcome and royal entertainment was ours from the time of arrival.

As this was by no means my first visit, I prepared her for the shock of seeing many, many saloons and other disreputable places for the purpose of robbing hundreds, nay, thousands of boys, far from home and mother, of their hard and scanty earnings. Nevertheless, there is an excellent Marine Y.M.C.A. in Vallejo, with a large membership; but they are in the minority. We saw scores pouring out of the saloons or hanging around their immediate vicinity; scores more that evening coming in or going out of the dance-halls and dens of iniquity and vice. Many were in dreadful stages of intoxication. Alas! the pity, the great pity of it, that Uncle Sam does not wake up to protect those ready to lay down their lives for home and country, not to speak of the hundreds of thousands, nay, millions of our floating population. Where will it all eventually end? where, oh! where?

I contend that the civic clubs of any community hold the key to the situation. If they would strive for the prevention of crime rather than for the reformation of the criminal, the resultant good would soon be tenfold that of the present regime.

The day following our arrival we were taken to inspect Mare Island. As heretofore, the prison-ship was filled with young men serving short terms or awaiting trial for some serious offense. *In almost every instance liquor was responsible for their being in trouble.* It was heartrending. We realized that, aside from speaking a kind word or giving some motherly advice, we could do little if anything. We were inadequate to cope with the situation. We could pray with them, poor lads; we could sympathize with them; but we were practically powerless in that or in any community that tolerates, licenses, and votes for the means of the downfall of men, women, and children. All we can do is pray and wait, wait and pray. God speed the day when the enemy of souls shall no longer reign over them and laugh at their calamity. God speed the day.

I again made it my business to visit many lost girls in that city, earnestly pleading with them to quit the downward path and stop dragging other souls down to hell along with their own. *Most of them appeared to be gospel hardened.* One girl, however, seriously impressed me. She was one of the few who would listen.

"I'll tell you how I'm situated," she said, "and then if you don't think I am to be pitied more than blamed, you're different from what I think you are. I've the dearest mother on earth. She lies, a hopeless cripple, in a little cottage in West Oakland. I also have a little brother not old enough to go to school yet. I hire a woman who has known us for many years to take care of them. She is elderly, and, for the sake of a good home, works for small wages. She knows how I live, but would rather die than betray me. Mother thinks I am working in a hotel where I get plenty of 'tips' besides my wages. I go home every Monday to see her. *Mother Roberts, I would give the world if I could be able to have my pure mother kiss lips that were clean instead of stained and stained with sin.*

"I won't send her to the hospital. I love her better than my life. She'd die there, for the need of nice little things they never provide, and other necessaries. My little brother would have to be reared in some charity institution. I couldn't stand it. I'm the most unhappy girl on earth because of the situation, and don't you forget it; but I can't, I can't earn sufficient honest money to support them and myself properly."

Later, the mother died, and *the poor daughter, who had ruined her life to support her, went insane and then took her life.*

Some of the girls told me that one man owned nearly all the dance-halls there as well as the girls, and that very few of them had any liberty or money. They were living in hope, but alas! many were dying in despair. Apparently little if any impression could be made on those we did have a chance to talk with. We could only sow the seed and trust our merciful God for results.

All the pastors invited us into the pulpits, where we endeavored faithfully to give such messages as God saw fit to lay on our hearts.

The next day we left for a visit to Alcatraz Island, the isolated military prison situated midway between San Francisco and Sausalito. Oh, what a gloomy, desolate place! Notwithstanding its beautiful situation, excellent discipline, etc., its atmosphere is most depressing. Even before one lands one feels weighted down, despondent for its prisoners, many of whom sit or stand with hats drawn low over their faces, breaking, ever breaking stones by the roadside. Nearly all are being punished for desertion. The sympathetic visitor longs to address them, but is not permitted to do so. He is allowed only a brief visit with whomsoever he has, after much trouble, received a permit for an interview, and then always in the presence and within hearing of the officer in charge. Surely the way of the transgressor is hard, and especially so with the violator of Uncle Sam's rigid army and navy rules and regulations. For this reason Uncle Sam ought to remove the stumbling-blocks that he countenances and legalizes and that cause so many of his otherwise obedient servants to fall into disrepute and, in numerous cases, into untimely graves.

The young man whom we had come to visit, though a refined, intelligent soldier, was a deserter. He had the usual sad story to relate—wine, women, then desertion. There was so little, with the exception of Christian sympathy, with which we could encourage him. The future looked gloomy. I made an effort, through one of my friends in Congress, to obtain this young man's parole, but as this was his second offense, the attempt was futile. It is hard, very hard on the missionary to have to be the bearer of discouraging, often heart-breaking, news; but as this is part of our office, we bear the cross as we alone can, always pointing the disappointed and heavy-hearted to the Savior, the Burden-bearer; sometimes, but not always, leaving them with the load somewhat lightened.

From this sad place we, with heavy hearts, proceeded to San Quentin. After spending two hours (for our time was limited) we then departed for San Francisco, where we visited various points of interest to the consecrated ones. Then, after an absence of ten days, we returned to beautiful Santa Barbara, where church and other engagements were awaiting me.

Thence I traveled up the Coast, ever with the one object in view—"the Master's service." I visited jails and the avenues that lead to that place, and held many meetings, always being well received by pastors of various denominations, civic societies, etc. In the name of the Lord, yet with the spirit of love, I endeavored to place the blame for the downfall of the masses where it belonged and belongs—at the door of the licensed saloon.

When I reached San Luis Obispo, I learned, to my great joy, that the Columbia Park Band Boys of San Francisco, forty of whom were on a walking tour from that city to Los Angeles, were due the following day. At Chittenden (my home), just before I left, my friends had delightfully entertained them with a picnic on their beautiful grounds. There we learned what an effectual (prevention) work was being carried on for the reputable lads of the public schools of San Francisco under the leadership of the Piexotto brothers, who arrange for entertainments, outings, and treats throughout the year, thus appealing to all the better instincts and qualities of many of the rising generation. It is truly a most practical, worthy enterprise, one which should be adopted in all large cities for the encouragement and the promotion of better citizenship.

A sad case was awaiting trial in this city—a fifteen-year-old girl prisoner accused of the murder of her babe. I visited her frequently. She was finally sent to Whittier Reform School. Much comment on this is out of the question; suffice it to say, the girl, because of her pre and post-natal environments, was far more to be pitied than blamed.

I was next due at Santa Maria. During my brief sojourn there I was the guest of the president of the Women's Improvement Club, who, with many others, was making a strenuous effort to abolish the saloon from their midst. I there became acquainted with a very enthusiastic, fearless child of God, a converted Jew, whose name I can not recall at the time of this writing, but whose help I greatly appreciated. He was leaving no stone unturned for the elimination of the local liquor traffic.

Returning to San Luis Obispo for a brief stay, I was much gratified in renewing the acquaintance of Dr. Bulgin, a successful evangelist, with whom, in various places, I have had the pleasure of being more or less associated in the work.

S——, the city where I was on the morning of the earthquake, was once more, for a short time, my stopping-place. As something that had just occurred, so dreadful yet so interesting, occupied all my time and attention during my stay there, and as it furnishes ample material for another story, I will relate it in the following chapter.

CHAPTER XLVII
IRENE'S AWFUL FATE—"THE WAGES OF SIN."

After very warmly greeting me, the landlady of the hotel in which I was staying at the time of the earthquake introduced me to several, with the remark, "This is the lady of whom I was speaking a while ago—the one who occupied the room in my house in which the plaster was not even broken on that morning of the earthquake. I've always claimed God had a hand in that, for every other room and everything else here was practically destroyed, as many can testify." This being corroborated by a number sitting or standing around, she next said:

"Did you come to investigate last night's murder?"

"What murder?" I inquired. "I have not as yet heard of it."

"The awful, cold-blooded murder of a young woman they call Irene, down on — — Street, by a drunken lad twenty years of age. It's the worst ever!" she exclaimed.

"Do you know the parties, either of them?" I asked.

"Not the girl, only by sight. She was about twenty, and as pretty as a picture. She and her sister were leading awful lives. One lies murdered, and, now that you are here, I guess it won't be hard to induce the other to quit. They have been well reared, in as nice a family as you could wish to know. It's too bad, too bad!" mourned my landlady.

"What about the lad who has committed this awful deed? Do you know him?" I inquired.

"Yes, almost ever since he was born. He is an only child. His mother is a widow, and one of the nicest women you ever met. But he always was bad, even when a small boy. Let me tell you what he once started to do. He took a kitten and was in the very act of skinning it alive, just as you would a rabbit, when he was caught, and the poor little animal quickly put out of its misery. He seemed to delight in being cruel to anything that came his way. He'd take a fly and pick a wing or a leg off at a time, and then turn it loose to enjoy watching it trying to move about. When he got older, his mother couldn't make him go to school much, although she did everything to coax or bribe him. He got beyond her control, and would leave home for days and weeks at a time, then suddenly put in his appearance and demand money from her, which she always gave him; otherwise she would have no peace. Then off he'd go again, to turn up again just as he did yesterday morning, when he came in on the train and began to make his brags that he meant to paint the town red before he left it, and he certainly has—with human blood."

"Is not his home here?" I inquired.

"Not now. It used to be, but they moved away to — — — — some time ago, all owing to his bad actions," she replied, and then added. "My but I'm awful sorry for his poor mother! One of the nicest Christian women you ever met, Mother Roberts. I can't understand how God could punish her with such a child. I can't, indeed!"

Inquiring my way, I soon found myself at the jail, where this twenty-year-old murderer was being held. The sheriff was very kind; but he considerately informed me that the lad was in such a shocking state of inebriety as to be loathsome even to them, and also that they preferred to let his mother, who had not yet arrived, have the first interview.

Thence I wended my way to the district in which this awful crime, at nearly midnight the previous night, had been perpetrated. I first called at a respectable house in the immediate neighborhood, in order to get my bearings and necessary preliminary information; then soon I rang the bell of the door where the poor murdered girl had been lodging, but received no response. Some one next door, however, heard and answered, then invited me in.

Five girls, all huddled together, their faces still blanched with horror, confronted me when I entered that room. Never was a missionary more warmly welcomed. Never was a better opportunity to comfort and warn, then point to the "Lamb of God, who taketh away the sin of the world." Never were more humble prayers or promises of reformation. Every one of them had homes to go to, and every one promised to go as soon as the funeral was over. Then I inquired where I could find the sister of the murdered girl. They told me. They also gave me particulars concerning the murder.

The lad, it appeared, loitered around that neighborhood before dark, apparently semi-intoxicated, and then went into one of the houses, where he still more freely indulged. Upon leaving, he pointed his pistol and carelessly fired, "just for fun," into a window up-stairs. The bullet missed a girl's head, singeing her pompadour. Returning at dark, he renewed his wild revelries. About midnight, because his victim would not continue to drink with him, he shot her without one word of warning. Screaming at the top of her voice, she ran through every room of the house, he after her, still shooting. He emptied every barrel of his weapon into her poor sinful body. Every girl and youth under that roof fled at the first shot. The murderer, after doing his worst, coolly walked out, went up-town, and entered a saloon. There, as he called for a drink, he laid his weapon on the bar, bragging as he did so of his terrible deed. He was immediately arrested.

When the officers arrived at the scene of the crime, they found the bloody trace of the victim in every room, and when they finally discovered her, she was quite dead. She was kneeling by her bedside, her head buried in the clothes, her hands tightly clasped as though she had been trying to pray as her poor soul passed out into eternity.

I found her sister and had a heart-to-heart, soul-to-soul talk with her—one that I shall never forget. She was so silent, so uncommunicative, yet I talked on until I felt the Spirit say, "Enough." I have seen her since. She was still leading the kind of life which had been instrumental in sending her sister's soul and others' souls by the thousands to eternal perdition. She received me kindly, but she would not heed, notwithstanding she admitted that she was haunted the livelong time. She would give no reason for continuing on the road to hell.

"Who were these sisters?" you ask. Daughters of parents who were in comfortable circumstances and stood well in their community. *I was told that both girls were inveterate novel-readers, patrons of every show that came to town, good dancers and dressers, and*—reader, it is the same old sad, sad story. They confided in any one rather than their parents; and hence were easily persuaded to take the first step downward.

And what about that boy, whose mother wept and mourned and questioned why this awful trouble should have been put upon her, *she who had never wronged anybody in all her lifetime.*

Listen! poor afflicted mother. You have forgotten that when you were young and newly married you did not want to be burdened with motherhood for a long time to come. You wanted to continue to enjoy social functions in the very pretty dresses your fond parents had provided toward your wedding trousseau; you had no intention for many a long day to settle down to the usual routine incident to motherhood; in fact, you purposed to have a good time for the next two or three years, before your pretty clothes went out of fashion; besides, you did not particularly take to children anyhow, and if you had had your own way, you would never have had any. You said it, and you know it, that a woman is so tied down who has babies to take care of.

The time came when the greatest boon conferred on woman was to be conferred on you. What did you do? How angry you were as you, for months nursed your grievance, because God was going to have his way in spite of all opposition. One day the little babe was laid in your arms. As he was a goodly child to look upon, you were resigned; but, oh! poor, poor, untutored mother! *you had unawares robbed your darling of his birthright, and, furthermore, you had brought into the world a being with murderous tendencies.* Yes, you were converted at that revival meeting, and knew that all your past sins were blotted out by the efficacy of the precious blood of Jesus. Yes, we know you are living a Christian life so far as you know how, but *"your sins have been visited upon"* your poor child. *The germ was in his being, and now he must pay the penalty for your crime of a little over twenty years ago.* For crime it was, and you can not call it by any other name. "Others have been alike guilty," you say. Alas, yes! by the thousands; but that never for a moment excuses you.

You didn't know? No; not altogether, for you were not taking a look, a long look into the future. You had no instruction from your own fond, indulgent, falsely modest mother regarding these God-given functions, capable of producing a soul, a wonderful soul; and so you ignorantly, selfishly erred.

Never was mortal sorrier for another than I am for you. Never was mortal more anxious to help bear another's burden than I am to help bear yours; but it is well-nigh impossible for me to do so. Only Jesus can ease your broken heart. Only Jesus can comfort you. Only Jesus can heal your terrible, terrible wound, poor, weeping, afflicted mother. All I am able to do is to sympathize with and pray for you.

After this heart-rending experience I was glad to rest a few days at Chittenden and enjoy the fellowship of its cherished owners. Ah! how kind, how very, very kind they were! but the mail was constantly bringing calls that were more or less, urgent; sometimes to quickly locate a wandering girl; sometimes to come to a juvenile court session, or perhaps to a hospital or jail; and one was to assist in the work at Portland, Ore. Whilst considering the latter call and praying for leadings, I took time to hold some meetings in an interior town. Following a mothers' meeting there a young lady urged me to visit her and have a confidential talk with her upon a matter which was of vital importance. I did so, and this is what she said:

"What I am about to betray would lose me my situation if it were known; therefore I shall rely on you to respect strictly the confidence I am about to place in you, as to the source from whence you received it. I have a position in the telephone-office, consequently, I hear many conversations, *some of which are utterly demoralising.*

"There is a certain woman in this city whose business it is, at least so I judge, to corrupt, morally and physically, young school and messenger boys, as you will surmise by a conversation which took place this very morning, and it is not her first offense. She called for her party, and as I could not get them at once, I asked for her number, so as to be able to call her as soon as I could. Presently I succeeded, and soon she was asking:

"'Is this Harry?'

"Some one at the other end of the line replied:

"'Yes. Is that you, Cora?'

"'Of course, you little dunce. When are you coming down again? Didn't you...?'

"'Dandy. But say, Cora, it's awful risky. I'm not fourteen yet. What if I should get nabbed?'

"'No, you won't if you'll mind me. Now listen. Come in at the lower side entrance. I'll give a tip to the bar-tender. If the coast is clear, you can come up the back stairs; if not, he'll hide you until I say so.'

"'What time?'

"'Tomorrow after you're out. You know. After three. So long.'"

The case was sickening, revolting; but it demanded immediate action. After prayerfully meditating for a few minutes, I called up the chief of police, asked for audience without delay, and soon thereafter was in his private office. After listening attentively to my recital, he at first thought to wait until the morrow and then arrest all parties concerned; but upon reflection he decided that that course would never do, as the boy's parents were of high social standing. The arrest would ruin them. Moreover, it would never do to wait until the morrow. One of his private detectives was immediately deputized to call on Miss Cora and give her twelve hours to leave town, bag and baggage. He was to tell her the real reason and to inform her that if she refused to go she would be arrested and severely punished for enticing and harboring minors. Short as the time was, she managed to dispose of her things. Her house was permanently closed, and the saloon soon afterward.

As to the boy, I waylaid him on his way home from school and told him what I had found out, so that he was perfectly willing to go with me to the chief of police, who, I am satisfied, gave him much fatherly advice as well as a thorough scare, calculated to last as long as he lived and also to aid him in warning his schoolmates and friends having similar evil tendencies.

But I must return to Chittenden. Several letters from Oregon had been forwarded. I felt that I must answer this call, God willing. I decided to help there, at least temporarily. Accordingly, one morning, bright and early, I started.

As I boarded the train, Mr. and Mrs. Chittenden handed me a letter, the reading of which brought tears of love and appreciation. Here it is, word for word:

Chittenden, Cal., Nov. 15, 1909. Dear Mrs. Roberts:

We do not wish you to cross the State line into Oregon without carrying a few words from home with you—that is our excuse for the writing of this letter.

You have been one of us at Chittenden since you were invited to make our home yours last spring. Our wish was, and is, that Chittenden should be your home in all that the name implies—a place to which you could always turn for rest and recuperation from your unselfish labors; and from which you could go forth again to your chosen task to battle against evil, cheered by kind words, and knowing that warm hearts and a warm welcome were waiting for you when you again needed rest.

You have been with us now for over half a year, and your presence here has been most agreeable to us. Our respect for you has ripened into regard, and our regard into affection, and now that you are leaving us, we realize how much the home spirit has worked to bind us all together, and we know that we shall miss you and shall often wish to have you with us again.

Well, Oregon can not claim you all the time. Some time you will feel weary and overworked—some time you will need rest—and when you do, just remember that there is a little green and flowery spot along the railway down in California—a place where the door stands always open, and where sincere friends are always waiting to welcome you—and—come home.

Sincerely your friends.

Ida H. Chittenden.

T. Chittenden.

I stopped off at several places: at San Jose and San Francisco, to visit the rescue homes and dear friends, particularly dear Sister Kauffman, whose house had been dynamited and destroyed at the time of the fire following the earthquake, but who still sheltered many a girl in temporary cottages on the land where the home had once stood; next Berkeley, where lives my hospitable friend, Mrs. J. T. Anderson, whose beautiful home I enjoy the freedom of whenever in her neighborhood; then Sacramento, to spend one night with dear Mrs. Trefren, already referred to as one of my warmest friends; then Redding, my old home, where I rescued little Rosa, and which was the scene of many battles and victories in the name of the Lord. At this latter place there awaited me a royal reception from my many former friends and associates. It had been more than a decade since I had held up on the rear platform of the train that Bible with its blessed parting message from Gal. 6:9. All through the interval the Master had graciously permitted me to sow and to reap. Though there had been much more sowing than reaping, yet there had not been a great deal of fainting, for the grace of God had been all sufficient. Hallelujah!

Before I had been many days in Portland, I received a telegram telling of the death of Mr. Roberts. (Reader, I have refrained from stating in this book under what circumstances and at what time Mr. Roberts came back into my life, simply because that matter has no direct reference to the title of the book and also because it recalls too much pain and distress of a private nature. This I will say: With the other duties an added heavy cross was mine, owing to his mental and physical condition—a cross which, I regret to say, I did not always bear as patiently or as cheerfully as I might have borne it. It lasted from February, 1905, to November, 1009.) A caved-in tunnel near the State line prohibited my return, but Pastor Harper, of San Jose, and other kind friends relieved me of all final responsibilities regarding my late husband.

Until my return to California three months later, in the direct interests of the prison commission work, I worked even more laboriously than ever before. As ever, the Lord raised up many friends for me in Portland and vicinity; yet, at the same time, I was bitterly opposed and well-nigh overwhelmed by the enemy, who resorted to all sorts of means and devices to crush both soul and body. Did he succeed? No, indeed; for God was "my refuge and strength, a very present help in trouble." His not the Lord promised that "when the enemy shall come in like a flood, the Spirit of the Lord shall lift up a standard against him" (Isa. 59:19)? What blessed assurance for those who truly love and try to serve him! Hallelujah!

My last meeting before leaving Oregon was under the auspices of the Woman's Christian Temperance Union in a suburb called St. John's. An account of the service was made in the local paper, The Review, Feb. 4, 1910, as follows:

The Woman's Christian Temperance Union of St Johns planned a treat for the women of this place which proved a grand success. Mrs. Florence Roberts, better known as "Mother Roberts," spoke for an hour to over one hundred and fifty women in Bickner's Hall Tuesday afternoon. The most strict attention as paid, for it was a most solemn message she gave to us.

After the meeting refreshments were served, and the ladies lingered a while to get acquainted. Five new members were added to the Union.

I left there that same night for California, and the next meeting that I shall mention was that held the following Sunday evening in the fine hall of the ex-prisoners' home, 110 Silver Street, San Francisco. On this occasion I had the prayers of many former prisoners that God would bless me as I went forth to interest the people in their behalf and to open hearts and purses to aid in lifting the mortgage on this home—"Golden Rule Hall." In this interest I remained in San Francisco for some time, being occupied exclusively in interviewing responsible business people and portraying the need of their cooperation, financially and otherwise. During this time I was the guest of Brother Charles Montgomery, president of the board of prison commissioners, at his hotel—The Brooklyn. Afterward I visited San Mateo and Burlingame, with the same object in view. At the former place the young pastor of the Methodist Episcopal church, Rev. C. B. Sylvester, was just commencing a series of revival meetings. Upon learning my errand to San Mateo, he and his wife urged my cooperation in the evening services, and to this end invited me to remain under their roof. As I acceded to their wishes, double duty for the kingdom now confronted me, but the realization that our Lord never imposed too heavy a burden was now demonstrated. Those precious meetings closed in two weeks, with most blessed results. This records my first active, actual revival work.

To the glory of God, let me make mention that hundreds of dollars was the result of the daytime labor for the payment of the ex-prisoners' home.

During July and August, 1910, I was in an interior town and was laboring under an indescribable burden for certain souls. I believe I know what untold soul-agony is. Whilst almost sinking beneath my load, I received a letter from one whom, with his bride, I had been brought into Christian fellowship with in the early days of rescue experience. The missive had followed me from one place to another until only the last address could be plainly deciphered, owing to numerous erasures. Other letters had often miscarried and failed to reach me. This one was, by the hand of God, safely guided through. The father, with four little helpless children on his hands, wrote of the mental derangement of their mother, of his inability to find help, and of his pleading to God to send some one consecrated enough to assist them in their time of trouble. He was a poor man, but had a home and was working industriously at his trade to support his little flock, the youngest of whom was not four years old, the eldest ten.

Positively I knew of no one to go to the rescue. Whilst I was praying earnestly for the Lord to find some good woman to mother those little ones pending their mother's recovering, I received the impression, "Go yourself." Surely there is work everywhere—just as much in that distant town as where I was. I admit I shrank from so trying an ordeal, but, do my best, I could not silence the impression, "Go yourself." I prayed that if no other door opened within the next three days, God would let me regard this as a sign that his voice was bidding me take up this cross. Such was his will. I wrote, saying, "Expect me [date] on evening train." For nine weeks my immediate duty was with those little ones. Still further to try me, there was added to my domestic labors, measles. No sooner had one child recovered than the next was taken with them, until all had been similarly afflicted.

Some of the neighbors, having learned that "Mother Roberts" was quietly sojourning at this brother's house, called; and soon I was assisted with very necessary sewing, etc. After the three oldest children were once more able to go to school. I received a unanimous invitation to hold revival meetings in that town. About this time God sent the brother a splendid housekeeper, an elderly Christian woman, who relieved me of domestic duties, so that I was able to accept the call mentioned.

On February 1 of this year (1911) I received from Wheeling, W. Va., a telegram which filled me with indescribable joy, for it informed me of the birth of a little grandson. (My first grandchild and little namesake I have never seen. God took her when she was nine months old.) I longed to hold this dear little one in my arms and prayed God to grant my heart's desire, if according to his will. And he did. Bless his holy name! Following the revival services already mentioned, came a call from another town not far distant. At the close of this meeting a free-will offering enabled me to take the desired trip. On March 7, 1911, in company with a lady who was going within a short distance of my destination, I boarded the train and before long was with my precious little family. My cup of happiness was now filled to the brim, my heart overflowing with gratitude to God, as I embraced my dear ones and their precious little son.

CHAPTER XLVIII
MY RETURN TO THE MISSIONARY FIELD

In a few weeks a longing to return to missionary work was again taking possession of me. In vain I sought for the undenominational rescue hall usually to be found in large cities. Apparently Wheeling had nothing of this kind, though surely very much needed. Moreover, the requisite encouragement for the starting of one was not forthcoming.

Sundays would find me with my treasured auto-harp in the jail, work house, or infirmary at the afternoon services, which for years have been conducted by consecrated Christians, longing as much, nay, even perhaps more than I, for the necessary places of refuge for discharged prisoners and others. God speed the day when these needed institutions shall be amply supplied.

A lengthy conversation with one of the local judges, who is specially interested in juvenile offenders, elicited the fact of there being no place of detention for erring children except with the professed or habitual criminals. Comment upon this is superfluous; it is sufficient to say that *in nine cases out of ten disastrous results are inevitable.* Owing to a lack of interest, of means, or of cooperation, perhaps of sufficient good citizenship, maybe of all four, the judge and his coworkers seem to be unable at present to cope with or improve the situation. In a few years hence, this and other cities similarly situated will be facing a problem well-nigh impossible to solve, unless unusual efforts are made to provide for detention homes and schools for the delinquent children, now so numerous everywhere, excepting in towns and States where the awful liquor octopus, so largely responsible for crime and criminal tendencies, is absolutely abolished. Let us not for a moment forget that these youthful offenders are, in the main, the offspring of lovers of drink and its accessories. Thus the sins of the parents are visited upon the children, and upon the children's children, unto the third and fourth generation of them that hate God; but he says that he will show mercy unto thousands of them that love him and keep his commandments (Deut. 5:9, 10).

A pastor, describing the situation, informed me with the tears in his eyes that, notwithstanding all the efforts put forth for children's spiritual instruction, the results were very meager, owing to the indifference of parents—fathers and mothers who send their little ones to Sunday-school in the morning and then undo all the good in the afternoon by supplying them with nickels and sending them unchaperoned to the moving-picture shows, in order that they (the parents) may be free to indulge in worldly pleasures and amusements. Fortunately, a Sunday-closing movement in this direction has recently been crowned with success.

Some time in April as I was taking a streetcar ride between Wheeling, W. Va., and an adjacent town just across the river in the State of Ohio, my soul was uplifted when my eyes alighted upon this sign: "City Gospel Mission." Upon getting off the car at the next corner, I soon learned from the one who was superintending this work of the need of more consecrated assistants. I therefore at once volunteered my services. God saw fit to keep me in this field for three months, or until the time came for him to trust me still further along in his glorious light and liberty, thus giving me greater realization than ever before of what "the steps to His throne" mean literally as well as spiritually. To explain: My attention was attracted to a little band of workers quietly, unostentatiously living remarkable lives of humility faith, and prayer, depending absolutely upon our heavenly Father for all necessities, health of body as well as of soul, and, in fact, literally following God's Word, in spirit and in truth. Investigation convinced me beyond a doubt that my Lord had very much more of his riches for my enjoyment here on earth than of what I had already partaken, if I would be willing still further to humble myself.

For days the adversary contended with my soul. Everything calculated to discourage me was brought to bear, but praise God forever for victory! On the day it was gained, I informed my loved ones that I was soon to leave them in order to answer the call of God in an entirely new field of labor, where opportunity would shortly be granted me to give the world the benefit of a *few* of the numerous experiences of the past fifteen years. Through the consecrated humble little band already referred to, I learned of the Gospel Trumpet Home and Publishing Company, situated at Anderson, Indiana. I wrote to them, and shortly afterwards received a cordial invitation to visit them for an indefinite period. About the middle of August I was lovingly greeted by a family of about two hundred and fifty children of God, mostly young people of both sexes, all consecrated faith workers; all cheerfully and gladly giving the Lord their time and talents in this beautiful spot and being abundantly provided for materially as well as spiritually.

Here, whilst writing these experiences, I am enjoying blessed rest of both soul and body, such as I had never dreamed of; for, like many, many others, I had no idea of there being such a foretaste of heaven oil earth as this which is being daily and hourly demonstrated by the many members of the church of God (Col. 1:18) sojourning under this roof of prevailing prayer and practical faith. Best of all, every one is given cordial invitation to investigate personally; to satisfy himself beyond a doubt that the God who so wonderfully fed the Israelites in the wilderness in Moses' time, and that the Christ who multiplied the loaves and fishes, who went about healing all manner of divers diseases as well as speaking the word of life to the sin-sick soul, is positively, absolutely, *just the same today.* These people, so I learn, are to be found scattered broadcast. Look them up. They are known as the church of God. They are those who have come out from confusion and sectarianism into the only church God will ever recognize—the body of his only begotten Son, Jesus Christ. I praise him with all my soul that through his wondrous grace I am now in this glorious light and liberty.

CHAPTER XLIX
SOME PRECIOUS LETTERS FROM PRECIOUS CHILDREN

Many poets have likened life to a dream. Reader, doubtless you are aware, as I am, that life is but too realistic for the masses, the great masses of suffering, sorrow-stricken humanity, with so few, comparatively speaking, so few to uplift, comfort, cheer, and sustain; so few to speak the blessed words of a bright hereafter. Especially is this so with regard to those of the underworld. We find but few of the home missionaries undertaking this line of work; still fewer who have the God-given grace and courage, coupled with soul-love, to go to the fallen sister and help her out of sin; very few who do not shrink from putting a foot across the threshold of a jail or prison; but many, very many quite willing to fill the easy places; quite ready to perform tasks, provided these will not cost much inconvenience, comfort, personal pride, sacrifice, or money. But some (are you among them?) were delegated to go out into the highways and hedges, the streets, and the lanes, and compel (by the power of divine love) those found there, to come to the King's banquet, in order that his supper might be furnished with guests. Most plainly does our Master emphasize the fact that the publicans and the outcasts will largely be represented on that great day, that day which will positively come, and which in these perilous times is seemingly right at our very thresholds.

I shall never forget going into the San Jose jail on one occasion and trying to impress a girl who, as she lay on her cot, seemed utterly indifferent to all advances; even turning her face to the wall and stopping her ears with her fingers. Imagine my great surprise months afterwards on receiving the following letter from her:

San Francisco, Cal.,

March 16, 1906.

My dear Mrs. Roberts:

I am feeling so lonesome and blue here tonight all alone in my room.... Somehow my thoughts turned to you, and I could not keep the tears from my eyes as I realized that I had one friend, because you were, oh! so kind to me during my imprisonment in San Jose.

Dear Mrs. Roberts, can you bring before your mind's eye this picture? Picture, if you can, the desolate darkness of the night extending on and on. For months not a ray of light, not one kind word, not one friendly face, until at last, when almost in despair, a gleam of sunshine shot across your pathway, a kind, loving voice said. "I will be your friend; I will help you." Such was my condition, and you, Mrs. Roberts, was that gleam of sunshine. Your voice was the one that cheered me until I took fresh courage. Mrs. Roberts, God has taken me back…. May God bless you in your work…. I wish I could see you and talk with you. You are indeed my spiritual mother. I hope you will allow me to call you so. I wanted to tell you how much you had helped me. I know you are very busy, but if you have time, please drop me one line. I am so hungry for a message from you to cheer me up. May God bless you and yours.

A— — M— —

San Francisco, Cal.,

March 20, 1900.

Dear Mrs. Roberts—My Spiritual Mother:

I cried from pure joy when I received your letter and photo. Yes, God is most wonderfully showing me his way, and at last my spirit is broken, and I am content to obey the voice of my Savior.

Praise God for his wonderful salvation that saves and keeps one enjoying his great blessings! Praise his name! I have nothing now to fear. Mrs. Roberts, I am glad I did that time in jail, because it taught me the lesson of patience and submission, and now it is much easier for me to live a Christian life. I now have a better experience than I could have had otherwise. Pray for me, Mother Roberts, and I will pray for you. May God give you success in your work.

May God bless you and yours is the prayer of your spiritual child,

A— — M— —

FROM A PRISON BOY

San Quentin, Cal.,

Sept. 13, — —.

My dear Friend Mother Roberts:

I received your letter of the 4th inst. and was very glad to get it, and will try and drop you a line in answer now, although there is not much in the way of news. I am much better now and am working outside around the warden's house, where I can get plenty of fresh air; so I think the time will pass much more pleasanter than if I was on the inside of the prison walls. I had quite a siege of sickness (pleuro-pneumonia the doctor pronounced it), but I am getting better all the time and think soon to be entirely strong again.

I think often of the kindness you showed me while I was in — — [a county jail], and I will never forget it or the advice you gave me. You started me on the right path to heaven, and I do pray to God that he will lead the rest of the way so that when I stand before him on the judgment-day he will claim me as one of his own children. There is one thing that worries me: my mother is quite sick, and writes me that she does not expect to live to see me set at liberty, but I pray to God to spare her until I am free and able to prove to her and every one else that I am a true child of God and worthy to take my place amongst honest Christian men. Don't think I can ever forget you, and my thoughts are with you when my words are not.

I will close now, hoping that God will take care of you, which is the prayer of your friend,

A— — G— —

FROM A RECLAIMED WIFE

San Francisco, Cal.,

Dec. 3, — —.

Dear Mother Roberts:

You don't know how glad I was to receive your kind and loving letter. Yes, I can praise God this very day for his loving-kindness and tender mercy. Yesterday I gave a testimony to some poor souls at San Quentin, and you don't know how much good it did them. Three gave their hearts to God. All that I am praying for now is that Jesus may make me a shining light for souls that know him not. There was one prisoner that knew me in my life of sin, and he told the others that I looked ten years younger....

Oh, may God forbid that it may ever be so again; for when I think how he has snatched me out from the pit of hell, oh, how I love my Jesus more and more, dear Mama Roberts!...

What God has done for me, surely he can do for others. *I only wish I could turn this wicked world upside down and make it new again.* In one of the Psalms I read, "My soul hath kept thy testimonies, and I love them exceedingly." May it always be so.

Mama Roberts, I will soon get a letter from Lucy. You don't know how I love to get her letters. I assure you that when I get blue I take and read one or two lines that her gentle hand has written, and it does me good.

Now, tomorrow night, you know, is prayer-meeting night, and I know you won't forget me. Pray that I may, by the grace of God, do some poor soul good by telling them of *the life that I led for twenty and one years* [drink, etc.]...

I will close with love from one that dearly loves you and who will always pray for you. I remain as ever,

Yours in Christ, E— — K— —.

P.S. My husband wishes to be remembered to you. I hope that you will come to see me soon. Write soon.

FROM A THIRTEEN-YEAR-OLD SINNED-AGAINST CHILD

Dear Mama Roberts:

I am learning about Jesus day by day. I hope you are well and strong.

The Lord will help you....

My little chick is growing, and its mother is showing her little chick to eat....

Pray for me. I am praying for you, too.

From your dear, F— — E— —.

FROM ONE IN A HOUSE OF SIN

M— —, Cal.

Mrs. Florence Roberts:

Your very kind letter received yesterday and am glad that your meeting at the church was successful. I also hope ere this that you have arrived safely in — — and that your trip was pleasant.

Mrs. Roberts, briefly concerning myself; words can not express my appreciation of the interest you are taking in me, and I hope I may be spared to prove to you that your efforts have not been in vain. I hope the day may not be far distant when I may make myself worthy of your friendship and interest—and hoping that you may think of whatever goodness I may possess, and not of what my life has been, I beg to remain,

Sincerely yours,

J— — W— —

The foregoing letter was written in a beautiful hand.

FROM A VERY YOUNG MOTHER

N— —. Cal.

My dear Mama Roberts:

I will now sit down to answer your most dear and welcome letter of so long ago, which has not been answered; but do not think I have forgotten you. You have been so kind and good to me that I will ever love you and not forget you.... The baby was pretty sick before the 4th of July, but he is well and fat now. I feed him on Mellin's food.... My stepfather says that the day I speak to the baby's father I will lose the home I have. He (the baby's father) does not give me five cents. All that the baby has I work good and hard to get. What he and I need, I earn honestly. I work whenever I have the opportunity, as my stepfather is the only one we can depend upon [she was only sixteen years old], and we are four boys and three girls, grandma, mama, the baby, and himself; so it is hard for him, and I haven't the heart to ask them for anything, no matter how bad I need it. I take in washing from the boarders at the two hotels, also sewing and ironing, or go out to do housework whenever I can.

I must close, as I must help mama to get the supper. With love and regards to Mama Roberts from all.... I don't forget my Bible and verse. Your loving,

L— — K— —

FROM A GRATEFUL MOTHER

S— —, July 28.

Mrs. Florence Roberts.

My dear Madam:

My darling daughter E— — has been home for a short time and has told me the kind interest you have taken in her welfare.

I wish to say for your pleasure (and certainly mine) that E— — is very much in earnest over your advice. I sincerely believe it will take only a little more persuasion on your part to fully convince her to give up her worldly ways and do as you wish her. Oh, how happy I shall be! My heart is breaking for my dear, sweet girl. She is bright and accomplished. She could help you so much in your noble work, which we both know would greatly help her. God is surely working in her heart. She says, "Mama, I can't get Mrs. Roberts out of my mind. All the time I was away [This girl used to leave home on periodical carousals], I could but think of her, and if it hadn't been Mrs. R—— talked so good to me, I would have had a big old time." Now, my dear friend, do you not think that encouraging? I shall pray every moment for your success. God surely will help us to save my darling child.

My dear Mrs. Roberts, please call and see me when you return to S——. So much I would like to say.

With my earnest prayer for your success, I am yours most sincerely,

C—— B——

FROM A GRATEFUL FATHER

K——. Cal.

Mrs. Florence Roberts:

May God forever bless you and reward you, dear madam, for being good to my poor boy. The board of prison directors have granted his parole, and if he behaves himself for two years, then he can apply to the governor for his pardon. I hope it will soon come my way to show you how much I appreciate how hard you worked to get his parole. God knows I do.... Please forgive my poor effort to thank you. I can find no words, but God forever bless you, and I'm sure he will.

Yours most gratefully, G—— F——.

The following is a reply to an anonymous letter introducing one who was undergoing a laborious effort to make good. I hope that this may teach its own lesson to all who would push the struggling ones still further down.

To —— ——. Dear Sir:

Kindly permit me space to answer an anonymous letter which came to me last Sunday concerning a young man in whom I am deeply interested, having been instrumental in procuring his parole recently, and who is in every way traduced to me by the writer, who styles himself or herself a Christian and signs the letter, "A friend to all."

Knowing this young man as I do, through officials, the sheriff of the county, and others in a position to make truthful statements concerning him; knowing of the terrible struggle he is enduring to live down an act of the past for which he was more to be pitied than blamed; knowing from the lips of those with whom he spent his youthful days that prior to his incarceration in San Quentin he had a character unsullied, I ask, How can any one claiming to be a Christian, thus hinder the cause of Christ by making unsubstantiated charges? 'Woe to you who offend one of these little, ones!' saith our Lord, who came, not to save the righteous, but to call sinners to repentance.

My varied experience proves that many are hindered from coming into the fold by just such reflections on the Master, as indicated in this letter.

Now I am perfectly willing to meet the writer of the aforesaid letter in the presence of two or more witnesses, in order that he (or she) may be given a chance to substantiate his statements; and until this is done, I shall continue to consider said letter the work of a coward instead of a "friend to all."

Most respectfully yours,

(Mrs.) Florence Roberts. From Warden W. H. Reilly,

State Prison at Folsom, Cal.,

Sept. 18, 1911.

Mrs. Florence Roberts, Gospel Trumpet Publishing Co.,

Anderson, Indiana. Dear Madam:

Upon my return from a little needed rest. I found your letter of the 7th inst., which surely afforded me pleasure.

We are very glad indeed that you are so pleasantly circumstanced, and wish you sincerely all manner of success in your good work.

Joe —- is here yet, and he was much pleased when I handed him your card. There are many fine points about the boy, and he surely appreciates your kindness.

Mrs. Reilly and the children are well and join me in kind remembrance.

Very respectfully,

W. H. Reilly.

Joe is the young man who was sentenced for ninety-nine years on circumstantial evidence, and whose story is in this book.

CHAPTER L
CONCLUSION

One morning a little lad was observed by his mother to be making great efforts to stretch his chubby limbs to such an extent as to place his feet in every one of his father's tracks.

"What are you trying to do, Sonny? Come into the house quick, or you'll catch cold," called the anxious mother.

"No, no, Mama; I don't want to; I want to follow papa. I'm trying to walk in his footsteps," replied the innocent child.

Does this cause the smoking, drinking, swearing, card-playing, Godless parents to halt and reflect? God knows; we hope so. Does this fill the mother of cherished, idolized little ones with remorse of conscience? Does it occasion her to take a retrospective view of the time when, during courtship days, she was warned and advised of the indiscreet marriage she was about to make, because of her sweetheart's well-known dissolute propensities? Yet all those warnings and pleadings were in vain.

The little innocent ones are trying to walk in their parents' footsteps. Myriads of mothers are weeping and wishing they had been firmer; that they had not so readily yielded to the ardent persuasions to marry, but had waited until such times as true reformation, repentance, and turning to the God they were then serving had taken place in their sweethearts' lives.

> Of all sad words of tongue or pen,
> The saddest are these—It might have been.

Poor, poor remorseful, unhappy wife and mother, my heart aches for you as you realize the sowing and weep over the prospective reaping. Long since you have grown cold in your Christian experience. You realize it today as never before. You wonder what you are going to do about it? The older children have outgrown your jurisdiction. Mary is running with company you do not approve of, to balls, theaters, and other demoralizing places; wanting finery you are not able to afford, although you do your best. You can't get any help from her; for, when not otherwise engaged, she is absorbed in novel-reading. It does no good to complain to her father; in fact, that seems only to make a bad matter worse. You haven't an atom of her confidence. When she was younger, you never really encouraged her to give it, and now, though but fifteen, she laughs at you because she thinks that she knows so much and that you know so little. All her confidence is given to those you do not approve of, and you are dreading the outcome, the inevitable.

Then there's thirteen-year-old Tom. While you sat up mending his torn coat the other night after he had gone to bed, you found some tobacco and cigarette paper in his pocket. When you quietly asked him next morning what it meant, he only laughed and replied, "That's nothing. All us kids smoke nowadays. *It won't hurt us any more than it will father. He smokes.*" You are wondering how you can find out whether he has contracted any more of his father's bad habits, and while searching his room, you come across a dirty pack of playing-cards hidden in the back part of one of the bureau drawers.

Awful vision of the future of these two older children is yours as you ponder what you can do to subvert the growing evil in your home. You indulge much in vain regrets—vain, indeed, so far as you are concerned. But listen, mother—you who would lay down your life to spare Mary from disgrace and eventually an ignominious death; you who love Tom so dearly you would give all the world were it yours to make him understand that the habits he is contracting lead only to impaired health and disgrace, ofttimes to imprisonment, sometimes to the scaffold. It is not too late yet, distressed mother, particularly with the two younger children, who are just beginning to ask leading questions. These you must, *you must answer*, so that your little son and daughter will find no need of inquiring of other children concerning the beautiful plan of life, which should never be imparted to them by any other than you yourself. "What must I do? What can I do?" you ask. Listen. I'm going to tell you.

Lose no time. Do as I did. Go to God, in your secret closet. Lay all your troubles and problems at his feet. Throw yourself on his loving mercy. Confess your backsliding, your sins, your errors, your weaknesses, everything—everything that is causing you, your husband, and your children to be held by the enemy of souls, and that will soon bring more misery into your life and their lives, unless God undertakes for you and them. Then, cost what it will, take the humble place before God and them. Tell them of your love for them; of the mistakes you have made, through false modesty, in not gaining their companionship, their confidence. Ask them to help you in the future by trusting you more than they do any other friend or acquaintance. Tell them how much you once loved God, and that now, after wandering far away, you have returned to him. Go with them to Sunday-school and to other religious services; set up, even in the face of all opposition, the family altar; ask a blessing at table; have an open Bible always.

The outcome. Probably at first, and maybe for some time to come, rebellion, even desertion, even more sin to battle with; more heartaches, more tears, more struggles than ever heretofore. But *"be thou faithful."* Thy loyalty, thine efforts, shall be rewarded. Watch, wait, pray always.

There is only one reason to be given why the children go wrong— *Godless homes.* "Train up a child in the way he should go; and when he is old, he will *not* depart from it." Prov. 22:6.

One day a clergyman handed me two very startling verses, the characters of which were all too true. I remarked that some day, God willing, I would add to the verses and set them to music. I have done so, and in His name, I herewith give them, under the awful title:

WANTED, RECRUITS FOR HELL

Johnson the drunkard is dying today,
  With traces of sin on his face;
He will be missed at the bar, at the play.
  Wanted, a boy for his place.

Ruby, poor Ruby is passing away,
  A victim of vice and disgrace.
Wanted, recruits for the houses of shame,
  Some mother's girl for her place.

Simons, a gambler, was killed in a fight;
  He died without pardon or grace.
Wanted, to train for his burden and blight,
  Somebody's boy for his place.

Wanted for dance-halls, for brothels, for bars,
  Girls attractive of form and of face,
Girls to decoy and boys to destroy;
  Have you a child for the place?

"Wanted," pleads Satan, "for service of mine,
  Some one to live without grace,
Some one to die without pardon divine;
  Please train me your child for the place."

That eminent writer, Mrs. Ella Wheeler Wilcox, says:

"Every person on earth is making some sort of a cell in his or her brain every waking moment of the day or night.

"Thoughts are things. Thought is energy. Thought is a creative power. That is why it is so important to direct the minds of human beings to good, kind, helpful thoughts. [Let me add, to direct them, from the very commencement, to the great, loving God and his Son, our Savior.]

"Parentage is the oldest profession of men and women in the world, but there are the smallest number of prize-winners in that profession of any in the world. [Why? because of a neglected, insulted God.]

"Real, good motherhood must include the universal motherhood. It must make a woman love her child *so unselfishly* that she is willing it should suffer while learning its lessons of kindness, thoughtfulness, and protection, rather than to enjoy itself while taking away the joys, the privileges, or the rights of other creatures, human or animal."

The warden of a certain State prison, who is a student of human nature, said to some visitors one day, "If a child is properly educated to the age of ten, no matter what its inheritance, it never becomes a criminal." His sentence includes all the needed preventatives of crime.

Oliver Wendell Holmes when asked, "When should a child's education begin?" promptly replied, "Two hundred years before it is born."

There would be little or no need of the rescue missionaries had parents and guardians but heeded these words in Deut. 6:5-7: "Hear, O Israel: The Lord our God is one Lord: and thou shalt love the Lord thy God with all thy heart, and with all thy soul, and with all thy might. And these words, which I command thee this day, shall be in thy heart: and thou shalt teach them diligently unto thy children, and shalt talk of them when thou sittest in thine house, and when thou walkest by the way, and when thou liest down, and when thou risest up. And thou shalt bind them for a sign upon thine hand, and they shall be as frontlets between thine eyes, and thou shalt write them upon the posts of thine houses, and on thy gates." "O that there were such an heart in them, that they would fear me, and keep all my commandments always, that it might be well with them, and with their children forever!" Deut. 5:29.

It is very, very blessed to undertake the part of a good Samaritan. It is far more blessed so to know and serve the Lord, that our present and future progeny, instead of sharing a destiny similar to many of these depicted between these pages, may, under any and all circumstances, enjoy the everlasting smile of His countenance, that peace and joy in their souls which this world can never give, neither take away.

Lord, we pray thee, "so teach us to number our days, that we may apply our hearts unto wisdom." Psa. 90:12.